The Darlings Are Forever

Melissa Kantor

HYPERION
New York

Printed in the United States of America

First Edition

1 3 5 7 9 10 8 6 4 2

V567-9638-5-10288

Reinforced binding

Library of Congress Cataloging-in-Publication Data
Kantor, Melissa.
The Darlings are forever / by Melissa Kantor.—1st ed.
p. cm.
Summary: Best friends Jane, Victoria, and Natalya, who call themselves the Darlings, find their relationship tested when they start their freshman year at three very different high schools.
ISBN-13: 978-1-4231-2368-2
ISBN-10: 1-4231-2368-9
[1. Interpersonal relations—Fiction. 2. Best friends—Fiction. 3. Friendship—Fiction. 4. High schools—Fiction. 5. Schools—Fiction. 6. New York (N.Y.)—Fiction.] I. Title.
PZ7.K11753Dar   2011
[Fic]—dc22   2010009767

Visit www.hyperionteens.com

THIS LABEL APPLIES TO TEXT STOCK

To Rebecca Friedman

It is one of the blessings of old friends that you can afford to be stupid with them.
—Ralph Waldo Emerson

Chapter One

THE LABOR DAY sun was scorching, and as Jane waited for the light to change, she could practically hear her dark hair frizzing. It had taken her longer than she'd expected to wrap the boxes, and racing along the few blocks between her house and Ga Ga Noodle, where she was meeting Natalya and Victoria, had made her sweaty. In Los Angeles, where she'd spent the past month with her dad, it was too dry to sweat. Still bleary-eyed from her overnight flight, she was surprised to be surrounded by plane trees wilting in the late morning sun instead of palm trees swaying in an arid breeze; to see the brick buildings of Greenwich Village instead of pink stucco Spanish-style villas.

Crossing Sixth Avenue, Jane looked down the block to her right. She couldn't see One Room, the school where she, Victoria, and Natalya had gone since they were five, but she could picture it in her mind's eye—the bright blue lobby, the walls of the main stairs covered in paintings and poems written by the littlest students. As memories of One Room flew through her head, her stomach turned over. And it wasn't just because tomorrow was the first day of school. Tomorrow was the first day of *high* school. That would be stomach-tightening enough if One Room had a high school. Which it didn't.

One Room only went through eighth grade.

Squeezing the bag of gifts to her side, she finished crossing the street and pushed tomorrow out of her mind. Through the plate-glass window of Ga Ga Noodle she could see Natalya and Victoria already sitting at their regular table. Just the sight of them comforted her, and she waved madly in the hopes of catching their attention. They saw her and waved back, grinning at her through the window. She hurried across the last squares of sidewalk and pushed at the heavy glass door.

Inside, the room was hushed and freezing. As usual, almost every table was empty. When the restaurant had first opened, the girls had worried it had so little business that it might have to close, but then they'd realized that two delivery guys were constantly running in and out with people's orders.

"I am sooo sorry I'm late." Jane practically leaped across the room as Victoria and Natalya screamed and jumped up to greet her. "I can't believe it's been a whole *month*!" she said as they hugged.

"Just to fill you in, we've decided you can't visit your father anymore," Natalya informed Jane, slipping back into her seat and tucking her straight brown hair behind her ears. She'd spent the past year growing out her bangs, and now it was finally possible to see her extraordinary, dark brown, almond-shaped eyes. "Unless it's just for a long weekend."

"Oh, and we agreed that Natalya can't go to Russian camp again," Victoria added, sitting down and dropping her napkin onto her lap. "She already knows enough about Russian culture."

"*Da.*" Natalya nodded.

Victoria shook her blond head. "It has been *so* boring here without you guys. I'm amazed I survived." Even in a pair of faded jean shorts and an ancient Harvard T-shirt of her mother's, Victoria was strikingly beautiful.

"Boring?!" Jane repeated doubtfully, pulling her bright green tank top away from where it was stuck to her stomach with sweat. "Your dad is like, a *rock star.* He was on the front page of the *LA Times.*"

Victoria sighed and put her elbows on the table, her chin in her hands. "It is *so* weird. Yesterday my dad was at a fund-raiser in the Hamptons with *the president!*"

Jane and Natalya stared slack-jawed at their friend. Ever since they'd been little, Victoria's father had run a nonprofit, working to provide national health insurance. A little over a year ago he'd gotten so aggravated by the state of the nation's health care system that he'd announced he was going to run for Senate, to go to DC and change things. The whole thing had been . . . well, not a joke, exactly, but almost. Only the joke was on Victoria's dad. Because in May, the front-runner, a hugely popular Democratic congressman from Long Island, dropped out of the race when it was discovered he'd been having an affair with his au pair.

And suddenly Andrew Harrison, Independent, became the Democrat's only chance of holding on to a Senate seat they'd never thought was in play.

"The president," Natalya breathed. "That is the coolest."

Victoria continued, shaking her head in amazement at her own life. "Saturday I went with my parents to this county fair and some girl asked for my autograph."

"I am *sooo* jealous," said Jane.

Victoria shook her head. "No, you're not. It's really *weird*. What if it's like that at school?" Tomorrow Victoria would be starting at The Morningside School, a magnet high school just a few blocks from her Upper West Side apartment.

At the mention of school, the girls looked at each other. "I'm freaking out," Victoria announced.

"We need a plan," said Natalya.

"Different high schools," Victoria reminded them. "Different high schools! We are going to be freshman at *different high schools* tomorrow."

"Vicks, we *know*," said Jane. In April she'd received a letter telling her she'd won a spot at The Academy for the Performing Arts, New York City's most competitive performing arts school.

"I mean, what were they thinking?" Victoria demanded, banging her fist on the table in indignation. "Why would they create a school that only goes through eighth grade? It should be *illegal*."

Tom, the ancient waiter who had been serving them ever since the beginning of eighth grade, which was when One Room students were allowed to go out for lunch, came over to their table.

"Hello. How are you girls?" He nodded and smiled.

"We're okay," said Natalya.

"The usual?" he asked.

"Oh my god, you remember us!" Victoria was amazed.

"Vicks, we came here like, every day from September to June," Jane reminded her. "Of course he remembers us. And yes, thank you, Tom, we'll have the usual."

Jane, Victoria, and Natalya had been drinking virgin piña coladas ever since Jane's ninth birthday, when their waiter at a bistro in Nolita had asked if the "pretty little girls" didn't want Shirley Temples. "We are *not* little girls," an irate Jane had informed the condescending waiter. That was when Jane's grandmother, Nana, had stepped in. "Maybe you would enjoy a virgin piña colada, darling." With its glamorous-sounding name, the drink suggestion had mollified Jane.

Now, as Tom stepped away from their table, smiling, Natalya giggled. "Do you remember when we found out what *virgin* means?"

"I don't know what I thought it was before." Victoria squinted at the effort of trying to remember. "I think I just thought it was an adjective. Virgin. Like . . ."

"Decaf?" offered Natalya, laughing.

"Exactly," said Victoria

Jane sighed. "I miss Nana."

Nana had always picked the girls up from school on Tuesdays, which was the day Jane's mother worked late. She'd taken them to art galleries in Chelsea and used-clothing stores in Williamsburg. They'd explored the neighborhood along the Gowanus Canal and seen old movies at the Film Forum.

"Mom," Jane's mother used to ask, "why don't you take them to a playground or something?"

Nana would shrug. "New York City *is* a playground."

Nana had lived all over the world—Zimbabwe, Paris, São Paolo (her third husband had worked for the State Department). Nana had climbed Mount Kilimanjaro. She knew how to do a dance called The Hustle, and she had been to Woodstock. She had ridden a camel in Morocco and an elephant in Jaipur, India.

Nana had had what she called a *real life*. She said every woman should have a real life.

Most people talked to Natalya, Jane, and Victoria like the children they were, but Nana talked to them like the grown-ups they would someday be.

And now she was gone. In July, the day after Nana had taken them out for Jane's fourteenth birthday, she had suffered a major stroke. An ambulance had brought her to the hospital, but she'd died that night without ever regaining consciousness.

"I miss her, too," said Natalya.

"Me three," agreed Victoria. "Nobody's going to call us *darling* anymore."

The girls sat in silence until the waiter placed their frothy drinks on the table. The piña coladas came straight out of a can, and the single cherries sank into the pale, creamy liquid, but they were still the girls' drink of choice.

6

Jane snapped out of her trance. "Wait!" She put her hand into her bag and pulled out three small boxes, wrapped in white and tied with blue ribbons.

Victoria looked at Jane, amazed. "Are these for us?"

"What are they?" asked Natalya. "How come there are three of them?"

"You'll see." Jane handed Victoria and Natalya each a box, then took one for herself. "Open."

Natalya and Jane slid the ribbons off their boxes, but Victoria untied hers carefully. Her friends waited until she got the ribbon off. Then they all opened them at the same time, and Natalya and Victoria gasped.

"Oh my god!" said Victoria.

"What *is* this?" asked Natalya. "It's *beautiful.*" Lying in the center of a small cotton square was a single pearl on a thin silver chain. Natalya took hers out to admire it. "Jane, where did you get these?"

Jane's smile was sad. "Remember Nana's necklace?"

Victoria and Natalya nodded. Of course they remembered Nana's necklace, with its six strands of pearls, its clasp a huge, shimmery opal surrounded by sapphires. Whenever Jane's mother had come home and seen that Nana was wearing the necklace with her jeans and sneakers, she would roll her eyes. "For heaven's sake, Mom, you shouldn't wear that thing while you're traipsing all over Manhattan. One of these days it's going to get lost or stolen, and you'll never see it again!"

"I'd rather lose something I've worn every day than keep something I never get to enjoy," Nana would answer. Then she'd wink at the girls. "Remember, darlings, everything can be replaced except people."

Sliding the thin silver chain along the back of her hand, Jane explained about the necklaces. "Well, my mom brought it to a jeweler to get it appraised, and he said she should have it restrung. So before she did, she asked me if I wanted the jeweler to remove one of the pearls and have it made into a necklace because Nana always wanted the whole necklace to be mine someday, but my mom didn't think I should have it until I'm older. She said this would be like a deposit on the whole necklace. So *I* asked her if she would do *three* necklaces, and she said technically the necklace is mine, so if I wanted her to do that, she would!"

"Your mom is *amazing*," Victoria breathed.

"Sometimes," Jane admitted. She opened the plain metal clasp and draped her necklace around her neck.

"It's beautiful." Victoria had already put her necklace on, and she pulled it away from her body to admire it. "Thank you, Jane."

"It's incredible," said Natalya, studying the simple pearl with its tiny hat of silver.

Victoria's eyes were suddenly damp as she looked around the table at her friends. "First Nana, now this. What if being at different schools changes everything?"

"What are you talking about?" asked Jane. Tom stepped toward the table to take their order, but Jane asked him for another minute.

Victoria shrugged. "I don't know." She toyed with the paper of her straw, not looking at her friends. "You guys are so much

8

better than me at meeting people. You'll probably have all these new friends. . . ."

"*WHAT?*" Jane glared at Victoria.

Natalya held up her hand to calm Jane down. "Vicks, you can't mean that. We're best friends. We're always going to be best friends. Going to different high schools isn't going to change that."

"Seriously," Jane said. "Look—" She whipped out her Sidekick. "I'm putting it down in my calendar right now. Tomorrow right after school . . ."

"What?" challenged Victoria. "We'll meet here for a late lunch? My parents aren't going to let me go from school to here and all the way back uptown." In the air in front of her, she traced the route she would have to take to meet her friends at Ga Ga Noodle and then go home again.

"Well . . ." Natalya began. But she couldn't come up with a plausible scenario in which they would be able to meet after school. The Gainsford Academy, an exclusive girls' school to which she'd received a full scholarship, was on the Upper East Side, and the trip back to Brighton Beach, Brooklyn, where she lived, would be a long one. Her parents were definitely going to want her to come right home at the end of the day.

"See?" Victoria said into Natalya's silence. "I'm scared."

Jane frowned, considering Victoria's despair. "We need Nana."

Victoria sighed.

"Guys," Natalya said. She was holding her pearl out away from her neck and studying it. "We *know* what Nana would say." She looked at her friends. For a second, their faces were puzzled,

9

and then they both realized exactly what she meant.

Knowing they had understood, Jane lifted her glass. Natalya raised hers to meet Jane's. Hesitantly, Victoria did the same.

Glasses touching, they recited together the toast Nana had made every year on Jane's birthday. "May you always do what you're afraid of doing,"

"Here's to us, darlings," said Natalya, her eyes shining.

"To us making Nana proud," Jane said, and her eyes were misty, too. "By doing all sorts of things we're afraid to do."

"Including going to high school," added Victoria.

Each wondering what tomorrow would bring, they clinked glasses, then sipped their watery but delicious piña coladas, the pearly liquid almost the exact same color as their new necklaces.

Chapter Two

NATALYA WAS PRETTY sure she was the only freshman at The Gainsford Academy who'd started her day getting spit on by her mother.

Spitting on someone for good luck was a tradition her parents had brought from Russia, where they'd lived before Natalya was born. The good thing was that over the two decades they'd lived in Brooklyn, her parents had eased up on the spitting a little. Natalya had a distinct memory of truly getting spit on when she'd started first grade, but now that she was heading off to high school, her mom just went *tu-tu-tu*, and no actual saliva emerged from her mouth. (Her dad had left for his job as a driver early that morning, so last night they'd played a game of speed chess together, and he'd done the fake-spitting thing before she'd gone to bed. Later, her brother, Alex, who was ten and still asleep now, had spit on his hand and tried to rub it on her, but she could still tackle him—just—and so his spit had ended up on his own cheek.)

"Look at you!" her mom exclaimed after she'd made the spitting noise. "You're a Gainsford girl!"

Natalya rolled her eyes, but she couldn't completely hide her smile. In her crisp, white, button-down shirt and short plaid skirt, she felt special, like she was part of something somehow larger than herself. Right now, every single Gainsford girl was (or would soon be) getting dressed in the same combination she was wearing. The only thing she'd had to choose was whether or not to wear socks with her shoes, and she'd gone with not.

Natalya's mother mimicked Natalya's eye roll, adding, "Oh, Mama, you're such a *drag*."

Natalya laughed at her mother's accented slang, then reached out and hugged her, taking in the sweet smell of her moisturizer and shampoo. The familiar combination plus the hug made it impossible for Natalya not to whisper into her mother's shoulder the secret fear that had kept her up much of the night. "What if everyone's smarter than I am?"

Her mom squeezed her back so tightly she made Natalya gasp. "You are *every bit* as smart as those girls." Her voice was fierce, and when she pulled away, Natalya thought for a second that she saw tears in her eyes.

"Mom?"

Her mother shook her head and sighed, waving away either her own emotion or Natalya's concern. "You're going so far away."

"It's just the Upper East Side." Natalya laughed a little: it wasn't like she was going away to college or anything.

"Well . . ." Her mom paused, then tapped her daughter lightly on the nose. "Just don't be surprised if it's further than you think."

Natalya was about to ask what she meant, but right then the cuckoo clock in the kitchen chimed the half hour.

"Oh, I've gotta go!" Natalya grabbed her backpack, momentarily panicking. "Bye, Mama. Love you!"

As she sped out the front door, Natalya's mom called, "Tu, tu, tu, I spit on you." And even though, objectively, the idea was gross, Natalya couldn't help laughing.

Her trip was a long one, and Natalya had plenty of opportunity for people-watching, which she loved. First were the Brighton Beach commuters: women with bright pink lipstick and enormous hair, men reading their Russian-language papers. Then came the Park Slope crowd: women in plain, pale, summer separates, parents holding hands with little kids carrying enormous backpacks. Almost everyone wearing a suit stepped off the crowded car at Wall Street, and Natalya studied the remaining passengers, wondering where they were headed. When she transferred to the 6, she thought she saw a Gainsford uniform, but it turned out to just be a girl in a similar skirt and a white shirt. She looked down at her new black Keds with the white piping and wondered if she'd been right to go without socks.

Stepping off the train at Seventy-seventh Street, Natalya felt the coming heat of the day lurking behind the early morning cool. The butterflies in her stomach had evolved into pterodactyls, and she grabbed her phone and sent Jane a text. Now I m freaking out. A minute later, her phone buzzed a reply. u have 2 do what ur scared 2 do, darling. Well, she was definitely scared to go to school. And it wasn't as if she could just not go. Natalya smiled at the double meaning in Jane's text.

As she approached the stately limestone mansion that housed The Gainsford Academy (formerly The Gainsford Academy for Young Women), Natalya was relieved to see that almost none of the other girls were wearing socks. Her first call, and she'd gotten it right! Once again she felt like part of a team—Team Gainsford.

Still, even if they were all part of the same team, as she climbed the steps, Natalya felt hyperconscious of being the newest member. Every girl she walked by seemed to be hugging at least one person, and often as many as two or three. Gainsford started in preschool, so most of the other freshman had been here since they were three years old. When Natalya had gotten the news that she was the only student from One Room who'd been accepted to Gainsford, she'd been so proud. Now she wouldn't have minded seeing a familiar face.

Pulling her backpack close to her side, she pushed open one of the heavy wooden doors and entered the lobby. Crossing the threshold brought all of Natalya's excitement rushing back. From the second she'd walked into the building for her interview last January, she'd dreamed of this moment. Gainsford was the most elegant, beautiful building she'd ever been in—a holy space dedicated to higher learning. The walls of the entryway were dark wood paneling; the ceilings, which seemed to hover hundreds of feet above the marble floor, were decorated with intricate plasterwork. Natalya felt her new shoes sink slightly into the thick Persian rug as she made her way to the office.

The main office at her old school had felt almost like an extension of the classrooms—there was always a huge pile of kids' backpacks and instruments in the corners, and the walls were covered in student artwork. The Gainsford office was nothing like that. There were real oil paintings in heavy frames, with lamps focused on them, and the desks were huge and old-looking and made of dark, shiny wood. At One Room, the assistants who worked in the office usually wore jeans and T-shirts. But here, the older woman who sat behind her fancy desk was wearing a suit, and she looked serious.

"Hi, I'm Natalya. I got a letter saying I should come to the office before my first class."

The woman smiled and shook Natalya's hand. "Hello, Natalya. I'm Mrs. Bradley. I'll get your schedule." Her voice was crisp, and there was something a little scary about her professional smile and handshake. Nervously, Natalya touched the small pearl at her throat, feeling better as she thought of Jane and Victoria wearing their necklaces in their distant corners of Manhattan.

Natalya's first-period class was Intro to Greek. Ever since she'd told her dad that Intro to Greek was a mandatory class for freshman, he'd been going around saying, "It's all Greek to me." As she slipped into an empty desk and looked around the room of unfamiliar faces, Natalya wouldn't have minded even a corny joke from her dad right about now.

Mr. Schweitzer barreled into the room, coffee dripping onto his hand from a paper cup as his bag swung wildly on the crook of his elbow. "Hello, hello!" he barked. "Let's see who's here and who's not."

As the girls in the room studied their teacher, Natalya took the opportunity to study them. For the first time she saw the downside of uniforms: it was pretty much impossible to figure people out when they were all dressed identically. Were these girls jocks? Nerds? Even stuff like shoes and jewelry didn't provide clues—Natalya was wearing Keds because she couldn't wear flip-flops (no open-toed shoes). Was that why the girl next to her was wearing simple black ballet flats? Or did she really love black ballet flats?

Mr. Schweitzer clearly saw taking attendance as a total waste of time, and called the roll way too fast for Natalya to catch most of her classmates' names. Then he dimmed the lights and flashed a map on the whiteboard at the front of the room.

"Welcome," he announced, pausing dramatically and shining a red light at a spot on the map, "to ancient Troy!"

Natalya leaned forward slightly in her seat. In third grade, her class had spent almost the whole year studying Greek mythology. Was that why she'd always thought of Troy as a mythological place, like Atlantis or Narnia? Had her third-grade teacher even told them Troy was *real*?

Out of the darkness behind her, a disembodied voice called,

"My family went to Troy last summer. We chartered a boat and went to a bunch of Greek islands."

Natalya whipped her head around, but before she could identify the speaker, a girl across the room announced, "We did that for my parents' twentieth wedding anniversary. It was a total bummer. They have this really cheesy fake Trojan horse." In the dim light, Natalya could just discern the outline of a small girl wearing glasses.

"I thought it was cool," the girl sitting next to the girl with the glasses corrected. "All that history. You could totally *feel* it."

In less time than it took Natalya to remember her trips on a plane—two, both to Florida—half the students had shared their opinions on Troy. Then someone said she'd liked seeing the sphinx and the pyramids more than Troy. By the time they'd compared Cairo to Istanbul, Istanbul to Jerusalem, and Jerusalem to Beijing, Natalya was positive she was the only girl who hadn't uttered a word.

Natalya wanted to say something. She always participated in class discussions. But it wasn't like Mr. Schweitzer was asking questions about something they'd studied for homework.

When the bell rang, she realized she hadn't spoken a word except to say thank you when Mr. Schweitzer handed her a textbook.

The hallways were packed with girls, all of whom seemed to have about a thousand friends. Natalya tried not to feel weird for having no one to walk with, and focused instead on finding her next class. She was sure English would be an improvement over Greek. After all, it wasn't like people had to go on vacation to exotic locations to speak English. People spoke plenty of English right there in New York City.

Instead of having individual desks, her English classroom had an enormous round wooden table. Ms. MacFadden, who didn't look much older than her students, took attendance more slowly than Mr. Schweitzer, and Natalya was able to get most of her classmates' names—she'd never met a girl named Jordan or Parker; the Parker in her class at One Room had been a boy—before Ms. MacFadden tucked away the list and said, "I'm going to hand out *Othello* today, so—"

Before she could finish, a beautiful, dark-haired girl named Katrina, who was sitting two seats away from Natalya, said, "I totally saw that in the Park this summer."

"Oh, did you?" asked Ms. MacFadden eagerly. "What'd you think of the production?"

Katrina stretched her lightly tanned arms lazily out in front of her. A slim silver bracelet slid from her wrist almost to her elbow. "It was okay. Morgan's mom's on the board, so we had really good seats." At the word *Morgan*, Katrina gestured slightly at the girl sitting between her and Natalya. Morgan had been digging around in an enormous leather bag, but at the sound of her name, she looked up. Her blue eyes sparkled between thick lashes straight out of a Maybelline commercial.

Across the table, a girl named Amy leaned forward eagerly. "I saw you guys there. After. At the cocktail party." Amy turned to Ms. MacFadden. "There's a patron's cocktail party opening night. I was there."

Neither Katrina nor Morgan acknowledged Amy's comment

or said anything to Amy about having seen *her* at the party. It was as though she hadn't even spoken.

"That must have been just wonderful," said Ms. MacFadden, and Natalya could tell their teacher was impressed that three of her students had gone to a show and then had drinks with the actors. Ms. MacFadden smiled at Morgan, who gave the tiniest shrug in response, as if having cocktails with famous actors was so not a big deal that she couldn't see why Ms. MacFadden even cared.

"Well . . ." began Ms. MacFadden. "I guess it's time to hand out the play." She stood up and walked to the bookcase at the back of the room, then returned to the table.

Morgan pushed her bag to the floor between her chair and Natalya's, and Natalya checked the label, betting that it would say *Coach* or *Marc Jacobs*, which were the bags all the richest girls at One Room had.

But the label read *Juniper Bush* in blocky print letters.

The words meant nothing to her. As Ms. MacFadden handed each girl a copy of the play, Natalya found herself thinking of her dad again.

So far, it was all Greek to her, too.

Chapter Three

IN HER HOT pink sundress and green sandals, Jane had been sure she'd stand out at The Academy for the Performing Arts, but apparently everyone else in the freshman class had also dressed to be noticed. Even the bright red toenail polish she'd gotten at her mother-daughter pedicure on Friday wasn't particularly eye-catching. She practically needed sunglasses just to look around her math class, where boys in shrieking-neon jams were sitting next to girls in bright floral patterns who sported shimmery neck-laces and bangles that clanked together every time they raised their hands. As much as she would have liked to be unique, Jane got a contact high from the palpable energy in the hallways and classrooms, the sense that people in the building were channeling their artistic energy into their clothes until next week, when auditions for the school's dozens of productions would start.

After class, as Jane shoved her new math textbook into her bag, she felt a hand touch her lightly on the shoulder. "I love your dress."

Jane looked up. Sitting at the desk next to hers, a girl in canary yellow baggy overalls was staring at Jane.

"Thanks," said Jane.

As the girl nodded eagerly, her enormous glasses slid slightly down her nose. "It's so pretty. I love pink." She pushed her glasses more firmly against her face. "It's kind of the perfect color, don't you think? And it looks so good on you."

"Thanks," Jane repeated. It wasn't that getting a compliment was *bad*, but the girl's enthusiasm felt a little over the top. Jane stood up and slung her already heavy bag over her shoulder.

"I'm Laurie," said the girl, standing up also. "Isn't this so exciting?" She looked around the emptying room and shivered with pleasure. "I totally can't believe it. When I got my acceptance letter, I was like"—and she sang—"*Oh my god!*" Turning back to Jane, she explained in a normal voice, "I'm a singer. I mean, I've always sung with a chorus, but I never thought I'd be accepted *here*." She giggled excitedly. "Do you sing?"

Jane shook her head. "I'm an actress."

"*Oh my god*, that is so *amazing!*" Laurie literally jumped up and down twice, following Jane out the door of the classroom and into the crowded hallway. "What did you audition with? I was like, *freaking out* about my audition. After it was over I went home and cried. Do you want to have lunch together?"

Listening to Laurie talk was like drinking a third orange soda. Jane's teeth hurt.

"Actually, I was going to find out about this improv group I saw a sign for." Jane hadn't exactly planned to look into the improv group her first day, but she figured she might as well. She had time now, and she didn't think she could sit through an entire lunch with Laurie.

Laurie's eyes grew huge. "Oh. Wow. That is really cool. Only, can I tell you one thing?" She made her voice so low, Jane could barely hear what she said next. "Just so you know, this guy Mark told me that group totally sucks."

It took Jane a second to piece together what Laurie had whispered, but once the sentence registered, she was curious. "How does Mark know?" She stopped walking, and Laurie stopped too.

Laurie shook her head, her eyes still wide with amazement. Or maybe it was just the glasses. "I don't know, actually. But he's in my history class, and this morning we walked by one of those posters they have up, and he told me they're"—she paused to indicate she was quoting Mark—"'totally talentless.'"

Totally talentless. Could people at the Academy *be* totally talentless? Wasn't the whole point of the school that *no one* was totally talentless?

Who, exactly, was this Mark person?

Jane looked around: they were just a few steps from the open doors of the enormous, slightly run-down cafeteria.

Laurie glanced toward the doors and shuddered. "It's kind of freakazoid not to know anyone."

Jane looked across the room. Somewhere in the crowd she was facing were the people she'd have to beat out for lead roles, boys she'd be playing opposite for four years' worth of plays, girls who would be her fellow cast members and understudies. Without being conscious of doing it, she toyed with the slim chain of her necklace.

Did this Mark, another freshman, really already know about the Academy's talent pool? Jane was intrigued.

"Let's find Mark," she said.

Laurie's eyes opened even wider. "Oh my *god*. I mean, I think—he seemed like he knew a bunch of people already. He's probably sitting with them."

Jane nodded. Laurie's words were all the more reason to find him.

They'd barely made it halfway around the chaotic lunchroom when Laurie spotted Mark. He was sitting with two other guys, neither of whom Jane recognized from her classes. After pointing him out, Laurie hesitated to approach the table, but Jane made her way right over to it. *Do what you're afraid to do.*

"Mind if we join you?" she asked.

Laurie materialized at her shoulder. "Hey, Mark." She waved.

"Oh, hey," said one of the guys. His black hair was gathered in a low ponytail, and he wore a T-shirt that said MEAN PEOPLE SUCK. One of the boys sitting opposite him also had long hair, and the other had a mop of curls that hid his face except for his nose.

Jane pulled out a chair across from Mark. "I'm Jane." She liked the way he looked—scruffy but not *too* scruffy.

"Hey," the guys said.

Laurie sat down but didn't introduce herself.

"We want the scoop," Jane announced, looking at Mark. The words were uttered almost as a challenge.

Mark stared at her for a moment, then grinned a slow, knowing grin. "Oh, you do, do you?"

Jane met his stare, flirtatiously raising an eyebrow. "I do."

Looking around, Mark said, "All right, ladies, you've requested a tour of the significant players at The Academy for the Performing Arts. My name is Mark and I'll be your guide."

The curly-headed guy stood up. "Much as I'd love to stay and enjoy the sights, I gotta find Moshinksy and drop Lighting," he announced.

"I thought we couldn't drop classes until next week," said the other guy.

Curly shook his head. "Nah, he said if I find him today he'll deal."

Other Guy stood up. "Wait, I'm going with you." He waved at the table. "See you."

"Later," said Mark.

Mark was cute. Mark was funny. Mark hung out with guys who knew how to get special dispensation to drop classes.

Jane had hit the mother lode.

Still searching the room, Mark said, "Let's see. What have I got, what have I got?" He stroked his chin, then nodded and gestured to his right. "Our resident model, Michael Thomas."

"Model?" Laurie gasped. She and Jane looked in the direction Mark was pointing. The African American boy they found themselves staring at was wearing a tight white T-shirt that showed off his well-defined pectoral muscles. His face was nice, but it was nowhere near as perfect as his body, and Jane wondered what he modeled.

"Underwear," Mark answered her unasked question. "When he's not attending classes here at the Academy, Michael Thomas can be found wearing Calvin Klein underwear in a magazine near you."

"Wow." Laurie's voice was a near whisper.

Jane pushed her hair away from her face and stared at Mark. "That's what you've got for me? An *underwear* model?"

"Hey, give me a break here. I'm doing my best." Mark threw out his hands in a gesture of helplessness, then announced, "There! Julia Rappaport. She's *Meryl Streep's* cousin. By marriage." He pointed directly behind Jane, but she didn't bother to turn around. "What, you're not even going to *look?*"

Jane crossed her arms and cocked her head. She liked Mark's smile. "When you point out Meryl Streep, I'll look."

Mark rubbed his thumb over his lips as he searched the room. Suddenly he snapped his fingers. "Here's something for you. Fran Sherman, four o'clock. Fran Sherman is *the* biggest star at the Academy. Last year she played Adelaide in *Guys and Dolls* and Nora in *A Doll's House.*"

Jane whipped her head around. A tall pale girl with long reddish hair stood at what would have been four o'clock from where Mark was sitting.

"Hey, way to be subtle," Mark chastised her. Jane looked over her shoulder at him and winked, then looked back at the girl, who waved to someone and made her way to the other side of the room. She was very thin, wearing a pair of slightly loose jeans that only made her look thinner. The girl wasn't exactly beautiful, but there was something about her that made Jane think she would have noticed Fran Sherman even if Mark hadn't pointed her out. Fran moved as if she were crossing a stage, not the cafeteria. When she waved to someone outside Jane's line of vision, it was a dramatic wave, one that said hello not only to whomever Fran was waving at but to the room at large.

Jane watched until Fran sat down. Then she turned back to Mark.

Mark pointed a finger in Jane's direction. "Someone's got her eyes on the prize, doesn't she?"

Jane nodded. It was cool how he could see that about her. "Someone does."

Mark smiled a slow grin that took its time to spread across his face. "I respect that." He leaned back and crossed his arms over his chest. "Here's a little tidbit for you: Fran's the only student who ever got a role in a main-stage production as a freshman."

"What's a main-stage production?" Jane asked.

Mark chuckled. "Wow, you don't know anything, do you? Every year there are three main-stage productions—a fall drama, a spring musical, and a wild card."

"A wild card?" Laurie repeated. Jane had completely forgotten she was even there.

"Dance recital, opera . . . You guys planning on being drama majors?"

Laurie nibbled her lower lip. "I don't know."

"I'm going to be a drama major," Jane announced. She totally could *not* understand people like Laurie. How could you ever get anywhere by being *intimidated*?

Mark looked at Jane, a long, penetrating stare. "I think I get you."

Jane couldn't believe it. Lunch on her first day and she'd already met the cutest, coolest guy in the freshman class. She returned his stare with one of her own.

Oh, you've got me, all right.

Chapter Four

THE GOOD NEWS was nobody at Morningside said anything to her about her father's running for senator even though at the newsstand across the street from her house, Victoria passed a *Time* magazine with his picture on the cover and the headline, "Could Andrew Harrison Be Health Care's Only Hope?"

It wasn't like she was *ashamed* of her dad. She was proud of him. *Really* proud. But it was so weird how now that he was becoming famous, everyone Victoria met acted strangely—both starstruck and familiar. She'd told Jane and Natalya about the girl who'd asked for her autograph at the county fair, but she hadn't told them the whole story, how the girl had called her Vicky, then immediately apologized. "I'm so sorry, my mom read on your dad's Web site that you're going to be a freshman too." Her long brown hair fell to her butt and she was wearing a pink tube top and tight black pants. "I totally feel like I *know you*, you know? Like we could be friends. Oh my god, we should be friends. Are you on Facebook?" She clutched the piece of paper Victoria had signed to her chest as if it were something truly precious.

Victoria didn't know what to say. She didn't know this girl. She didn't feel like they were friends. And her dad's scary new campaign manager had warned her not to have *any* activity on her Facebook page until after the election. *Anything you do or say can and will be used against your father—even if to you it seems perfectly innocent.*

"Um, I don't really check Facebook that much," Victoria stammered, just as Ellen, whose job title was assistant or associate something, swept over and slipped her arm around Victoria's waist.

"I'm sorry, we need to go." Ellen smiled smoothly at the girl. "Thank you so much for your support."

The girl, still clutching the paper with Victoria's name scrawled across it, waved and called, "Bye, Vicky!"

Victoria realized she had no idea what the girl's name was. "Bye," she called simply, and then she and Ellen turned around and were swallowed up by a crowd of Andrew Harrison's supporters.

What if that happened at school? What if the kids at Morningside asked for her autograph or called her Vicky or wanted to be friends with her just because her dad was running for Senate?

And what if, as the campaign manager had warned, anything she did or said was used against her father?

To Victoria's relief, no one at Morningside seemed remotely interested in getting her autograph. Actually, her dad was the least of her problems. Victoria's first- and second-period teachers asked not if she was Andrew Harrison's daughter, but if she was Emily Harrison's sister. Both times she said yes, and the teachers got special smiles on their faces. The smiles said, *I'm so lucky. I know I have at least one outgoing, articulate, engaged student in my class this year.*

Victoria gave them her own special smile in return. Her smile said, *No, you don't.*

Emily was now a freshman at Princeton. Victoria, having followed her sister all through One Room, knew how bad the first month of class was going to be. When Nana had died, Jane's mother had taught the girls about the five stages of dealing with death: denial, anger, bargaining, depression, acceptance.

That trajectory perfectly described how teachers who had once taught Exemplary Emily Harrison responded to having Average Victoria in their class.

Except for her teachers asking if Victoria was Emily's sister, everyone else pretty much ignored her. Was it her imagination or did all the other freshmen already have a friend? People sat down strangers, something magical happened that Victoria could neither see nor hear, and they walked out of the class practically holding hands.

Twice Victoria opened her mouth to talk to people, but then

she shut it before saying anything. Every sentence she formulated in her mind sounded too stupid and obvious to utter.

How's it going?

Oh, you're in this class too?

So, high school. Wow.

She had just given up on anyone talking to her when Chloe, a redheaded girl who sat next to her in English, turned toward her after the bell rang and asked, "You want to get lunch at Rick's, that place across the street?" Victoria was in such a state of shock that her "Okay, sure" sounded less desperately grateful (which she was) and more blasé (which she wasn't).

"Great," said Chloe. She shoved *The Catcher in the Rye* into her bag and flipped it shut. "See you there."

It was as if Victoria had won the lottery. She sat in her chair for a minute, trying to make sense of her amazing luck.

Her next and last class before lunch was History, where her teacher introduced himself by saying, "This is my first year at Morningside too, so we are *all* freshmen in a way."

Okay, she was definitely experiencing some kind of miracle: someone to eat lunch with *and* a teacher who hadn't taught her sister.

More relaxed than she'd been since lunch at Ga Ga Noodle yesterday, Victoria glanced around the room, checking out the kids as Mr. Mazetti called their names. Michael Bronner, Alissa Confessore, Sean Hamil. From what she'd seen so far, she'd picked a good first-day outfit. In her pale yellow T-shirt and cropped blue pants, she looked like most of the other girls.

"Victoria Harrison?"

She gave Mr. Mazetti a smile and raised her hand slightly. He continued to look at her, almost like he knew her from somewhere, then checked his class list and ever so slightly straightened his already straight tie. "Are you by any chance related to Andrew Harrison?"

Victoria's heart sank, and for a second she considered lying. *Andrew Harrison? Who is that?*

"Um, he's my dad."

A few kids shifted in their seats. Was she imagining it, or was Alissa Confessore glaring in her direction? She imagined Alissa's parents listening to Rush Limbaugh or one of the other conservatives who hated her father.

Mr. Mazetti smiled so broadly it was amazing his face didn't split in two. "Very exciting."

"Mmmmm," she agreed. By then everyone in the class was staring at her. If she'd been Emily Harrison instead of Victoria Harrison, she would have parlayed their curiosity into the presidency of the debate club, a dozen invitations to hang out after school, a boyfriend, the dean's list. But she wasn't Emily Harrison. She was Victoria Harrison, and all she was doing was smiling an awkward please-stop-looking-at-me smile.

Her fingers fluttered up to her necklace, and she slid the pearl up and down the chain, finding comfort in the gentle *zzziiipp* it made as it moved.

Victoria almost ran out of History and across the street to Rick's. The small space was already crowded with Morningside students. At first she didn't see Chloe, but then someone called her name, and a second later, she spotted her. "Come!" Chloe mouthed, beckoning.

"The wraps are awesome," she said as Victoria reached her side. "I live like, two blocks away, so I'm here pretty much every day. This is Grace, by the way." A tall girl with braces and black hair in neat braids gave a little wave, and Victoria said hi, then looked up at the wrap menu printed above the counter. There must have been a hundred different options. Chloe ordered the Al Capone, while Grace and Victoria chose the Carol Channing. Victoria recognized the names but couldn't see how Al Capone equaled roast beef or Carol Channing, Swiss cheese. As the three of them paid for their sandwiches and made their way back to school, talking about what classes they had, Victoria couldn't believe how lucky she was to have found the only people at Morningside who weren't obsessed with a member of her family.

"These tables are so cute," Grace observed, sitting down at one of the café-style tables sprinkled among the bigger, more traditional cafeteria tables.

"Totally," Victoria agreed, unwrapping her sandwich.

Chloe glanced at the table, shook her head in amazement, then announced, "Can I just say that my dad is *going to freak out* that we're friends. My parents are really into your dad's campaign. They'll want to come to an election night party. JK!" she added quickly. She smiled at Victoria and took a bite of her wrap, as Victoria felt her chair seem to drop out from under her. Was that why Chloe had wanted to have lunch with her—because Chloe's parents were Andrew Harrison supporters?

"Oh," Victoria managed to say. "That's . . . yeah."

They were the last words she uttered for the rest of the lunch, but Grace and Chloe didn't seem to notice her silence any more than they noticed that when the bell had rung, Victoria's uneaten wrap was still sitting on the table in front of her.

Standing at her open locker, the metal door shielding her from the rest of the world, Victoria closed her eyes and took a deep breath. Her stomach growled and she was going to be late for her next class. Perfect. Just perfect. She dug around in her bag for her phone to text Natalya and Jane what had happened. Jane would definitely have the perfect comeback for her to use next time that Chloe girl talked to her.

As her fingers found her phone, she heard the sound she'd come to dread more than any other these past few months.

It was the snap of a picture being taken.

She spun around. A few feet down the hallway, a boy she thought she recognized from Biology class had a camera aimed at her.

Nooo!

Was this what the rest of her year was going to be like?

Was this what the rest of her *life* was going to be like?

"Wait, what is that?" she cried, taking two giant steps toward him.

The boy slowly lowered the camera. His shaggy brown hair fell across his forehead, and he pushed it out of his eyes. "Um, it's a camera." He held it up for her to see. "Are you not familiar with this piece of equipment? Because if you're worried about my stealing your soul—"

"I can't—I mean, you have to . . . You're taking a picture of *me*."

The boy paused for a minute, considering her fairly obvious observation. "Okay, I can see how it would be a little creepy to turn around and see some guy snapping your picture. I'll start over." He pointed at himself. "I'm Jack, and it's my job to take as many photos as possible in the next"—he checked his watch—"three hours. *The Scoop*'s running a photomontage of the first day for the back-to-school issue. And don't worry. You're totally photogenic. Which you probably know already." He spun the viewfinder toward Victoria, pushed a button, and showed her a photo of herself standing at her locker.

Was he telling the truth? Was this picture really just for *The Scoop*? She took her eyes off the camera and squinted at Jack. He was wearing a faded blue T-shirt and a pair of cargo pants. With his easy smile and scuffed sneakers, he didn't exactly look like a political operative. Still. "I want you to delete it. Please," she added at the last second.

He wrinkled his forehead at her, confused. "Okay." He paused. "Um, can I ask why?"

What could she say?

Because this girl I thought wanted to be my friend doesn't.

Because everyone in my family is more important than I am.

Because Natalya and Jane are really far away.

Brilliant, Vicks. While you're at it, you can bulk order some World's Biggest Loser shirts.

When she didn't answer him, Jack said, "Is this the part where I tell you that it's a totally good shot and you look awesome so you—"

"You think I'm being *vain*?" Victoria stamped her foot in frustration. Jack looked at her like she might possibly be insane, and Victoria had the feeling he wasn't wrong. "Look, just delete it, okay?"

He stared at her for a long minute. Finally, he turned the camera toward himself, pushed a button, then turned the view-finder back to Victoria. The picture of her had been replaced by one of a guy with a bright neon backpack leaping the last two steps of the main stairs.

"Happy?" he asked.

"I . . ." Was she happy? Mostly she just felt stupid. "Yeah, thanks," she muttered. And then she sped down the hall as quickly as she could.

Chapter
Five

QV210024: It only sounds OK bc u weren't there. Trust me. I acted INSANE. I should have just let him keep the stupid picture.

RUSKIGIRLNAT: U did the right thing.

ASTARIZBORNJS: Was he cute?

QV210024: IDK

ASTARIZBORNJS: UDK?!?! If UDK, that means he wasn't.

QV210024: Was it weird being @ school w/o any guys?

RUSKIGIRLNAT: I didn't notice. Do U know what, tho? There were limos lined up outside after school. No joke.

ASTARIZBORNJS: When IM rich & famous, I'll buy us 3 limos.

RUSKIGIRLNAT: I NEED limo. I've got a sick blister. I should have worn socks.

QV210024: I've got vocab quiz *and* history paper. And guy who thinks IM insane. High school sucks.

ASTARIZBORNJS: U R *all wrong*. Think. I've got friend & crush. Do u know what that means?

RUSKIGIRLNAT: U R ditching us?

QV210024: We R even lamer than we thought?

ASTARIZBORNJS: AS IF, DARLINGS! It means there is hope.

Chapter Six

RIGHT AWAY, Natalya could tell that Biology was different.

First of all, everyone filed in silently. Second of all, nobody looked happy to be there. And not just because it was the first class of the day.

"Is Dr. Clover a man or a woman?" Natalya whispered to the girl who had taken the other seat at her lab table.

The girl had the shortest ponytail Natalya had ever seen. "Neither," she said.

Neither? There was no such thing as neither.

Natalya leaned toward the girl. "Neither?" she repeated. "You mean literally?"

The girl laughed briefly and whispered, "I guess she's literally a woman, but—" A noise at the back of the room made both girls turn in that direction.

A woman who couldn't have been more than four and a half feet tall was coming through the glass door. She was wearing a white lab coat and thick, ugly plastic glasses. Her black hair looked greasy, and it hugged her scalp in an unflattering bowl shape.

She half walked, half marched to a wooden podium at the front of the room. Centering herself behind it, she placed a roll book on top and began speaking, addressing the class list in front of her rather than the actual class. "Welcome to Biology. We meet three times a week, twice for a double lab period. Each class will begin with a quiz on the previous night's reading. If you are late, you will get a zero on the quiz, which will be factored into your average." Dr. Clover raised her eyes and looked around the room. "These quizzes, plus weekly lab reports and unit exams, will equal fifty percent of your grade. Another twenty-five percent will be other homework and class participation. Finally, you will write a term paper on a topical scientific issue, and this paper will be the final twenty-five percent of your grade. Are there any questions?"

Nobody had any questions.

"Good. Let us begin. Tell me"—Dr. Clover surveyed the room—"what is biology?"

"Um, torture?" someone whispered, and a few girls on the other side of the room, including Amy, the girl from Natalya's English class, giggled. Dr. Clover did not respond; she simply stared at the girls.

Natalya raised her hand.

"Yes?" Dr. Clover looked at her. "Please state your name."

"I'm Natalya." It was a little intense to announce herself like that, but Natalya focused on the question. "It's the study of life."

Dr. Clover appeared unimpressed. "And what is life?"

It took a moment for Natalya to realize the question was directed not at the class in general but at her. "Well . . ." She'd never thought about this exact question before. "Living things are born."

"What else?" asked Dr. Clover, her face completely expressionless.

Natalya waited to see if someone else would step in to answer. When no one else volunteered, she added, "They eat."

Dr. Clover nodded briefly. "And?" she continued.

"They grow." Natalya glanced around the room. People were looking at her, but still nobody said a word or raised her hand.

"And?"

Was Dr. Clover waiting for her to give the right answer? Was everything she'd said so far wrong?

Natalya tried to picture living things from different categories. Her mother's plants. Her brother's fish.

Remembering what had happened to Chekhov the goldfish right before they'd flushed him down the toilet, Natalya added, "They die."

"And what do they do between being born and dying?" asked Dr. Clover. "For example, if you eat, what else must you do?"

Natalya felt simultaneously excited and nervous. It was like Dr. Clover was giving her a test.

"They excrete," Natalya said. Her word generated a giggle from several girls, and Natalya forced herself not to make eye contact with anyone but her teacher.

Dr. Clover responded simply, "And . . ."

Well, she'd spoken the word *excrete* out loud. What did she have to lose?

"They reproduce," said Natalya. Her voice was firm, as if there was nothing embarrassing about what she'd just said. "Sometimes," she added quickly, finding it hard to imagine a *Mr.* Clover with whom Dr. Clover was reproducing.

This time Dr. Clover didn't say *and*. Instead, she said simply, "Thank you, Natalya." She looked around the classroom. "I see none of you has a pencil or pen out, which is truly a shame, as Natalya has just given us an excellent working definition of life." There was the sound of fifteen girls scrambling to get pens out of their bags. Dr. Clover walked to the board and began writing the words Natalya had spoken. At *grow*, she turned to face the class. "In the future, I suggest you all take notes the *first* time we discuss something in this class."

When the bell rang, Dr. Clover assigned the homework, then marched back to her office. The girl who'd been sitting at Natalya's table gave a dramatic exhalation.

"You were awesome. I can't *believe* you survived that. I'm Jordan, by the way."

"Oh," said Natalya. "Thanks." As they packed their bags, then fell into step heading toward the lunchroom, she didn't add that being questioned by Dr. Clover had been the best thing that had happened to her in a class since she'd been at One Room.

Question. Answer.

She could work with that.

Chapter
Seven

"VICTORIA?"

Ms. Kalman was standing with her back to the board, her right arm extended and her hand pointing to something she had clearly drawn, while Victoria's mind was elsewhere. She'd been thinking about how there were exactly two months until the election. Two months until her life went back to normal.

Or didn't.

"Ummm . . ." Victoria contemplated the blackboard. Had that blobby thing with the little hairs sticking out of it been up there before?

"We were talking about paramecia," Ms. Kalman explained.

She had a confused this-isn't-how-Emily-would-act look on her face.

Ms. Kalman was clearly deep in the denial stage of teaching Victoria.

Victoria wondered what it would be like if she went to a school from which her superstar sister *hadn't* just graduated. Would she magically find herself comfortable talking in class? Would she speak less than she did now? Could a person speak less than Victoria did now and still be considered *alive*?

When Victoria remained silent, Ms. Kalman continued. "I was asking if you remembered from last night's reading how they reproduce."

Okay, why was her teacher asking her a question about reproduction? Was it because her dad was running for Senate? Was this really a question about *abortion*? Or, wait, that was completely paranoid. No one cared who her dad was. Except her history teacher. And Chloe's parents.

Victoria's eyes darted around desperately, as if the answer might be printed on one of the walls of the bio lab. She was sitting at a table near the back of the room, and people had turned around in their seats to look at her. One girl stopped staring long enough to write something on a slip of paper and slide it to her lab partner—Victoria was so not being paranoid when she imagined it said, *Is Victoria Harrison stupid or what?*

Her father's campaign manager's words came back to her. *Remember, Victoria, anything you say or do will be held against your father.*

How about what she *didn't* say?

At the front of the room, expertly twirling his pencil, sat Jack, the guy with the camera from yesterday. As she looked at him, desperately trying to remember how paramecium reproduced, Victoria remembered Jane's question.

Is he cute?

She hadn't had an answer then, but she had one now. Jack was cute. Jack was *very* cute. The eyes that were staring into hers were a deep, dark gray. His skin was pale with a hint of pink at the cheeks, like even though it was September and a million degrees out, he'd somehow just come in from the cold. He was wearing a short-sleeved brown T-shirt, and his shoulders were broad and defined. Could he be a swimmer? His hair wasn't long exactly, but it was slightly tousled. That was the word for it. *Tousled.* With those shoulders and that hair, Jack wasn't just cute. He was sexy.

Jack is sexy, Victoria thought, and as the sentence ran across her brain, like one of those advertisements that planes pull across the sky, the answer to Ms. Kalman's question came to her.

"Asexually!" she blurted out. "They reproduce asexually." Only after she'd said the words did Victoria realize she was still staring deeply into Jack's eyes.

"Excellent!" said Ms. Kalman, turning to write the word on the board.

Jack held Victoria's look for a long beat; the corner of his mouth turned up. And then, slowly and silently, he clapped for her.

When she got home, Victoria was shocked to hear her dad call out, "Hi, honey! We're in the office!"

"Hi," she yelled back. Lately she and her parents texted and left each other voice mails more than they actually saw one another. Yesterday, the first day of school, she'd come home to an empty apartment.

She walked through the living room, nearly falling over one of the baskets of fruit that arrived at the campaign office or the apartment nearly daily. Every lobbyist in the state was interested in her father's campaign, and the law forbade their spending more than a certain amount on gifts. Since this was about the fiftieth identical basket they'd received from a place called Harry & David, Victoria had the feeling it cost exactly whatever it was people were allowed to spend.

Her dad's "office" was a small alcove off the living room that they'd put a sliding door on a few years ago. It was just big enough for his desk, where he was standing, and a chair, which her mom was in, one leg thrown over the arm. In the very few feet of available floor space, campaign literature was piled high— pictures of her dad smiling out at her from familiar, dark green borders.

Her mom reached an arm up, and Victoria bent down to embrace her. "We're playing hooky," she whispered. "Everyone thinks we're sick." She made her voice mock stern. "But don't you tell lies. Do as we preach, not as we do." Victoria laughed and hugged her. She hadn't seen her mother in jeans and a ponytail since May; it was good to see her dressed like this instead of in the suits she wore to campaign events.

Without taking his eyes off the screen of his computer, Victoria's father gestured for her to come to him. She did, and he put his arm around her waist and gave her a squeeze. She looked at the page he was reading: . . . *good are life, liberty, and the pursuit of happiness without health, the unspoken assumption on which all quests rely?*

"That's great," she said, coming to the end of the sentence. She stepped back to her mom's chair and sat down on the free arm. "Did you write that?"

Still reading, her father shook his head. "I haven't gotten to write a speech of my own in about twelve weeks. Now that I might win, nobody trusts me to speak for myself." He cocked his head to consider what he'd just said. "What a strange country we live in."

"How was school today?" her mom asked, stroking Victoria's arm.

"It was okay."

Her dad ran his hand through his salt-and-pepper hair. "This is . . . I can't see myself saying half of this."

Sometimes Victoria got the feeling that her parents were a little afraid of the campaign staff. Before, when her dad had been a nobody, and her family and all their friends had spent weekends standing on street corners with petitions until they'd finally managed to get the thousands of signatures he'd needed to be on the ballot, the campaign had seemed really fun. But ever since Congressman Dowers had left politics to "devote" himself to his family (instead of their au pair), Victoria's dad's campaign had been staffed by professionals, people who had worked for Obama, Clinton (Hillary *and* Bill), people who knew a million times more about politics and running for office than her parents or the friends who'd staffed the campaign before. Lately she'd noticed that if Steven, the campaign manager, thought something should be done, it got done. *Steven thought it would be a good idea* was a refrain Victoria had heard a lot in the past three months. *Steven thought it would be a good idea if you'd come campaigning with us. Steven thought it would be a good idea to let some press come down to Princeton when we drop Emily off. Steven thought it would be a good idea if you wore a dress instead of shorts.*

She'd started substituting *Satan* whenever she heard his name.

"So," said her dad, slapping his thighs with his hands and stepping back slightly from his computer to stare at Victoria, "does everyone at that school of yours know how wonderful you are yet?"

Victoria thought of how she'd practically cried in front of Jack yesterday, then stared at him and half shouted *"ASEXU- ALLY"* right in his face today. Not to mention Chloe and her *"JK!"* Oh, and the girl who'd passed a note to her friend in bio that probably said how stupid Victoria was. "Um . . . not exactly."

"They will," her dad assured her. He gave her a warm smile. "You're the nicest Harrison. It's not even a contest."

"Thanks." Victoria tried to return his smile. She knew her dad meant what he was saying as a compliment, but she couldn't help thinking he called her "nice" because Emily had already taken all the good adjectives like *driven* and *talented.*

He stood up and raised an eyebrow at her. "Feel like baking something?"

"Seriously?" People who knew that Victoria liked to bake always assumed her mother had taught her, but it was actually her father who was the cook in the family. He said making a complicated recipe was the only way he could shut his brain down and relax after a hard day of work. Her mom, on the other hand, despite being a tenured professor at Columbia Law School, couldn't boil water without taking antianxiety medication.

Her mother clapped once. "Yes! I vote for you two baking something. If you bake dessert, I volunteer to clean up. And I'll order dinner."

"Are you sure, honey?" her dad teased. "You can handle ordering?" He leaned down to kiss his wife, who kissed him back, then gave him a mock salute.

"Aye, aye, captain. I'm on it."

Victoria followed her dad through the living room. "What are we making?" Before he'd entered the Senate race, Victoria and her dad had made a dessert together at least once a week—they took turns finding evermore elaborate recipes for cakes, pies, tarts, cookies, sometimes even savory foods like quiches or cheese soufflés. Now, as they walked to the kitchen, Victoria tried to remember the last time she and her dad had baked together.

They stood side by side and looked around the room. Clearly the fruit basket she'd nearly tripped over wasn't the only one that had been delivered since she'd left for school this morning.

"Um, how about something with fruit?" he suggested.

"Sounds like a plan," she agreed. And as they circled the kitchen, gathering the necessary ingredients and supplies, debating which recipe for peach tart was their favorite, Victoria could practically feel memories of Chloe and Jack and asexual paramecium fading away.

Chapter Eight

MARK WAS NO longer Jane's crush.

In fact, Jane hated him.

He talked to Jane and Laurie as though he knew everyone and everything worth knowing at the Academy, but the only person he knew who wasn't a clueless freshman like the rest of them was some random sophomore in his set design elective, a guy who'd gone to Mark's junior high. Though Mark repeated what he heard from this person as if it were highly classified information that he'd received from multiple high-level sources, careful questioning on Jane's part slowly revealed his "sources" were really just *a* source. Singular.

Then there was the way he dressed. His Vans, hooded sweatshirts, and ponytail made him appear to be a skater punk, but Mark didn't seem to own a skateboard. And he was completely uptight, nothing like the laid-back skater dudes at her old school. As far as Jane could tell, Mark had read an article: "How to Dress Like a Hipster Skater Punk—Without Actually Being One."

"What are you going to audition for?" asked Laurie as the three of them sat at lunch on Friday.

"Not sure yet," answered Jane. She didn't exactly hate Laurie, but she was tired of her relentless enthusiasm. She had more pep than a cheerleading squad.

Laurie's eyes bulged with excitement. "What if we all try out together? It would be so fun to be cast in the same show, don't you think? Does either of you sing?"

Mark leaned forward and gave Laurie and Jane a significant look, like he had a major secret to share, one they were doubtless dying to hear. Laurie bent her head across the table toward him, but Jane stayed where she was as Mark whispered, sotto voce, "Okay, don't freak out on me, but I'm thinking of trying out for *Midsummer.*"

Laurie gasped. Jane felt the blood rush from her head. *Midsummer.* The fall drama.

Though she'd been at the school less than a week, Jane knew there were dozens of upcoming auditions at the Academy—for dance performances, for student-directed plays, for video productions. It was, after all, The Academy for the Performing Arts, and the hallways were already wallpapered with flyers offering students a chance to try out in the coming weeks.

Most of the shows were small ones: they'd have tiny casts and crews and would be held in one of several black-box or other little theaters in the building. But the fall drama and the musical were both directed by the head of the theater department, Mr. Robbins, and staged in the school's only proscenium auditorium, which had a capacity of almost a thousand people.

This year's fall drama was *A Midsummer Night's Dream*.

"Oh my god," squealed Laurie. "I can't believe you're going to try out for *Midsummer*, Mark. That's like, the bravest." She turned to Jane. "Can you imagine? I didn't even know freshman *could* audition for the main-stage productions. Or, wait, you said Fran Sherman got a part when she was a freshman, so I guess I did know."

Mark shrugged, trying and failing to hide a grin.

If only he'd acknowledged the hugeness of what he was doing; if only he'd said, *I know, isn't it crazy!* or *I'm totally freaking out*, Jane could have been happy for him. As it was, his feigned nonchalance felt condescending, like to Mark, Jane and Laurie were just a couple of starstruck freshmen who couldn't understand the decisions made by *real* stars.

"That's just the kind of guy I am," Mark explained. "I'm not afraid to put myself out there." He gave them both a vaguely stern look. "And you shouldn't be either. Anyway, it's no big deal. I'm sure I won't get a big part. Not one of the lovers, for example."

Despite her irritation with him, Jane had to make herself not giggle when Mark said the word *lovers*. She'd read *A Midsummer Night's Dream* in eighth-grade English, and she thought of Hermia and Helena and Lysander and Demetrius as *couples*, not lovers. But clearly that was babyish.

"Who do you think will be cast as the, um, lovers?" The way Laurie pushed her glasses up on her nose and hesitated over the word made Jane pretty sure she, too, was using it for the first time.

"Well, Fran Sherman, obviously," said Mark.

"Obviously," echoed Jane.

Mark, who had missed the sarcasm in her voice, leaned back in his chair and took a bite of the chocolate chip cookie that was his lunch. "Len, like, loves her."

"Len?" Jane had never heard of Mr. Len. Was he the assistant to Mr. Robbins, the director?

For a second, Mark had the good grace to look uncomfortable. "Leonard Robbins," he explained. "He directs the dramas. But everyone in the plays calls him Len. Or, I mean, he tells you that if you get in." Jane tried to get a mental picture of Leonard Robbins—the old-fashioned name made her picture someone gray-haired and dignified, maybe with a cane and an ascot.

Mark hurriedly took another bite of his cookie and looked around. "Don't tell anyone I told you this, but I happen to know that he chose the play because Fran wants to be Helena." He pursed his lips together. "I probably shouldn't have said anything. I hope I can trust you."

The only thing Jane hated more than not knowing the inside scoop was being condescended to by someone who claimed *he* knew the inside scoop.

"Oh, please," she snorted. How could she have had a crush on this guy? What had she possibly been *thinking*?

"What?" Mark shot back.

"Just . . . if you're going to audition, fine, but don't be all"—she gestured in a way that was meant to convey the totality of his idiocy—"you know about it."

Mark gave Laurie a look like, *Can you believe her?*

Laurie studied the table.

"Well, whatever," said Mark, giving a tense laugh. "I think if you were brave enough to audition for a main-stage production, you'd be talking about it too."

Do what you're afraid to do.

Jane stood up. "As a matter of fact, I *am* going to audition for the main-stage production. I'm just not making a major deal out of it."

The look Laurie gave Jane was one of sheer amazement. "You are?!"

Mark's look was significantly less excited, but he couldn't completely hide how impressed he was. "Okay, well, that's great."

"Yeah," Jane said. She suddenly felt light-headed, as if there weren't enough oxygen in the room. "Well, actually, I have to go."

"See you," said Laurie.

Mark didn't say good-bye to Jane, and Jane didn't say good-bye to Mark. Would they ever sit together at lunch again? Jane highly doubted it.

Jane's mom had texted her before she left work, and they'd agreed to meet at the restaurant right across the street from their Greenwich Village apartment building. Panne e Vino was the kind of neighborhood place where the maître d' remembered your name and said "Good evening," as though your walking into his restaurant was the best thing that had happened to him all day.

When Jane told people her parents were divorced, they always responded as if it were a bad thing, and when they learned her parents were divorced *and* she was an only child, they acted as if she were some kind of ward of the state.

But as far as Jane was concerned, being the only child of a divorced couple was the best. She loved flying out to LA by herself to go visit her dad. She loved meeting her mom for dinner, like they were friends, not mother and daughter. Natalya and Victoria talked about their parents as Their Parents—people who made decisions based on information their children had no access to. They didn't mind, either—Natalya and Victoria were okay with sitting at the kids' table.

But Jane liked sitting with the grown-ups.

Her mother had been listening to Jane's story about Mark since she'd arrived, and now Jane was almost done. "So I signed up for a Tuesday audition slot," she finished. "Needless to say, Mark's name was *nowhere* on the list." As she finished telling her mother what had happened, Jane ripped at a piece of bread as if it were something Mark valued that she was destroying.

Her mom danced her long, elegant fingers through the bread basket, finally settling on a sesame bread stick. "Well, I guess you should thank Mark if you get a part." She took a bite. "If he hadn't irritated you so much, you might not have gotten the idea to audition."

Jane snorted. "Yeah, I can see that conversation now: *'Hey, Mark, thanks for being so totally full of it. If you hadn't lied about planning to audition, I never would have put myself out there!'"* She had a sudden realization. "Nana would have *hated* him."

The waiter arrived with their drinks—a bottle of sparkling water for the table and a glass of red wine for Jane's mom.

Her mother pushed her black, fashionably short hair off her face, then picked up her wineglass. "Oh, I don't know. I think Nana was pretty understanding in some ways."

Sometimes Jane felt as if her mother hadn't known Nana at all, even though they'd been mother and daughter. "Mom, you don't understand, Nana *hated* cowards. She believed in facing your fears."

Her mother laughed and sipped at her drink. "Jane, Nana had a lot of sympathy for all different kinds of people. Don't turn her into Lady Macbeth, okay?"

Touching the pearl at her throat, Jane knew her mother was wrong. Nana *would* have loathed Mark, she was sure of it.

Still, her mother's reference to Lady Macbeth gave her an idea, and for the rest of their dinner it percolated in the back of her mind.

Chapter Nine

THE PEOPLE-WATCHING THAT Natalya did on the subway was nothing compared to the people-watching she did at Gainsford. It was as if she were an anthropologist and her classmates were a mysterious tribe she traveled to the Upper East Side to study.

Her favorite place to observe her fellow students was the lunchroom; with its black-and-white marble floor, its tall chairs and heavy wooden tables, the room was without a doubt the most elegant place she'd ever eaten a meal. Sitting there watching her peers, it didn't take long for her to see that the girls weren't nearly as similar as they first appeared—tiny variations in their uniforms indicated enormous differences between them. There were the bags, for example. A few girls carried regular nylon backpacks, the kind most of the kids at One Room had, the kind Natalya still used. These seemed to be the girls who stayed after school for sports—familiar games, like soccer, and other games that were completely foreign-sounding. Hearing announcements about lacrosse and field hockey, Natalya felt as if she were in New Delhi or Oxford, not Manhattan. She wouldn't have been surprised to see a cricket match schedule. Or Quidditch, for that matter.

Other girls had actual leather briefcases. These girls were always pulling flyers out of their bags and tacking them up in the stairwells. *Check out Model UN!* and *Robotics Club Meets Thursday in Room 4-3.* They consulted tiny, laminated copies of their schedules, and hung out exclusively with each other. The artsy girls carried bags made of fabrics that had probably originated in Africa or Latin America—brightly colored cottons that clashed in an on-purpose way with the plaid of their skirts.

Natalya had had lunch with Jordan every single day since their exchange in the bio lab, and she wondered if part of the reason Jordan and her friends seemed so familiar was because they all carried the same nylon backpacks as she did.

"I can't believe you got the mac and cheese," said Catherine, who had long brown hair and played on the soccer team with Jordan.

It was Wednesday, and Natalya had been psyched to see that they were serving elbow macaroni and cheese—one of her favorite meals.

"Don't worry, I know CPR," Jordan assured her.

Natalya swallowed the bite on her fork. It tasted fine to her, but she looked around and saw that all the other girls were eating sandwiches they'd made from the cold-food bar.

"The hot food's always super lame, but the mac and cheese is the worst," explained Perry, another teammate of Jordan's.

"Sorry. I should have warned you," Jordan apologized.

"Oh, that's okay," said Natalya. "It's actually not so bad. I kind of like it."

Jordan, Catherine, and Perry all looked surprised, but before they could respond, Perry whispered, "Oh god, here comes Her Majesty."

Natalya looked up. Walking down the center aisle was Morgan Prewitt, flanked by Katrina Worthington and a girl Natalya hadn't seen before. The three looked like models in a photo shoot. Morgan's long wavy blond hair was up in a loose ponytail, and Katrina's dark, equally perfect hair framed her pale face. Did these girls have stylists or something? Even their uniforms, which were technically comprised of the same skirt and blouse every other girl at Gainsford was wearing, looked nothing like the other uniforms. Their white shirts were chicly rumpled, their shoes grown-up and sexy without violating the no-heels, no-open-toes rule. The third girl's hair was strawberry blond, almost but not quite red, and it gleamed as if she had her own personal ray of sunshine following her.

"Morgan and Katrina are in my English class," Natalya said when the girls had passed. "They went to a really fancy party with some actors this summer."

"Let me guess." Jordan pretended to consult a crystal ball, then closed her eyes and pressed her index fingers to her temples. "I see that one of their moms is on the board of The Public Theater."

Natalya could not have been more amazed if Jordan had turned her sandwich into a bird and set it free to fly around the high ceiling of the cafeteria. "How did you know?"

"Please." Perry rolled her baby blue eyes. "Their moms are like, on the boards of everything in New York."

"They pretty much run the city," Jordan continued. Then she gave Natalya a significant look and said, "Morgan?"

Natalya had no idea what Jordan was getting at. "Okay, you lost me."

"Morgan," Catherine prompted. "Like, J. P. Morgan."

"Like the Morgan Library," Jordan continued.

"Sloane Gainsford," added Perry. She gestured meaningfully around the room. "As in the school we are currently attending. Her like, great-great-great-something started it."

"And if you go to pretty much any museum in New York, you'll find the Worthington Wing," added Jordan. "Just so you don't, you know, feel bad for Katrina or anything."

"Morgan Prewitt, Katrina Worthington, and Sloane Gainsford," said Catherine, her voice low and deep, like a radio announcer's. "They don't just *act* like they own New York."

"They do!" Jordan, Catherine, and Perry finished together. Then the three of them collapsed in laughter.

Natalya watched Morgan, Katrina, and Sloane as they disappeared into the crowd around the salad bar. Morgan was related to *J. P. Morgan*? They'd studied J. P. Morgan in fifth grade, when they did New York City history. He was a robber baron. Or was he a steel magnate? Or was it railroads? She couldn't remember; he got confused with Rockefeller and Vanderbilt in her mind. Still, J. P. Morgan had been in their *history* book. And someone related to that girl Sloane had *founded* Natalya's school. That meant . . .

Natalya stared around the table. "Her family must have lived here," she informed them. "When it was a *house*."

"I never thought about that." Catherine surveyed the palatial room.

Jordan did the same, then arched an eyebrow at her friends. "Well, for their sake, I sure hope the food was better back then."

"*Totally*," agreed Natalya, and this time she joined Catherine, Perry, and Jordan when they laughed.

Natalya had English class right after lunch today. Morgan was sitting next to her again, with Katrina on Morgan's other side, and Natalya found herself watching them, trying to see if there was a way she could have guessed how rich and powerful the girls' families were if Jordan hadn't told her. Where she lived, in Brighton Beach, people with a lot of money practically dripped diamonds, and even at One Room the rich students had way nicer stuff than the other kids—iPhones and Marc Jacobs bags and J Brand jeans. But except for Katrina's plain bracelet, the only jewelry she and Morgan were wearing were simple earrings—Katrina's were silver balls and Morgan's were tiny silver knots. And they both had really ugly bags, big satchels in colors that were just a shade away from a nice color—Katrina's near purple, Morgan's near red. They looked like purses the old Russian ladies in Natayla's neighborhood would carry.

As Natalya watched, Morgan whispered something to Katrina, who shook her head. A second later, Morgan turned to Natalya. "Do you have an extra pencil I can borrow?"

Natalya felt hot and cold at the same time, and instead of responding to Morgan's question, she just stared at her. Morgan was practically a celebrity. More than a celebrity. She was *history*.

When Natalya didn't respond, Morgan held up her mechanical pencil and shook it ever so slightly, as if pantomiming to a non-English speaker what "empty" meant.

"Do you have an extra pencil?" Morgan repeated.

Natalya snapped out of her trance and flipped to the pencil case at the front of her binder. "Oh, yeah, sure. Here you go."

"Thanks," Morgan whispered. "I'll give it back at the end of class." She turned to face the board, where Ms. MacFadden was writing *Discuss the qualities of Othello's that Desdemona falls in love with in two well-organized paragraphs.*

"Don't worry about it," said Natalya to the side of Morgan's head.

After school, when Natalya stepped out of the building, it was raining. Morgan, Sloane, and another girl were standing below her on the sidewalk with a group of guys from Thompson, their brother school. The boys were getting rained on, but the girls all held clear bubble umbrellas that came down over their faces, the kind Natalya remembered having as a kid. Rather than childish, the umbrellas—each of which had a stripe of color around the rim, Morgan's bright green, Sloane's orange, and the third girl's red—made the girls look chic, as if they were posing for a photo shoot.

Natalya realized she was staring, and she was about to turn away when Morgan raised her hand and waved in Natalya's direction.

For a second Natalya froze, but then she felt a surge of warmth run through her body.

Morgan Prewitt was waving.

Waving at *her*.

What should she do? Should she stop and wave back? Wave back and keep walking? Maybe this was about her pencil and she should head toward Morgan.

Hesitantly, Natalya lifted her hand to return Morgan's wave. But just then, Katrina, who must have been standing right behind Natalya, and who had obviously been the person Morgan was *actually* waving at, shouted, "I thought you said we were meeting inside!" A second later, she dashed past Natalya and toward Morgan, opening her clear bubble umbrella with a band of white at the bottom.

Natalya turned away as quickly as possible and practically ran down the steps, away from Morgan and her friends, into the street, where she stepped into the path of an oncoming town car. The driver blasted his horn at her before veering sharply to the right and skidding past. Natalya was too embarrassed to look back, but she wondered whether the crowd on the steps had noticed.

Chapter Ten

SATURDAY MORNING, WHEN she came out of her bedroom, Victoria felt as if she'd gone to sleep in her apartment and woken up in her father's campaign headquarters.

From the dining room came the sound of what must have been fifty people having a heated debate about Facebook. As she put two scoops of sugar into her milky coffee, Victoria heard her sister's voice. "Yes, but I'm not the only out-of-state college student who's registered to vote in New York. So are a lot of my friends."

A lot of my friends. Of course Emily, who had started college one week before Victoria had started high school, already had *a lot* of friends. She'd probably also written a major exposé for the Princeton paper and been asked by a professor to help him with some groundbreaking research project. Emily was so good it was incredible. Even when she was *bad* she was incredible. When Emily wasn't being perfect, she was being horrible—she'd failed the only class in which she didn't get an A (a health course called Modern Teenage Ethical Dilemmas, which she'd described as "beyond a waste of time"). Junior year she'd lied to their parents and spent an entire weekend at her boyfriend's apartment, and two summers ago, before she'd even had her driver's license, she'd taken the car out one night when their family was on vacation upstate.

It was as if Emily had two temperatures: boiling and freezing. Victoria, on the other hand, had one: lukewarm.

A gravelly male voice—maybe their dad's—said something Victoria couldn't quite hear, and then Emily responded, "A few thousand kids is a few thousand votes." Even from the other room Victoria could hear her sister's confidence and poise. She didn't sound like a kid sitting with a table of grown-ups, a table of *professionals*. She sounded like a member of the campaign team, someone who knew she had something worthwhile to say and wasn't afraid to say it.

Victoria knew she should probably say good morning to her father and welcome home to her sister, but no *way* was she going into the dining room; she'd rather walk into the lions' cage at the Bronx Zoo. Instead she took her coffee over to the small table by the window, and as she drank it, she glanced through the Welcome Back issue of *The Morningside Scoop*. There weren't many articles, probably because it was only the beginning of school. The middle of the paper was a two-page spread titled "ONE DOWN, ONE HUNDRED SEVENTY-NINE TO GO!" There were about fifty photographs jumbled together, but Victoria easily spotted the one of the boy and his backpack that Jack had shown her on his camera. The boy was jumping the last two steps, his hair floating up behind him, his feet almost but not quite touching the floor. It was cool how Jack had caught the boy *just* before he landed. Along the side of the photo was Jack's name printed in small type. PHOTO: JACK HASTINGS.

She read it again. Jack Hastings. She liked his name. Was that weird? Was it weird to like someone's name?

No weirder than it was to stare at a person you never spoke to. Every day Victoria spent Biology with her eyes glued to Jack's back, as if he were a magnet and she were a piece of metal. Each time he raised his hand, Victoria would feel her heart pounding in her chest until Ms. Kalman called on him, as if it were her hand that was in the air.

It was cool how Jack talked in class—sometimes his hand was up because he had the right answer, but sometimes he'd say he was confused, or he'd offer his understanding of a concept and ask Ms. Kalman if it was right. He was never embarrassed when he did that. If Victoria didn't get what Ms. Kalman said, she tried to make herself invisible, sitting as still as possible and pretending to take notes so she wouldn't get called on. Jack seemed totally comfortable asking the teacher to explain what she meant.

Victoria couldn't imagine being like that.

Whenever Ms. Kalman was speaking from the back of the

room, Jack would turn around, and each time, Victoria let herself think that maybe he was looking at her and not their teacher. But the likelihood of his checking her out was pretty small; whenever she saw Jack around school, he was with a crowd of people, and they always seemed to be having a great time, as if they'd been best buddies for years. Yesterday she'd walked by him and his friends in the hallway just as one of the guys asked, "You coming this weekend, Hastings?" Jack had answered, "If I can," like he had so many plans he really couldn't commit to one more.

The scenario in which a cute, popular guy like Jack was interested in the strange deaf mute at the back of the bio lab was hard to imagine.

To get her mind off Jack, she flipped the page of the newspaper.

"JOIN A CLUB!" read the headline. Below that, a smaller announcement read, "OR START ONE." There was the astronomy club, the debate team, the rocketry club, the chess club (Natalya could join that), the video club, the mock trial club, and the science club. There were clubs for poets and actors (Jane!), future diplomats and entrepreneurs. Victoria skimmed the list, but there weren't any cooking or baking clubs.

"Morning, Vicks. You haven't seen my BlackBerry, have you?" Victoria's dad stuck his head into the kitchen. Standing next to and slightly behind him was his campaign manager, Satan.

Victoria looked up, but before she could answer, her mother, entering from the other end of the room, said, "I think it's on your desk." She kissed Victoria briefly on the head and went to pour herself a cup of coffee.

"Hello, Steven," her mom said.

Satan was wearing a pale blue button-down shirt and a pair of crisp khakis. Every time Victoria saw him, he had on the exact same outfit, yet it was never wrinkled or dirty. Since the campaign seemed to run twenty-four hours a day, seven days a week, and since Steven was never not working, Victoria took his pristine appearance as further evidence that he was involved in the dark arts.

"Hello, Jennifer." Satan nodded to Victoria's mom, then glanced at Victoria, who was wearing a red-and-purple-flowered skirt and a red T-shirt. *People* magazine was coming to do a photo shoot in a little while, and her mom had told her to wear something nice. She tensed as Satan looked at her, but all he said was, "Hello, Victoria."

"Hello," said Victoria, mentally adding *Satan*.

"Just to let you know, the *People* team is running a little late. They'll be here closer to noon," Steven informed them.

Victoria thought about how she was supposed to meet Jane and Natalya at one o'clock at Act Two, their favorite vintage clothing store. Now she was going to be late.

But there was no way she was going to complain. "Okay," she said.

Her mother came over and placed her hand on Victoria's shoulder. "Thanks for always being so accommodating, honey." She gave her shoulder a gentle squeeze.

To Victoria, *accommodating* sounded a little too much like *nice*, but with her sister confidently rattling off statistics to a room full of professional campaign staffers, she'd take what she could get.

Her calm response even earned her a smile from the devil himself. "Thanks, Victoria. You're a champ." Satan handed her mother a manila folder.

Victoria's mom sat down and looked through it for a minute, then clucked her tongue with annoyance. "Excuse me a sec, hon. I think this campaign literally has me in two places at the same time on Wednesday morning." She stood up and headed toward the dining room. "Steven, can I ask you about something?"

Victoria wasn't sure what she was supposed to do for the next two hours. She didn't really feel like doing homework on a Saturday morning. Through the door of the kitchen she could hear the intensity of the discussion in the dining room. Listening to it reminded her of the early days of her dad's campaign, how exciting it had been to hear her mom and her dad write speeches together and argue over his positions. Sometimes, when it was just her parents, or her parents and Uncle Bob, their old campaign manager, they'd even asked her opinion. She remembered one time, right after her dad had gotten on the ballot and he'd been invited to give a speech to the Lambda Legal Fund.

"Quick, Vicks," he'd said, coming into the living room, where she was watching the cooking channel. "Give me one good reason I should support gay marriage."

Victoria hadn't even had to think. Without turning around, she said, "You and mom always say you can't wait to dance at your daughters' weddings. What if we're gay? Where would you dance?"

Her dad had laughed, clapped his hands, and said, "That's it! You've just given me the opening line of my speech."

She missed those moments, but she couldn't imagine just barging in and telling this new, scary staff what she thought. Victoria remembered the last time she'd tried to articulate her ideas about politics. In August, *The Washington Post* had interviewed and photographed the family for an article in the Sunday magazine.

REPORTER: Emily, do you think kids today are apathetic about politics?

EMILY: You know, Ellis, I hear that said all the time by people of your generation.

REPORTER: (*laughing*) Old fogies, you mean?

EMILY: (*also laughing*) Your phrase, not mine. (*more serious*) But have you ever gone to a Princeton Model Congress weekend? You can *feel* the excitement. The students are thrilled to be there, totally engaged with the political process. Honestly, no one who's seen that could accuse my generation of being apathetic.

REPORTER: (*nodding appreciatively as he frantically jots down every word Emily has uttered*) What about you, Victoria. Do you think kids today are interested in politics?

VICTORIA: Oh, definitely.

(*Reporter waits eagerly, pen poised, for the rest of Victoria's response.*)

VICTORIA: I really do.

SATAN: Well, Ellis, I think that's just about all the time we have for today. Do you want a few more minutes with Andrew?

Yeah, it was probably better that she not try to involve herself in major policy discussions.

Instead, she would bake something. That would fill the time. Without consciously settling on a recipe, she found herself digging through the cabinets for flour, sugar, vanilla, baking powder—all the ingredients to make chocolate chip cookies. They were simple to make; she'd been following the same recipe since she was about six. Still, it was easy to get lost in the rhythm of measuring and sifting, the gentle effort of pressing the butter into the brown sugar, cracking the eggs over the crunchy, slippery mix.

Thirty minutes later, as she was placing the second batch of perfectly bronzed cookies onto a cooling rack, a voice from the dining room called out, "I can't take it anymore. You've got to bring us some of those cookies." It was Julia, the communications director, the only person on the campaign Victoria remotely liked. Maybe because she was a little older than most of the staffers, or maybe because she'd been born and raised in North Carolina and (as she put it) could turn on that *little ole Southern charm*, Julia never seemed impatient or frustrated with Victoria the way the rest of the staff did. Every time Victoria answered a reporter's question or came off the stage after a rally, Julia gave her a thumbs-up and an enormous smile.

Now she called, "I'm serious. Victoria, I know it's you baking in there. Get in here immediately, honey, or I'll be forced to do something drastic."

Victoria put two dozen cooled cookies on a plate and made her way across the kitchen. At the door to the dining room she took a deep breath. *There's nothing to be scared of. There's nothing to be scared of.*

She pushed open the door and found herself staring into what felt like a thousand unblinking eyes.

"Hi," she said quietly, stupidly.

"You are the best thing to happen to campaigning since the attack ad!" Julia called from the other side of the table. The Harrisons' dining room with its black-and-white photographs of Mount Marcy, which Victoria's mom had taken a few summers ago, wasn't big, but somehow there were almost twenty people squeezed around the circular table. Luckily, Julia was wearing a bright green jacket that clashed beautifully with her bright red hair. Victoria forced herself to stare only at the splash of color that was Julia.

"Would you like some cookies?"

From her perch on the radiator, Emily called out, "Women and children first!" She smiled and waved hello to Victoria, and Victoria smiled back. Emily was wearing a PRINCETON T-shirt that Victoria had never seen before, and a pair of slim, black cotton pants. If Victoria hadn't known who she really was, she would definitely have assumed Emily was a member of the campaign staff. It was half depressing, half amazing to have a sister who was confident enough to hold her own with all these adults.

"Here you go." She'd hoped to emulate Emily's confident call, but her voice was thin and quiet, and when she looked down, she saw she'd forgotten to take off the apron she'd put on to save her dress for the photo shoot.

If only Jack Hastings could see her now.

Chapter
Eleven

AS SOON AS they'd finished breakfast Saturday morning, Natalya's father rubbed his hands together and took a last swig of the bitter black tea he loved. "Let's get this show on the road!" he announced. Natalya giggled at her father's careful pronunciation of the expression. Unlike her mother, who spoke English with her clients all day, Natalya's father was a driver for a wealthy Russian investment banker; several of the man's employees were Russian, and so her dad spoke Russian all day, and his English was way less polished than her mom's.

"*Ti gotova?*" he asked, looking at Natalya from under his bushy eyebrows that were just touched with gray. *Ready?*

"*Ya gotova!*" she answered, meeting his stare with brown eyes that were almost identical to his own. She glanced up at the clock. "I'm going to meet Mom at eleven for coffee, and then I'm meeting Victoria and Jane in the West Village." She'd been talking to and texting her friends constantly since school started, but it felt like they hadn't actually seen each other in a lifetime.

"*Prikrasna.* Just enough time for me to teach you a thing or two."

Natalya rolled her eyes but followed her dad into the living room. Her brother was sitting at the computer at their father's desk, playing a video game.

"Alex!" their dad bellowed. "How many times do I have to tell you? No video games until you finish your homework."

Alex groaned and kept his eyes on the screen, jerking not just the controller but his entire body to the side as he moved. "Nobody does homework on Saturday. I'll do it tomorrow."

"Fine," said their dad. "But shhh." He put his finger to his lips. "I mean it. We need absolute silence."

"Like I *don't*?" Alex responded, eyes on the screen. "World of Warcraft is a *very* demanding game, okay?"

Laughing, Natalya crossed the room and pulled her father's old wooden chess set off the shelf, then went to sit at the small table in the corner of the crowded living room. Her father finished filling the pipe he only smoked when he played chess, and sat down across from her, handling the pieces in a way that was simultaneously familiar and respectful. Once their pieces were in position, he grunted briefly and looked across the board at her. She nodded, and in response, he moved a pawn.

The game had begun.

Natalya loved chess. She loved the order of the board, the steady pace of the game, how her dad made warning clucks with his tongue when she was in danger of executing a foolish move or grunted his approval when she avoided one. She loved the demands it made on its players, how you had to think one, two, three moves ahead of where you actually were, how you had to get inside your opponent's brain using clues he provided with every move he made. Was he bold, willing to risk an important piece for future gain? Did he hesitate when confidence was called for, losing by inaction rather than action?

She and her dad played silently for a while, the cloud of his pipe smoke seeming to grow thicker with each move. They were well matched, having played together since she was a little girl. Natalya's father got one of her rooks, but almost immediately after, she took a bishop and a knight. Sighing, he gently stroked his beard.

"*Chort!* I have taught you too well." He tapped his pipe against his front teeth and stared at the board.

As he studied his options, Natalya pointed at the top right corner. "Bishop to E-five."

"Then won't you simply . . ." He pointed to her queen and moved his finger forward half a dozen squares.

"Wow, I've really got you boxed in, don't I?" Natalya hadn't even considered the move her father predicted she would make.

He laughed. "You have, my dear." After another minute he moved his bishop, but not where Natalya had indicated he should.

Natalya studied the changes her father's move had made to the board. As if he'd just thought of the idea, her father announced, "It's like life, chess. You always need to be thinking how your decision will play out in the future."

Natalya laughed. Sometimes it seemed her dad made this statement once a day, but each time he said it as if he'd never uttered the sentence before.

"Yes, Dad, I know," she said. She looked up at her father, who was shaking his head at the wisdom of this familiar proverb.

"So," he continued, "we haven't had a real chance to talk yet. How is this new school of yours?"

"Yeah," Alex called from across the room. "When are you going to bring some of your superfly new friends home in their uniforms?"

"Alex!" her father called a warning. *"Molchi."*

"It's . . ." Natalya knew her father would love hearing about her question and answer session with Dr. Clover, but it was hard to figure out how to put it in the context of everything else that had happened since the first day of school. Finally she said, "Let's just say I'm definitely a pawn."

Her father didn't say anything for a long minute, and Natalya wasn't sure if he was considering the board or her comment. But then he reached over and gently squeezed her hand. "Not for long, my dear," he assured her.

The dorky wave she'd given Morgan came back to her, and Natalya pushed it out of her mind, focusing on the game in front of her.

As far as Natalya was concerned, the neighborhood around Interlude, the upscale spa near the southeastern corner of Central

Park, where her mom worked, was the most beautiful and elegant in the entire city. She was early, and she took her time looking in the windows of Bergdorf Goodman, Henri Bendel, and Tiffany, laughing at how strange and even ugly so much of the merchandise was. One mannequin was wearing a coat that looked like it was made out of discarded sofa pillows, and the weird bag she held aloft was shaped like a popcorn container. Natalya took a picture of the display and was about to send it to Victoria and Jane, when she noticed the writing in the corner of the window: JUNIPER BUSH, FIRST FLOOR.

Juniper Bush! Was this weird stuff in the window by the same company that made the ugly bag Morgan Prewitt carried?

Natalya checked the time and then pushed through the heavy door. Immediately she was in another world, one that smelled of delicate perfume and felt soft to the touch. She stroked a pile of impossibly thin silk scarves and a pair of bright pink earmuffs. It was so weird how everything that wasn't ugly was beautiful— did the same person who decided the store would carry the tiny embroidered change purses also order the strange, octagonal, plastic sunglasses? Or maybe there were two people with opposite tastes. Natalya liked the idea of their scowling at each other across their desks, rolling their eyes at whatever the other one said was the season's must-have.

The bags were at the back of the store, by the staircase. Natalya saw the one that had been in the window, but it was in a locked case. She breathed in the heavy, delicious smell of leather all around her, then lightly touched a few bags that weren't locked up. One was a tiny clutch, and it was actually kind of cute. She tucked it under her arm, feeling the cool leather, soft against her skin.

There *was* something to holding this bag. She caught a glimpse of herself in the mirrored wall across from her and walked toward the reflection, first turning her left side to the mirror, then her right. When she faced left, the mirror reflected the faded tote bag that carried what she'd packed for her sleepover at Jane's. Staring at her reflection, she just felt . . . blah. Regular. But when she turned to the side that sported the Juniper Bush clutch, she felt . . . sleek. That was the only word for it. Her own bag, which she'd gotten for her tenth birthday, was green cotton with blue piping. She'd always loved it, but now it seemed dingy and babyish. The Juniper Bush bag made her look as if she'd stepped out of a movie or a magazine.

Was she branding herself a total wannabe if she got the same bag as Morgan and Katrina? But it wasn't like it was the same *bag*. It was just the same *brand*. Probably lots of people at school had Juniper Bush bags. She could ask for it for her birthday, which was how she'd gotten the small Coach purse that she wore on special occasions.

Natalya slipped her hand into the tiny pocket of the clutch and felt what she'd been looking for—the slip of a price tag. The bag wasn't big, but she bet it cost at least a hundred dollars. As she pulled the price out of the pocket, she played a little game. If the bag cost under a hundred dollars, she'd save up and buy it with her allowance. If it cost more than a hundred dollars, she'd ask for it for her birthday.

The price tag slid easily out of the bag, connected to the

zipper by a delicate ribbon. Natalya looked down at it.

Juniper Bush Clutch was written in delicate, looping script.

Beneath it was the bag's price.

Nine hundred and fifty dollars.

As Natalya rode up in the elevator to meet her mother, her heart was pounding. Somehow she felt as if she'd done something wrong, but all she'd done was look at the price of a bag. It wasn't like that was *illegal*. Her parents were always talking about the importance of freedom. *In America, you are free.* It was the dream of freedom that had gotten them from Moscow to New York, a city where their daughter would be free to look at a clutch purse that cost almost a thousand dollars.

A thousand dollars for a bag! A *tiny* bag. The bag she'd looked at was easily one-quarter the size of Morgan's. Was it one-quarter the price? Natalya felt weird thinking about how much Morgan's bag cost. It was like thinking about how much Morgan weighed or what her bra size was. It was worse. Natalya knew what size bra Jane and Victoria wore, but she had no idea how much money their parents made. She touched her necklace. Could Jane's mom have spent a thousand dollars on the necklaces? No, that was impossible. Last year, Jane and her mom had had a *mondo* fight because her mother wouldn't buy her an iPhone. *Even I don't have an iPhone, Jane. You don't need one and it's a waste of money.*

Would a mother who said an iPhone was a waste of money think a thousand dollar bag *wasn't*?

No way.

Right?

In the Interlude reception area, the woman sitting behind the modular desk gave Natalya a huge smile. "Natalya." Her accent was thick; most of the people who worked at the spa were Russian.

"Hi," Natalya said. She forced herself to put the clutch out of her mind, and smiled at Ana.

Ana patted her hair, which was big with hair spray. "Your mother's running a little late, but she'll be ready in a few minutes. How's school?"

"It's okay." The last thing Natalya felt like doing was explaining all the complexities of her life at Gainsford to Ana. She could barely understand them herself. And what was Ana supposed to do if Natalya suddenly started spewing about some bag that cost a thousand dollars, and how she'd waved at a girl who hadn't waved back?

Better to say nothing. Natalya sat down, relieved to hear her phone buzz. She took it out of her bag, the bag she'd barely thought about when she'd left her apartment that morning, the bag she now hated.

Family photo thing running late. I'll text when it's over. Waaah! Your darling V

Natalya was still replying when her mother pushed open the glass door between the reception area and the spa proper.

"Sorry, sweetheart." In her white pants and top, her mom nearly blended into the white wall behind her. "I'll be ready in just a few minutes."

"It's okay, Mom."

Her mother blew her a kiss, then slipped back into the spa.

Behind her, Natalya heard the elevator doors open, and then a tall blond girl walked past the couch Natalya was sitting on and said something quietly to the receptionist, before taking a seat on the other side of the room.

Natalya had only half noticed the girl's entrance, but when she sat down and picked up a magazine, Natalya realized she went to Gainsford. She wasn't a freshman, but Natalya had definitely seen her in the hallways. Pretending to read *Vogue*, Natalya kept looking over at the other girl. Her skin was perfect; she definitely did *not* need a facial. So what was she there for—laser hair removal? A leg waxing? Jane's mom had taken Jane, Natalya, and Victoria to get their legs waxed right before the summer, and Natalya had vowed *never* to do that again. It was one thing to do what you were afraid to do.

It was another to get your legs waxed.

The girl glanced up just as Natalya was looking her way. Natalya felt bad. What if the girl had some weird, unsightly, body-hair thing, and the sight of a fellow student made her totally embarrassed? But she just gave Natalya a vague smile, as though she couldn't quite place her. Then she slipped her iPhone out of her Marc Jacobs bag and dialed a number.

"Hi, it's me," she said.

As the girl talked, Natalya realized that her mother could come back at any second. What if, since she was going back to work after their coffee break, she hadn't changed out of her uniform into her street clothes? What if the girl sitting here was a *client* of her mom's? Would she say something to people at school? How weird would that be, if some random girls came up to her in class or at lunch and said, *Your mom waxes my eyebrows.*

Natalya felt sick, sicker even than she'd felt when she saw the price of the Juniper Bush purse. Her heart was pounding and her hands were sticking to the magazine, and for a second she was afraid she might actually vomit. She stood up and made her way towards Ana's desk.

"Yes, dear?" Ana turned to her with the same warm expression she'd worn before, but this time Natalya couldn't fake a smile.

"Um, could you tell my mom—" her voice was a whisper.

"I'm sorry, I didn't hear you."

Behind her, Natalya could hear the Gainsford girl still talking into her phone. She risked raising her voice a notch. "Could you tell my mom I'll meet her at the Starbucks on the corner?"

"Of course. Do you want me to ask her to come out?" Ana's hand was on the phone.

"No!" Natalya's voice was sharper than she'd meant it to be. "I mean, don't bother her," she added quickly, already moving toward the elevator. "I'll wait for her there."

"Okay, dear. Have a nice day."

Natalya frantically pressed the down arrow. "Thanks," she called over her shoulder as the doors mercifully opened.

Only when she was out of the building and standing on the bustling Fifty-ninth Street sidewalk did she realize that, in addition to everything else, she'd just stolen a copy of *Vogue* from her mother's place of business.

Chapter
Twelve

VICTORIA FELT AS if the photo shoot had lasted until midnight, even though her phone told her it was only two o'clock in the afternoon. The *People* photographer and the campaign's press liaison had pushed and prodded her and moved her from one end of the couch to the other, told her to look up at her father "lovingly," talk to her sister "seriously," and sit with her mother "comfortably." At the very end of the photo shoot they'd asked her to put on an apron and mime serving chocolate chip cookies to her family, and she knew *that* was the photo they were going to use.

She could see the copy now. *Though the candidate is only in his late forties, he somehow has a daughter who's a 1950s housewife.*

When Victoria finally reached the Fourteenth Street station, she climbed the stairs and turned south, toward Act Two, where Jane and Natalya had been waiting for her for the past two hours. As she took out her phone to tell them she was just a couple of blocks away, she saw someone walking down the block ahead of her. He had shaggy brown hair and was wearing a pair of faded jeans and an old-school leather bomber jacket against the chilly, overcast day.

Slung over his left shoulder was a camera.

Victoria felt her heart begin to race in her chest.

Could it be . . . Jack?

Doing a quick mental check of her outfit (white skinny jeans, long-sleeved green T-shirt, blue hoodie, blue Chuck Taylors— nothing memorable but nothing to be ashamed of), she walked a little faster, but not too fast. Jack (or the person who looked very much like Jack from behind) was walking slowly, as if he had nowhere in particular he had to be. Finally he stopped and turned slightly in her direction.

Victoria gasped.

It *was* Jack.

Had he seen her? She froze as he lifted his camera to his eye and focused on a spot across the street. He adjusted the lens, then took the picture. A second later, he started walking again. He hadn't seen her.

Victoria followed him.

Her phone buzzed and she glanced down at the screen. It was a text from Jane.

Just bought awesome T-shirts! Where r u?

Victoria looked up. Jack had turned the corner, and she hurried to follow him. He was walking faster now, as though he had someplace to be.

Victoria hit Reply, then typed back. I m heading west on Christopher.

A second later her phone buzzed.

?????

Jack was taller than Victoria, and he had long legs, so she was practically running to keep up with him. He had a great walk, relaxed and confident, as if he were strolling through a city he didn't just live in but that he *belonged* in. The street was crowded, and Victoria let people come between them, so if he turned around he wouldn't see her. But then she let him get too far ahead, and she actually had to sprint to keep him in sight.

Her phone buzzed again.

V!!!????

She risked losing him in order to type back a response.

I m stalking Jack.

Hustling to catch up with him, she nearly tripped on the uneven sidewalk as she read Natalya's text.

Who is Jack?

She barely slowed down to type an answer.

Camera boy.

It took a second for the reply to come, but when it did, she knew Jane had written it, even though it was sent from Natalya's phone.

So he IS cute.

Victoria grinned at her screen. There was no need to answer

that. Instead, she texted, I m heading south on eighth.

Was this what it was like to be a spy? Victoria liked the feeling of trailing Jack, knowing where he was without his knowing where she was. Not that he would have cared, exactly. *Who's on Eighth Avenue? Victoria Harrison? Oh, isn't she that weird silent girl in my bio class?*

We r heading w on bleecker, Jane texted.

Eighth Avenue was less crowded than Christopher Street, but there were still a lot of people around. She noticed a couple of men look at Jack. She smiled to herself as she imagined calling after them, *Hey, I saw him first!*

As they headed south, the crowds thinned until there was almost no one on the sidewalk between Jack and her. If he turned around he would definitely see her. She was debating the risk of letting the distance between them grow, when he made a sudden left turn.

Victoria followed him. They were on a small block with brownstones on one side and a basketball court on the other. This must have been Jack's destination, because he slowed down and crossed the street, leaning against the fence to watch the game.

There were literally no other pedestrians on the block, and Victoria ducked back to Eighth Avenue to avoid being seen. She reached for her phone again.

Meet me @ corner of 8 & Leonard.

She stayed on the Eighth Avenue side of the corner for a long minute before realizing that maybe Jack had just *paused* to check out the game and was planning to continue on. In that case, standing where she was, she would have no idea that he'd left. There had to be a way for her to watch him without standing on Leonard Street, where he would absolutely see her.

She leaned forward to peer around the corner.

If Jack *had* turned around, the bewildering sight that would have met his eyes was a girl in his bio class, wrapped around the corner of a building, her legs on Eighth Avenue, her torso on Leonard Street. Luckily, he didn't turn. Instead, he pressed his camera to his eye and began shooting pictures of the game.

Victoria studied him, barely aware of her uncomfortable position. Jack was utterly focused, as if the chaos of the city didn't exist for him. As he moved closer to the fence, following the play by crouching and kneeling, he seemed to be engaged in a beautiful dance, one for which only he could hear the music.

Suddenly, there was a voice whispering in her ear. "Agent Jane Sterling reporting for duty, sir. Do you have the target in your sights?"

Victoria giggled and, without turning, pointed toward Jack. Jane leaned past her, gave Jack a quick glance, then swung back to Eighth Avenue, her back pressed against the building. Without speaking, she gestured for Natalya to take a look, but Natalya was doubled over with laughter.

"Shhh!" warned Victoria, even though Natalya was miraculously managing to keep her laughter perfectly silent.

"What's the plan?" whispered Jane, her back still up against the wall.

Victoria turned to face her. "I don't know. I don't have a plan. This is a no-plan situation."

"Roger that," said Natalya, and then she began laughing hysterically.

"Stop!" said Victoria, but now she was laughing too. Only Jane kept a straight face.

"Okay, then, this is the plan," Jane whispered. "On my signal, we're going to turn the corner, and we're going to walk down the block really, *really, really slowly*. Got it?"

Victoria nodded.

Natalya nodded.

Jane gave them the thumbs-up, and they turned and began walking down Leonard Street at a snail's pace.

"What if he doesn't see us?" asked Natalya, eyes focused straight down the block.

"What if he *does* see us, you mean?" corrected Victoria, eyes equally focused on a point ahead of her.

"Wait, we want him to see us, don't we? I mean, you want him to see us. I mean, see *you*, right?" asked Jane. She stopped walking.

Victoria stopped walking also. She turned to face Jane, keeping her back to Jack. "I don't know!" she hissed, grabbing Jane's forearms.

"You better decide quick," Natalya whispered, barely moving her lips. "I think he's coming this way."

"Act natural," Jane ordered. She reached into her bag and pulled out something pink. Then she spoke in a completely normal voice. "So I bought this shirt for you. We each get one."

Victoria couldn't focus at all on the piece of material Jane was holding in her direction.

"It's okay," Natalya muttered. "He turned around again."

"Do you like it?" asked Jane calmly.

Without actually being aware of what she was doing, Victoria unfolded the pink T-shirt. Scrawled across the front in hot pink lacy letters dotted with rhinestones were the words FOXY LADY. She cracked up. "I can*not* wear this!"

"Of course you can," Jane insisted. "If we can wear it, you can wear it. Because we are all *foxy ladies!*" She snapped her fingers and spun around. "I'm thinking of wearing it to my audition Tuesday."

"Oh my god, he *is* coming!" Natalya yelped.

"Act natural!" Jane warned.

Victoria bunched the shirt up like it was a piece of incriminating evidence and, not knowing what else to do, shoved it in her purse. Her heart was pounding so fast she was sure it was using up beats it should have been saving for later, as if these moments of stalking Jack were literally taking days or maybe even years off her life.

"He's definitely coming this way," muttered Jane, and at that moment she spun Victoria around so she was facing the direction Jack was coming from.

Victoria felt her hair fan out around her, then settle across her face as she came to a stop. She looked out at Jack as though through a picket fence.

He was crossing Leonard Street at an angle, and when he saw the girls, he hesitated, then squinted at Victoria. From the middle of the street, he waved. "Hey."

Victoria swiped at her hair. "Hey."

He was still standing in the street. She couldn't decide which would be worse: if Jack realized she'd been stalking him or if he got hit by a car.

"You're Victoria," he said.

Should she say, *You're Jack?* Or did that make it obvious that she liked him? But he'd just said *her* name. So maybe she should say his.

"Do you guys know each other?" Jane sounded so natural, Victoria actually believed Jane didn't know the answer to her question. It was amazing. She glanced at her friend. Jane's face was open, curious. She was smiling at Jack as though she were prepared to be friendly if he turned out to be someone Victoria knew.

No wonder Jane had been accepted to The Academy for the Performing Arts.

Jack closed the distance between them, and Victoria felt a sense of relief as he stepped out of the street and onto the sidewalk. "I don't know. Do we know each other?" he asked, smiling at Victoria as if they were in on some private joke.

Victoria felt herself smiling back, even though she had no idea what the joke was. "We go to school together," she told Jane and Natalya, who already knew.

"Oh," said Natalya and Jane together.

For a second Victoria was scared they were going to start cracking up. Then she was scared *she* was going to start cracking up.

"We have Biology together," added Jack. He put one foot up on a low fence surrounding a tree and placed his camera on his knee.

"Biology," Jane repeated, and now Victoria could hear in her friend's voice that she was about to lose it.

Jack cocked his head to the side as he studied Victoria. She could *not* get over how cute he was. His skin was perfect, and his eyes were the color of the Caribbean on a cloudy day. "So, let's see: I know your name. And I know that you don't like to have your picture taken." He looked up at the sky, then snapped his fingers. "And I know that you know how paramecium reproduce."

Victoria blushed so fiercely she could practically hear her cheeks sizzle. She couldn't have thought of something to say if her life depended on it.

Once again, Jane came to her rescue. "Do you live near here?"

Jack shook his head. "I'm doing a photo assignment." Without turning around, he gestured toward the basketball court with his elbow. "We're supposed to take action shots with a wide depth of field."

"Cool," said Victoria.

Cool?! Had she really just said "Cool"?

But Jack didn't seem to think her response was the lamest ever. "Yeah," he agreed. "I thought so too."

A quiet beeping made him reach into his pocket and take out his phone. He touched it, and the beeping stopped. "That means I have to go," he explained.

"Oh," said Victoria. Was it obvious from her voice how disappointed she was?

"Where are you going?" asked Jane.

Victoria was half embarrassed that Jane had asked, half glad. She wanted to know the answer.

"Lincoln Center," he answered.

"Are you going to a concert?" asked Jane.

"Jane!" Natalya said, slapping her lightly on the shoulder.

"Sorry," said Jane. "I'm just really nosy."

Jack shrugged. "I don't mind. Yes, I'm going to a concert." He looked at the three of them, his eyes lingering on Victoria. "If I had an extra ticket, I'd invite you."

Oh my god. Oh my god. OH MY GOD! "Oh." She hesitated, then just said it. "If you had an extra ticket, I'd go."

Jack smiled at Victoria. Victoria smiled at Jack.

She could have stood there smiling at him for the rest of her life.

Finally, he dropped his foot from the fence. "Good to know." He gave a little wave to Jane and Natalya. "Nice to meet you."

"You, too," said Jane.

"Oh . . . yes," said Natalya. "Very nice." Though her back was to Natalya, Victoria could tell that Natalya was doing all she could not to crack up.

"Bye," said Jack, looking into Victoria's eyes with his own deep gray ones. "I'll look for you Monday."

"Bye," said Victoria. She couldn't bring herself to say she'd look for him Monday.

It was too true to speak out loud.

As Jack headed down the block, Jane and Natalya, standing behind her, burst into laughter.

"Guys!" Victoria hissed, slapping at them without turning around. "He'll *hear* you!"

"Sorry," mumbled Natalya, still laughing.

"Sorry," agreed Jane, also laughing.

By now Victoria was laughing too. The three of them collapsed onto the steps of the nearest brownstone.

"Oh my god," Victoria sighed. She leaned her head against Jane's knee. "Oh my god."

"Totally," agreed Natalya. "Jane, you were amazing! 'Do you two know each other?'" At the memory, she cracked up again.

"He said he would have invited you if he had an extra ticket!" Natalya shrieked. "That is *such* a good sign!"

"You think so?" asked Victoria, though she knew it was.

"Totally," said Natalya.

"Definitely," said Jane. Then she leaned over to look down at Victoria. "Oh, and for the record?"

Victoria tilted her head back so she could meet Jane's look. "Yeah?"

"That—" She pointed down the block in the direction Jack had disappeared.

"Yeah?" asked Victoria again.

"—is cute, darling," Jane concluded.

And the three of them just lost it completely.

Chapter
Thirteen

TUESDAY AFTER SCHOOL, Jane had planned to hang around the theater with the other kids who were auditioning. But seeing a crowd of people who wanted what she wanted just as badly as she wanted it made her feel utterly pathetic, a cliché of a little girl writing Santa to ask for a pony. She walked across the street to Starbucks and waited in an enormous line for what felt like hours, before realizing all a latte would do was make her jittery and need to pee.

Back at the Academy she slipped into a first floor bathroom. The light was bad and the mirror small, but her hair looked reasonably tame. She'd decided the Foxy Lady shirt was too much, but she thought her bright red T-shirt would be memorable to a casting committee. Slipping into a stall, she took out her phone and called Natalya. Without bothering to say hello, Jane announced, "I swear to god, Mark told *every single freshman* that I'm auditioning." She described how two girls had come up to her in French that morning to ask if it was true that she was trying out for *A Midsummer Night's Dream*. When she'd said that it was, they'd backed slowly away from her, as though whatever she had might be contagious.

"Stop," said Natalya, laughing at Jane's description. "They're totally rooting for you."

Jane shook her head. "No, they want me to fail."

"Realistically, half of them might," Natalya acknowledged. "But the other half are hoping you'll get a part."

Jane traced her fingers thoughtfully along a heart someone had carved into the old wooden door of the stall. "No, they *all* want me to fail. I know they do because it's what *I* would want if *I* were them and *they* were me, darling."

"Maybe you're meaner than other people," offered Natalya.

Jane considered the possibility. "I think I'm just more honest than other people."

"Either way, it's four forty," Natalya said. "Do you know where your audition is?"

"Are you serious?" Almost half an hour had passed since she'd gone across the street to kill time by getting a latte. Was it possible that now she was actually going to be *late*? "Oh god, I gotta go!"

Before she slapped her phone shut, Jane heard Natalya shout, "Vicks and I will bring the roses!"

Jane smiled sadly to herself. Nana had always brought Jane a beautiful bouquet of long-stemmed roses on opening night. It was weird to think that even if Jane *did* get cast, Nana wouldn't be there to hand her flowers.

Jane was panting when she arrived at the theater seconds before four forty-five. A boy she didn't know was sitting nearby, leaning against the wall, and when he saw her frantic approach, he immediately said, "Don't worry, they're running late."

Jane stood where she'd stopped and took a deep breath. "Thanks." She slid down the wall to sit across the corridor from him. Less than a minute later, as if she'd been conjured by Jane's arrival, the door to the theater opened and Fran Sherman came out. Her cheeks were flushed, and she had a look of triumph on her face that made Jane think of Lady Macbeth. She didn't stop to look at Jane and the guy in the hallway, just swept past them and out of sight. Jane wondered if she'd even seen them sitting there.

A girl Jane didn't recognize stepped out and said, "Come on in, Nate."

After Nate said good-bye, Jane was still having trouble catching her breath. It had been a long time since she'd had to prove herself. Sure, she'd auditioned for parts at One Room. But had there ever been a doubt she'd land the lead?

"Jane?" The door opened as the girl said her name, and Jane sprang to her feet. Without speaking, she passed into the theater.

It was dark, with just a few spots on so that the middle of the stage was well lit. There at a table sat four people, all of whom, from a distance, looked like students. Was the director even here?

"Jane, welcome," said a male voice. The person speaking sat at the far end of the table, one ankle crossed over the opposite knee.

Jane made her way onto the stage. As she got closer, she saw that he was clearly an adult, though she could see why she'd mistaken him for a student—even close up, he looked pretty young, and the jeans and T-shirt he was wearing made him seem that much younger.

"Sorry we kept you waiting," he said. "I'm Len Robbins."

Jane couldn't hide her surprise at how . . . well, handsome Len Robbins was.

"Hi, Len." It felt right to call him Len.

"Hi, Jane. This is Sharon, Larnel, and Wendy. They're producing the show."

He indicated the students at the table with him, and Jane nodded at them as if she'd registered who they were, though she'd forgotten their names as soon as Mr. Robbins said them. She had a second to wonder what it meant to produce a show before Mr. Robbins asked, "So, what do you have for us today?" He leaned forward slightly in his seat, as if despite the fact that he'd been watching people audition for two afternoons in a row, he was thrilled at the prospect of yet another student reciting yet another monologue for him.

"I'm going to do one of Lady Macbeth's speeches." Jane was relieved her voice wasn't quivering like her hands.

"A bold choice," Mr. Robbins said. Then he leaned back in his chair. "Whenever you're ready."

Jane fluttered her fingers against her necklace, then took a deep breath and began, imagining, as she spoke, the dark power of Shakespeare's witches running through her blood.

"'The raven himself is hoarse that croaks the fatal entrance of Duncan.'" As the rhythm and magic of the lines pulsed through her body, she felt completely present in the words she was speaking. Halfway through, she was positive she'd nailed the speech—her voice was sure and booming, and she raised up her arms to the sky, letting the power of Shakespeare's language carry her through the final line, which she nearly shouted.

She felt as triumphant as Fran Sherman had looked.

When the last syllable of *instant* had died out, the silence was deafening. She dropped her hands.

The three students made notes on the pads in front of them. Nobody said anything, and she realized she was probably supposed to leave.

"Well, thanks," she said. It had been a good audition. She *knew* it had been a good audition. So why wasn't anyone saying anything to her? Even a careless *Nice job* would have been appreciated.

"Just a second," said Mr. Robbins. He rubbed his chin thoughtfully, staring at her. One by one the students finished what they were writing and looked up at her.

"How old is Lady Macbeth?" he asked.

She'd never thought about it before, but she figured Lady Macbeth was probably pretty old. Did it ever say in the play? "Fifty?" she guessed.

Now Mr. Robbins had his elbows on his knees, and he was leaning toward her. His stare was intense, his sandy brown hair chicly cut, and his jawbone was stubbled like a model's.

Okay, he was *way* cuter than any teacher she'd ever had.

"So you see her as a middle-aged woman?" he prompted.

"Actually, I see her as old," Jane said before she could stop herself. Was it possible that Mr. Robbins was *fifty*? She hoped she hadn't offended him.

Mr. Robbins laughed. "Right." He leaned back and crossed his arms over his chest. "What if she's young? The text never actually gives her age."

"Young?" she asked. This was starting to feel more like an English class than an audition.

"Young. Young and gorgeous and sexy and standing there in a revealing nightgown, raising her arms to the heavens and demanding of the spirits that they *unsex* her?"

Again, Jane spoke before she could think about what she was saying. "It's more significant to unsex a sexy woman."

His pleased smile told Jane that Mr. Robbins knew she'd gotten his point. He nodded at what she'd said before expanding on it. "If she's older, if she's, say, Judi Dench, it doesn't mean much to degender her. But if she's young and hot, it's a powerful request. Why don't you try it again, and this time, make her sexier. Make her a woman who's used to getting what she wants because she's hot."

Jane nodded. She was a professional. No way would she allow her expression to belie any weirdness she felt talking about being sexy with Mr. Robbins.

"Got it," said Jane.

"When you're ready," Mr. Robbins said again.

Jane began again, but halfway through the first sentence, she realized she was saying the line exactly the way she'd said it before.

"Sorry," she interrupted herself. "Can I try that again?"

"As many times as you want," said Mr. Robbins.

Jane wasn't sure she really had an infinite number of times to screw this up. She took a deep breath and thought to herself, *Sexy. I'm sexy. I'm totally hot and sexy.* Jane pictured Fran's flushed, triumphant face as she'd exited the theater. Fran wasn't hot, exactly, but she looked like she thought she was.

"'Unsex me here, and fill me from the crown to the toe topfull of direst cruelty,'" Jane said again, and she tried to visualize herself in a sexy nightgown, the silk swishing against her bare feet as she paced the floor. Now when she got to the line about "come to my women's breasts," she felt self-conscious, and she stumbled her way through the sentence. Her cheeks were burning. As fast as she could, she raced to the end of the speech. When it was over, she looked down, unable to meet anyone's eyes.

Into the silence, Mr. Robbins said, "That's a lot to ask someone to do at an audition. You were a sport."

"No problem," Jane lied.

"Thanks so much," said one of the girls at the table, either Wendy or Sharon.

"Thanks for humoring me," said Mr. Robbins. "It was a great attempt."

Your attempt to be sexy was hilarious.

Your attempt to play Lady Macbeth was amusing.

Your attempt to be cast in this play was admirable.

"The cast list will be posted on the door to the main theater on Monday morning."

But your name so clearly will not be on it.

Chapter
Fourteen

WITH ITS INTRICATE inlaid floor, thick Persian rugs, glass-topped display cases of yellowing manuscripts, and enormous old wooden tables, the library at Gainsford should have been lit by flickering candles, not lightbulbs, as if it existed in a time and place where electricity hadn't yet been invented. But when the librarian gave Natalya the book she'd asked for, he added, "You can't check this out since it's on reserve, but you can copy the chapter over there," and pointed at a very twenty-first-century-looking Xerox machine.

"Thanks," said Natalya. She took the heavy book over to the corner and flipped it open to "The Spread of the Cool." In Bio last period, they'd talked about how bacteria and viruses spread, and Dr. Clover had said cryptically that illnesses weren't the only things that could be contagious. She'd told the class that anyone who wanted to learn more about the subject could check out an article she'd put on reserve in the library.

"Will we get extra credit if we read the article?" asked a girl sitting at the front lab table.

Dr. Clover shoved her hands in the pockets of her lab coat and pivoted in the direction of the questioner. "You will get extra knowledge, Louisa. I would hope that would be of more interest to you than extra credit."

As they were walking out of class, Natalya asked Jordan if she was going to read the article.

Jordan held her hands out in front of her, as if they were a scale. "Let's see: read incredibly boring article for terrifying science teacher, or enjoy fabulous lunch with friends." She dropped her right hand almost to her knee, as if something heavy had suddenly been dumped on it. "And we have a winner!"

Natalya laughed. "I think . . . I'll meet you in a minute. I just have to do something."

"'Kay," said Jordan. "I'll save you a seat."

Now, as she stood in the library copying the article no one but she would know she'd read, Natalya couldn't help wondering if she was stupid for adding this reading to her already massive quantity of homework. She had a bio lab due Friday and a history essay that she'd just been assigned this morning due Monday, not to mention Greek verbs to conjugate by tomorrow and *Othello* scenes to read and answer questions on by the end of the day.

Still, she found herself standing by the Xerox machine glancing through the article she'd just copied. The book was called *You Know You Want It: Modern Advertising and the Myth of Need.* Natalya skimmed the first page. *The challenge for marketers is how to take advantage of the moment before a trend becomes passé, to ride the wave of the new and exciting all the way to the bank.* . . .

Natalya felt someone hip-check her, and without looking up, she knew it had to be Jordan.

"Give me one sec—" She snapped the book shut, slipped the copy of the article out of the tray, turned around, and found herself staring directly at Morgan Prewitt's face.

Everything about Morgan radiated light—her white teeth shone, her silky hair shimmered, her small pearl earrings gleamed. Natalya stood staring at her, tongue-tied, like Morgan was some guy she had a crush on.

"Hey!" Morgan smiled at Natalya as if Natalya were the person she most wanted to talk to in the entire universe. "You're Natalya. And we have *never* hung out, which is completely insane."

A warm glow spread through Natalya's entire body. Morgan's smile was so genuine, her enthusiasm for having found Natalya standing at the Xerox machine so palpable. It made Natalya feel special, as if, like viruses and trends, Morgan's sparkliness was also contagious.

"Are you busy?" asked Morgan, nodding at the book Natalya was holding.

"No, I just . . . I have to give this back to the librarian." She made her way over to the librarian's desk, handed him the book, then took the article and folded it into her backpack. Incredibly enough, when she was done, Morgan was still waiting for her.

"Come." Morgan gestured for Natalya to follow, and despite being completely bewildered about what was happening, Natalya did. Together they walked through the central part of the library, a grand arched room with enormous reading tables; dictionaries on intricately carved iron stands; and ancient-looking, brightly colored maps of the world hanging on the walls. When they were halfway across the room, Morgan made an abrupt right along a narrow passage between two high bookcases, then entered a small alcove Natalya hadn't noticed before. Morgan crossed the alcove and pushed through a door that looked like part of the paneled wall. Following her, Natalya found herself standing in a small room with a love seat and two armchairs. On the floor was a worn Persian carpet with a light floral design. Despite how tiny the room was, on one wall was a stone fireplace so tall, Natalya could have stood in it without bumping her head.

"Oh my god." She looked around her. High up on the outer wall, a series of stained-glass windows let in ruby and lemon light.

Morgan flopped onto the love seat and surveyed her surroundings as if seeing them through Natalya's eyes. "I know," she agreed, "isn't it awesome? There are a whole bunch of these little rooms, but this is the best one—none of the others have a fireplace. It's too bad there's no fire."

Natalya nodded.

"I just can't deal with the lunchroom anymore." Stretching out on the love seat, Morgan sighed contentedly. "Katrina and Sloane should be here soon. We've been having lunch here all week. Isn't this a million times better than those crappy chairs?"

"Oh definitely," Natalya agreed. And even though she thought the lunchroom was beautiful, it wasn't a lie. Sitting in the cafeteria wasn't nearly as thrilling as sitting in this tiny room having a private conversation with the most popular girl in her grade. After all, anyone could eat in the cafeteria.

Only she had been invited here.

But why? What could she possibly have that Morgan Prewitt wanted?

At the impossibility of *anything* of hers being even remotely interesting to Morgan, her heart sank. Maybe Morgan wanted to copy her English homework. But why would Morgan want Natalya's homework? The girl had gotten a ten out of ten on her vocab quiz (Natalya had seen the sheet when Ms. MacFadden returned it).

Natalya forced herself to stop thinking that Morgan wanted something from her. It really was paranoid. She reached up to her necklace and slid the pearl back and forth on its chain. The gentle *ziiiip, ziip* of metal on metal was soothing, and she felt her excitement about being singled out by Morgan return as Sloane Gainsford poked her head through the doorway.

"Hey," said the girl, "I'm Sloane." Her thick reddish-blond hair swirled around her face.

Natalya knew it would be uncool to say *I know*, so she just said, "Hi."

Sloane smiled at Natalya, then said to Morgan, "You found her."

"Totally," said Morgan as Sloane dropped into the free armchair.

Natalya couldn't believe it. Sloane and Morgan had talked about her. Morgan had been *trying* to find her. These amazing, sophisticated girls whose families had owned New York City for *centuries* wanted to be friends with her.

The door banged open, and Katrina flew into the room, her black hair streaming behind her. "Thanks a lot for coming with me," she complained to her friends.

Morgan rolled her eyes. "Oh yeah, I'm really going to drop by the bio lab when I don't have to." She adjusted her neck against the arm of the couch.

"It's not my fault Clover wanted to talk to me," Katrina complained. She walked over to the couch and pushed Morgan's legs so she could sit down. Morgan barked a protest but tucked her legs out of Katrina's way.

"You have Dr. Clover?" asked Natalya. She was about to add, *I like her*, when Katrina interrupted without answering.

"She is *such* an unfair bitch," Katrina announced.

Natalya was glad she hadn't gotten a chance to share her opinion.

"A bitch, yes. Unfair, no," corrected Morgan. "What'd you want to see her about, anyway?"

"This stupid term paper. My dad knows the head of neurosurgery at Weill Cornell, and he said I can shadow him for a day for my research project."

"You can follow a neurosurgeon around? That's amazing!" Years ago Jane's dad, who was an orthopedic surgeon, had told

Natalya she could come watch him operate when she was older. Of course, that had been before he moved out to LA.

Katrina waved away Natalya's enthusiasm. "Well, it's not happening. Clover was all, 'But, Ms. Worthington, I fail to see the hypothesis you will be proving or disproving.'" She snorted. "How about if I just prove Clover's a bitch, okay? Is that a good enough hypothesis?"

Morgan shook her head. "How could you disprove it?"

"Why don't you just write about outer space?" offered Sloane. "That's what everyone else does." She reached into her purse (which Natalya was pretty sure was *not* a Juniper Bush) and pulled out a small cloth version of a brown paper bag. She put the bag on the low wooden table between the chairs and the sofa and removed a little wooden box that she opened to reveal a collection of elaborately cut vegetables.

"God, outer space is so boring," Morgan sighed, reaching over to pull a carrot cut like a comb from Sloane's collection.

"I was just looking at this article Clover recommended," Natalya said. "It was about how trends spread."

"You *did* the extra *credit*?" asked Katrina, shocked. She took an apple from her Juniper Bush bag. "God, way to kiss ass."

"Um," Natalya was embarrassed. She'd meant to offer up a possible term paper topic, not show off.

"Maybe she's just *curious*. Not every person in the world is as lazy as you, Kat." Without sitting up, Morgan reached her arm out and dug around in her purse briefly before pulling out the most elegant white paper bag Natalya had ever seen. It had a blue-and-white ribbon around its twine handle. From the bag, Morgan removed an equally elegant white parcel and a blue-and-white napkin that was either cloth or extremely thick paper—Natalya couldn't tell.

"Do you want some of my sandwich?" asked Morgan. "It's totally veggie. Are you a vegetarian?"

Natalya thought about last night's dinner, her mother's cabbage stuffed with beef and secret, mouth-watering seasoning. It was, hands down, her favorite meal in the world. "Um . . . I think about becoming one sometimes."

Morgan unwrapped her sandwich and handed half to Natalya along with one of her napkins. A few sprouts hung over the side. "You know what you have to do? You have to picture the animal actually *being* killed. Then you won't want to eat it."

"Or eat *anything*, for that matter." Katrina lobbed her half-eaten apple into a small metal garbage can at the end of the couch. "Thanks. My appetite's shot."

Natalya giggled. Nervous as she was to be here, it was exciting to listen to Morgan and her friends talk. "This is fun," she observed, spreading the thick paper napkin over her lap.

"This is nothing," said Morgan. She sat up, put her sandwich half on the table in front of her, and crossed her legs, not seeming to care that her shoes were on the couch. "You and Victoria have *got* to come to the party my brother and I are throwing in a few weeks."

Natalya had just taken a bite of Morgan's sandwich, and she barely had time to swallow the unchewed mouthful before asking. "Victoria?" How did these girls know Victoria?

Now it was Morgan's turn to sound confused. "Wait, aren't

you friends with Victoria Harrison?"

"Yeah, but I didn't know *you* were." In what universe did Victoria secretly know Morgan Prewitt?

Morgan placed her hand against the side of her face and shook her head. "Duh. Sorry. Okay. So, my mom is like, *obsessed* with Andrew Harrison." As she talked, she pulled her honey blond hair down and casually twisted it back up into a loose bun. "She was at this fund-raiser for him, and I guess my mom and Victoria's mom were talking and my mom said I go to Gainsford and Victoria's mom said Victoria's best friend goes to Gainsford and she wrote down your name and I was like, wait, she's in my English class." Morgan beamed across the room at Natalya. "And here we are."

The warm glow she'd been feeling since Morgan's approach disappeared, and a chill washed over her. Morgan hadn't come looking for her because she was special. She'd come looking for her because Victoria was special.

Morgan smiled broadly at her. "So, can you guys come?"

"You really should," Katrina added, picking a sliver of invisible nail polish off her pinky nail. "Grant's at Thompson, and *all* of his friends will be there."

"Oh yes, *Graaaant*," Morgan trilled. She rolled her eyes in Natalya's direction. "Katrina's in love with my brother."

They'd never liked her. They'd never thought she was worth hanging out with.

Katrina blushed. "Well, he's got to go out with *someone*, doesn't he? Why shouldn't it be me?"

Morgan looked at Natalya and shook her head, mouthing, *Never.*

Morgan, Sloane, and Katrina could be friends with any girl in the school. Probably any girl in the *world*. How stupid was she to have thought they wanted to be friends with *her*?

Sloane ignored Morgan and Katrina's bickering. "It's basically going to be the party of the century."

Was she really going to say no to an invitation to the party of the century just because that invitation depended on her bringing Victoria? Even if Morgan had invited Natalya for her own sake, Natalya would have asked to bring Victoria along.

Was this so different?

But Victoria was *not* going to be into it. She'd never go to some party a girl had invited her to just because of who her dad was.

Katrina took a lipstick out of her purse and applied it expertly. When she finished, Morgan extended her hand, and without their exchanging a single word, Katrina placed the silver tube into it with a practiced snap that made Natalya think of hospital shows where surgeons barked *Scalpel!* at their assistants.

After she'd applied the pale pink to her own lips, Morgan arched an eyebrow at Natalya and nodded toward the lipstick she was holding. Natalya stared at it for a minute, not sure what Morgan meant for her to do. Morgan held up the shiny tube. "You want?"

Natalya hesitated for a second. Was it sanitary to share lipstick with girls she didn't even know? But then Morgan was holding it toward her, and she found herself reaching out to take it.

As she slid the soft, sweet-smelling lipstick across her lips, Natalya remembered Jane. Even if Victoria said she'd come, which was pretty much impossible to imagine, what was she going to do about Jane? Should she ask if it was okay to bring a second friend?

"Oh my god, you were *born* to wear that color!" Morgan announced, and Sloane and Katrina nodded in her direction.

"Thanks." Natalya licked at her lips. Was it possible for something to not just feel but to actually *taste* smooth?

She looked around the room at Morgan, Sloane, and Katrina. It wasn't that they *didn't* want her to come to the party. They did. It was just that they hadn't noticed her before. And now they had.

Did it really matter why?

And then, in a tumble, she said, "I . . . Could our friend Jane come too?" There was a strange buzzing in her ears.

Morgan pressed her shiny lips together. Natalya was positive she was about to say, *You know, that's pretty uncool, Natalya. We don't even want you there, just Victoria. Now you want to bring this Jane person?*

"Sure," said Morgan. "The more the merrier." And then, as if she hadn't just issued the most monumental party invitation in the history of the world, Morgan took another veggie from Sloane's lunch box and asked Natalya if she liked the sandwich.

Chapter
Fifteen

VICTORIA WASN'T INTO IT.

Saturday morning, Jane, Natalya, and Victoria had the apartment to themselves; Victoria's parents had just left to campaign at an apple-picking festival in Columbia County. Victoria stood by the stove wearing a pair of Old Navy pajama bottoms and a ROCK THE VOTE T-shirt, waiting for the apple popovers she'd made to finish baking.

"I just don't see my parents saying yes," said Victoria. "I mean, I *think* they would have said yes before the campaign, but now they'll definitely say no. Or they'll say maybe but then run it by Satan, and *he'll* say no."

Natalya studied the table, tracing some words in the headline of *The New York Times* so absently she didn't even notice they had to do with Andrew Harrison's Senate race. "You could ask, and then even if they say no, go anyway. Just like, sneak out."

Jane was shaking her head. "No plausible deniability if we do that, darling."

"What's plausible deniability?" asked Victoria, checking the timer on the stove.

"It's being able to claim you didn't know that what you were doing was wrong. Like, *Mom, Dad, I'm sooo sorry. I had no idea you wouldn't want me to go to the party of the century.*"

"Party of the century," Victoria echoed. "Does that make either of you see the words *parental supervision?*"

"Yeah, not so much," said Jane.

Leaning her hip against the stove, Victoria sighed. "Maybe you two should go without me."

"But don't you *want* to go?" Natalya asked. "I mean"—she looked around the room—"I think we all want to go."

Jane shrugged. "I can take it or leave it."

Natalya spread her hands in amazement. "Guys, *hello!* Isn't this what high school is *about?* Cool parties."

"Since when are you so into parties?" Jane laughed, then stood up and stretched. "Okay, what about this: Honesty is the best policy, right? You could just *tell* them. Just say, *Mom, Dad, I want to go to this party. There won't be parents there, but I'll be responsible. You can trust me.*" Hands high above her head, back arched, Jane shook her fingers. "Voilà! That's what I'm going to tell my mom, and she'll totally—"

"We *know!*" Natalya and Victoria said at the same time, exasperated.

Victoria took the popovers out of the oven and dropped them into a napkin-lined cloth basket, then turned to Natalya. "What are you telling *your* parents?"

Natalya picked at an invisible piece of thread on her FOXY LADY T-shirt. "I don't know . . . I'll think of something."

Victoria brought the basket over to the table, already set with half a dozen different jellies and butters, as Natalya jammed her index fingers into her forehead. "Okay, how about this . . ." She reached across the table and took Victoria's hand. "How about if you don't tell your parents *anything?*"

"You mean, lie?" A worried crease appeared on Victoria's forehead, and she put down her butter knife.

"Not *lie*, exactly," Natalya corrected her quickly.

Jane took a popover out of the basket, then danced it between her hands. "Hot. Hot. Hot."

Natalya continued. "I'm just saying, what if you ask your parents if you can stay at my house or Jane's house and then just . . . don't mention that we might go out briefly to the party of the century?"

"You mean, lie," Victoria translated. "I don't know . . . And won't *your* parents ask where we're going?"

Natalya dropped her head back, exasperated.

"Wait!" Jane said suddenly. "Why can't we just all sleep here that night? Aren't you always saying your parents are never home?"

Victoria considered Jane's point. "It's true," she acknowledged.

"Just think about all the things *Emily* gets away with," Natalya reminded her.

At Natalya's words, Victoria sat for a minute, staring off into the air above the table. Then she disappeared into the dining room.

"Where are you going?" called Jane, taking a bite of her popover. "Wow, Vicks, this is really good. I'd definitely pay money for one of these."

There was no answer. Jane looked at Natalya and shrugged. Natalya took a popover out of the basket and ripped off a piece but didn't eat it.

A minute later, Victoria reappeared, holding a manila folder open in front of her. "This is it."

"And this would be . . ." Jane prompted, wiping some jam from her upper lip

"Tentative schedule, blah blah blah September . . . September . . . October, October . . ." Victoria ran her index finger down the page, then announced, her voice inflectionless, "They have a fund-raiser in Rockland County the night of the party." She raised her eyes to her friends. "ETA Manhattan, midnight."

Natalya screamed and jumped out of her chair. "Oh my god, this is a *sign*. It's like a *fairy tale*: we have to be home by midnight."

"*If* we go," Victoria said.

"You have no *idea* how fun this is going to be." The words tumbled out of Natalya's mouth. "They're like . . . the coolest people."

"Hey!" Jane interrupted.

"Not cool like *you guys*," Natalya said quickly. Her cheeks were flushed with excitement. "But this party is going to be *really* fun."

Victoria traced her finger along the edge of the paper. "Do you think there's going to be drinking?"

"Hmm . . ." Jane pretended to consider the question. "High school kids. No parents. Party of the century . . . Nah."

"If there's drinking, we'll leave," Natalya promised.

Victoria nibbled her lower lip. "It *does* sound kind of fun," she admitted. There was the slightest hint of a gleam in her eyes.

Natalya crossed the kitchen to stand beside Victoria. Both girls were smiling, Natalya a bit more broadly than her friend.

"Our first high school party," said Jane, looking over at them, and her face broke into a grin, too.

"We're really going, aren't we?" Natalya breathed.

"Looks like it," Jane agreed. "Vicks?"

Slowly, slowly, Victoria nodded. Natalya jumped up and down and hugged her. "Oh my god, this is going to be soooo much fun!"

"I'm scared," Victoria whispered, but she was still smiling. "This is *so* bad." She slipped the schedule carefully back in the folder. "If they find out I went to a party without telling them, my parents will *kill* me."

"No they won't," Jane promised as Victoria and Natalya joined her at the table.

"How can you be so sure?" asked Victoria.

Jane handed them each a popover. "Because. Four out of five registered voters say they would be unlikely to vote for a candidate who'd killed a member of his immediate family."

Victoria lifted her glass of orange juice. "To registered voters, darling."

Jane and Natalya clinked their glasses against hers. "To registered voters," they echoed.

Chapter
Sixteen

SUNDAY, AFTER JANE and Natalya left, Victoria was sitting at her desk trying to figure out the area of a triangle, when her sister poked her head into her room.

"Hey," said Emily, coming in and plopping down on Victoria's bed. "Whatcha up to?"

Victoria nodded at the open textbook. "Math. Zipple."

At the name of her former math teacher, Emily rolled her eyes. "God, haven't they retired him yet? He *has* to be at least a hundred years old."

"Sometimes when he drops a piece of chalk and bends down to get it, I'm scared he won't be able to stand up," Victoria admitted.

"Perhaps not an idle fear," said Emily. As she stretched out across the bed on her stomach, Victoria realized it was a little weird to see her sister in the apartment on a random Sunday afternoon, and even weirder that it was weird.

Last month Emily had lived here. Now she lived in Princeton.

Emily looked around the room, taking in the white lacy bedspread and the white wallpaper with the pattern of tiny strawberries. "I think it might be time for a new look."

Victoria followed her sister's gaze. For the past year she'd felt more and more like she was living in the wrong room, like the rose-colored rug and tiny white desk and dresser she'd picked out in fourth grade had nothing to do with the person she was now. "Yeah, I guess it's a little babyish." Victoria scooted her feet onto the chair and hugged her knees; she had the urge to tell Emily about the party she'd been invited to, how she was going to lie to their parents about going. Emily had totally done things like that in high school—she'd probably think it was cool of Victoria.

But what if Emily felt some strange and sudden urge to tell their parents about Victoria's plans? That would mean no plausible deniability for sure. Best to keep her mouth shut.

The Scoop was lying on Victoria's bed, and Emily propped herself up on her elbows and thumbed through it. "Aaah, *The Scoop*. I so remember this."

"It's not like you're *thirty*," Victoria pointed out. "You only graduated in June."

Emily slowly turned the pages. "Oh, this is a good shot." She turned the paper sideways and read aloud. "Jack Hastings."

Victoria felt her stomach flip at the sound of Jack's name coming out of her sister's mouth. *I totally like him*, she almost said, only managing not to utter the words by literally biting hard on her lower lip. Emily had had two serious boyfriends already. She'd gotten caught spending the night with one of them. Did Victoria seriously think Emily would be impressed by her stalking Jack through the West Village last Saturday, then barely having the courage to wave at him each time they'd passed in the hall since then?

Folding the paper in half, Emily sat up with her legs tucked behind her. "You know, Vicks, I hope you won't take this the wrong way, but I could give you some talking points if you want. Just a few basic answers to questions reporters are likely to ask."

Victoria felt bad. Was this why Emily had come into her room, to offer *talking points*? "What, you mean that sixty percent of all bankruptcies are the result of medical costs charged to people who *had health insurance*?"

Emily perked up. "See, you *do* know things. You're just too shy to say them. Maybe you should do debate!" She lifted the paper slightly so Victoria could see that it was open to the JOIN A CLUB page. "That's really how I learned to speak in public."

This was so embarrassing. To think she'd almost confessed to Emily that she had a crush on Jack. Would Emily have offered her talking points on that, too? Victoria glared at her sister. "Did it ever occur to you that you need *not*-talking points? That people find it incredibly *annoying* to have to listen to some college girl's ideas about how to run a campaign when they're *professionals*?"

"Oh, please." Emily waved away Victoria's accusation. "When they feel that way they tell me."

Victoria stood up and put her hands on her hips. "I think you should go now. I have a lot of homework to do."

"Fine," said Emily. She glanced down at the paper one last time, then got off Victoria's bed. "But if Dad wins this election, you'd better be prepared for every reporter in this country to refer to you as the *quiet, pretty one.*"

"Better than being the *annoying, won't-shut-up one!*" Victoria yelled after her sister's retreating back.

"Later, Betty Crocker." And with that, Emily, who hadn't bothered to shut Victoria's door, slammed her own.

Victoria marched over to her door and tried to slam it, but the edge caught on the rug, and it just sort of sagged shut. Of *course* Emily's door slammed and hers didn't. Of course Emily had a better parting insult than Victoria had.

Victoria went back to her desk and her math problem, but what had been difficult before was impossible now. The numbers swirled around on the page, and the longer she stared at them, the more completely they refused to stay put.

Closing her pencil in her book, Victoria walked aimlessly around the room. Emily got her *so* mad. Why was it that everything her sister did well was stuff her family valued, while everything Victoria did well was totally irrelevant? Even baking. Baking was what her dad did after a hard day of *real* work; it wasn't the work itself. And her mother's feeling was that if you were important and busy enough, baking was just something you hired someone else to do, like cleaning the apartment.

Her eye caught *The Scoop*. Even her school didn't value the one thing she was good at. There were a million different clubs that boiled down to public speaking—oratory, debate, mock trial, model congress, model UN. But was there a baking club? No. Why had she even *gone* to Morningside? Natalya went to Gainsford because she was a genius, and Gainsford was the most prestigious, competitive school in New York. And Jane went to The Academy for the Performing Arts because she was a great actress.

Why did Victoria go to Morningside?

Because her sister had gone there.

Just thinking about how unfair her situation was made her even more furious. She grabbed the paper, spun around, and carried it over to her desk. Then she flipped open her computer and entered the Web address at the bottom of the page listing all the clubs. A minute later, the Morningside typeface filled her screen.

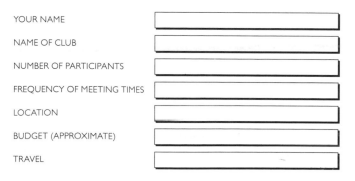

We're thrilled that you'd like to start a club! Please take a moment to fill out the following form. When you are done, send it to your class dean. And remember: the more you tell us, the more likely it is that we will approve your request.

YOUR NAME	
NAME OF CLUB	
NUMBER OF PARTICIPANTS	
FREQUENCY OF MEETING TIMES	
LOCATION	
BUDGET (APPROXIMATE)	
TRAVEL	

She stared at the screen for several minutes. Most of the answers were easy—the club could meet once a week. And it wasn't that hard to figure out how much ingredients would cost. Obviously they'd meet in the school's kitchen. *Number of participants. Number of participants.* The phrase made her feel cold and hot all at once. What if you formed a club and nobody came? She imagined the school's industrial kitchen, then pictured herself standing there, the president of a club that nobody wanted to join.

She was about to shut her computer when her fingers found her necklace. *Do what you're scared to do.*

Hands shaking, Victoria began typing, forcing herself not to add a sound track to the image of herself standing all alone at the first meeting of her baking club.

The sound track of Emily saying, *I told you so, Betty Crocker.*

Chapter
Seventeen

SITTING IN HISTORY on Monday morning, the day the cast list for *A Midsummer Night's Dream* was going to be posted, Jane barely listened to Mr. Chinowitz dissect the importance of the upcoming election, and it wasn't just because she always found it weird to hear people talk about Andrew Harrison's campaign when his daughter was her best friend.

". . . which is why you can see the history of this Senate seat as a history of *both* the Democratic *and* Republican parties in this country. Now, why is that unusual? Robert Hancock."

For reasons he had not bothered to explain, Mr. Chinowitz called all the students by both their first and last names. Jane wondered if it had something to do with teaching an academic subject at a school where everyone cared more about creativity than history. Maybe this was his weird way of being creative.

Robert Hancock, who'd been tapping out a beat with his thumbs on his blank notebook, was now looking up at Mr. Chinowitz, a bewildered expression on his face. "Wait, can you ask that question again?"

Jane looked down at her desk. Every Tuesday the school put out *Variety*, a calendar of all the upcoming performances and auditions. In anticipation of not getting a part in *A Midsummer Night's Dream*, Jane had slipped a copy into her notebook. She thumbed through it, checking to see what plays were holding auditions this week. Okay, they weren't seriously doing *The Vagina Monologues*, were they? The thought of trying out for a play when she would be actively hoping she *didn't* get a part was too much to bear. For the ten millionth time she relived her *Midsummer* audition—how she'd totally frozen on the second go-round, how she'd stumbled over *breast* like it was a dirty word she was embarrassed to utter in public. Maybe she deserved to audition for *The Vagina Monologues*. Maybe that would teach her to grow up and be less of a wuss.

English passed in a blur. Her phone buzzed and she looked down at the screen. J—what r we going 2 wear 2 the party?!?! N

Jane turned her phone to silent without responding. Did Natalya even remember that today was the day they were posting the cast list? Okay, so the most popular girl at her school had invited Natalya to a party at her house. It wasn't like Jane wasn't happy for her. But right now she had other things on her mind.

She glanced at the clock—it was eleven. The list was almost certainly posted; soon, people who weren't free this period would know who'd been cast. She would have to play it breezy. Cool.

Hey, I figured I wouldn't get cast.

Just getting some good audition experience.

Um, Shakespeare's kind of five minutes ago, don't you think?

As Mr. Stewart assigned the class two paragraphs comparing and contrasting George and Lennie, Jane stared at the cover of *Of Mice and Men* and tried to make her expression a study in blasé. Looking at the book as if it were a sympathetic classmate, she gave a small smile and shrugged in a way that felt worldly wise. By the time the bell rang she felt she'd hit on an acceptable expression of resigned pluckiness.

Walking out of English class, she literally bumped into either Wendy or Sharon, who was turning down the corridor at a trot. Would she remember Jane and her humiliating audition?

"Oops," Wendy/Sharon said, swerving aside at the last second.

"Sorry," said Jane as Wendy/Sharon continued down the hall.

"Later," called Wendy/Sharon over her shoulder.

Jane's response was automatic. "Later." She was grateful to Wendy/Sharon for being so chill.

The list had been posted, she was sure of it. Two freshman girls she didn't know walked by her, glanced her way, then looked at each other and whispered something.

"I'm not *blind*," she muttered as they passed. For the ten millionth time she thought about how awesome it would be if she'd had a great audition, if she were the only freshman to be cast.

Suddenly there was an arm around her waist.

"What the—"

She turned to face her attacker. There was Laurie. *Oh god, sympathy from Laurie. LAURIE. Laurie who she'd ditched for being so annoying.*

This moment had to be the low point of her life.

"Who's the bravest?!" Laurie chanted.

"I am!" Jane chanted back.

"You are!" Laurie echoed.

Right then, Mark came out of the classroom Laurie had just exited. Jane steeled herself for whatever condescending comment he was going to make, but he just gave a brief thumbs-up, then pointed at his watch and quickened his pace.

"Gotta motor!" he called as he passed.

"Oh my god," she said quietly.

Because Mark hadn't just given her the thumbs-up, he'd also *avoided* her.

And there was only one reason on earth Mark would have passed up this opportunity to gloat over her failure:

She hadn't failed.

"Oh my god," she repeated.

Laurie looked at her, confused, and Jane spun around to check the hallway clock. Her next class started in two and a half minutes. "Laurie, I've gotta run." She wanted to see with her own eyes, didn't want to hear another word from Laurie or Wendy/ Sharon or anyone. She turned in the direction of the theater and started booking down the hall.

"See you later!" Laurie called after her.

And for the second time that day, Jane responded, "Later!"

No matter what happened to her for the rest of her life (if she really did win an Academy Award or a Tony or get her own miniseries on A&E), Jane was positive she would never, ever forget the moment when she saw her name on the cast list for *A Midsummer Night's Dream*.

HELENA: Fran Sherman

HERMIA: Bethany Morales

DEMETRIUS: Hugh Price

LYSANDER: Daniel Milosch

TITANIA: Emily Chang

OBERON: Josh Fox

PUCK: Willis Avery

NICK BOTTOM: Jay McDonald

PETER QUINCE: Mark Alley

HIPPOLYTA: Jane Sterling

PEASEBLOSSOM: Dahlia Long

Jane had never known what people meant when they said they were so excited they couldn't recognize their own name, but now she did. It wasn't that you literally couldn't read the individual letters. It was that they didn't add up to anything. She saw the words *Jane Sterling* and had to remind herself that Jane Sterling was her. She was Jane. *That's me!* she kept saying to herself. *Me! My name is up there. I'm Hippolyta.* She remembered the character of Hippolyta from reading the play in English. It was a good part. Not a lead role, but not a tiny one either.

There was a ringing in her ears. As she read and reread her name, the door opened, and whichever Wendy/Sharon she hadn't run into earlier emerged. Jane had to fight the urge to throw her arms around the girl and say, *I love you, Wendy/Sharon!*

Wendy/Sharon gave her a nod. "Hey." She looked behind her at the list, as if checking to make sure it was still up, then waited to hear the click of the door locking behind her.

"Hey," Jane answered.

Wendy/Sharon headed down the corridor, then turned back briefly. "See you at two forty-five," she reminded Jane. "Don't be late."

Rehearsal. She had *rehearsal* after school. And as the reality of what she'd accomplished sank in, Jane felt her eyes welling up. She reached into her bag to get her phone, and when she took it out she saw she had seven missed calls.

No sooner had she switched her phone off silent than it started to buzz almost angrily.

This time she picked up. "Vicks!"

"I've only been calling all *morning*!" Victoria's voice was half relieved, half peeved.

"Let's just say you'd better be free October thirtieth because it's opening night."

Victoria screamed. "Oh my god!!! I knew it. You got a part. What's the part? Oh my god! Oh my god! Oh my *god*! You *did it, darling!*"

And somehow, even though it was Victoria talking to her, Jane felt like the words came straight from Nana.

Chapter
Eighteen

SITTING IN FRENCH class after getting off the phone with Jane, Victoria couldn't help thinking about what a dismal start her high school career had gotten off to. Natalya had been invited to a party by the coolest girl in her grade. Jane was the only freshman who had gotten a part in her school's major fall production. Could Victoria at least . . .

    A. talk to the boy she couldn't stop thinking about?

    B. stop thinking about the boy she couldn't talk to?

    C. impress all of her teachers with her superb command of the subject matter?

    D. none of the above.

Victoria drew a huge *D* on the blank page in front of her, then traced tiny *D*'s inside of it. Then she wrote *Jack* in loopy script and quickly crossed it out, drawing lines through the word hard enough to rip the paper.

She didn't know what she'd thought would happen after they'd run into each other in (okay, after she'd *stalked him through*) the West Village, but that Monday morning when she'd arrived at the bio lab seconds behind him, she'd been sure *something* would be different between them.

"Hey," Jack had said, seeing her come through the door. He'd smiled at her.

"Hey," Victoria had said. She'd smiled at him and then . . . Jack had gone to his lab table.

Victoria had gone to her lab table.

The. End.

U should have asked him how the concert wuz! Jane had texted her.

Its not 2 L8! Natalya reminded her.

Except that it was. Each time she saw him in the halls, or as they were walking into class, she'd tell herself, *Now. Now. Ask him now.*

Hey, Jack would say.

Hey, Victoria would say.

Lather. Rinse. Repeat.

"*Non, non, Maeve. Ce n'est pas 'je suis le livre.' J'ai le livre. Répétez. J'ai le livre.*"

Maeve, who usually sat toward the edge of the room and who never spoke unless Madame called on her, echoed what Madame

Desbonnet had just said, and Madame said, "*Bravo, mademoiselle.*" Maeve looked down at her desk.

Maeve seemed quiet but nice, and Victoria had the feeling they could be friends. But so far she'd been too shy to approach Maeve.

Hmmm. Perhaps this was the problem with two shy people becoming friends: neither one was brave enough to make the first move.

There was a knock on the classroom door, and a moment later it swung open and Madame Desbonnet took a slip of paper from an older woman Victoria didn't recognize. Madame Desbonnet glanced at it, then looked around the room until her eyes found Victoria. "*Mademoiselle, va parler avec Dean Gordon après la classe.*"

Totally confused, Victoria managed to nod calmly in response. It sounded like Madame Desbonnet had just told her to go talk to the freshman dean after class. But why? Was she in trouble for something? She stared down at the *D*'s she'd been drawing. Were her grades bad enough that she was going to get some kind of a warning? But she'd only had a handful of quizzes so far, and on each she'd gotten her usual eighty-something. Could Dean Gordon have somehow found out about her plans to sneak out to a party without telling her parents? Her heart raced at the possibility, but not even her father's campaign manager could have made Victoria believe such a paranoid theory. Dean Gordon was a pudgy balding man in khakis and rumpled sweaters who, when it came to saying hello to students in the hallway, favored the greeting, "How ya doin', tiger?" This did not strike Victoria as a man with the power to read teenage minds.

• • •

Victoria was about to push open the door labeled DEAN GORDON when she had a terrible thought. What if this *was* about her father? What if the dean was going to ask her to invite her dad to speak at Morningside? *Also, Victoria, we were hoping you'd introduce him. Your sister was always* such *a talented public speaker.*

The thought of standing frozen at a podium in front of the entire school made Victoria need to lean her forehead against the cool plaster of the wall. But then she took a deep breath. Her father was busy. *Really* busy. So busy she barely saw him. Normally that was a bad thing, but right now, it was a completely legitimate excuse. *He travels a lot, Dean. I don't think he can come speak.*

Before she could come up with another scenario with which to terrify herself, Victoria twirled her fingers through the chain of her necklace, then knocked crisply on the door. "Come in!" called a male voice.

Pushing the heavy wooden door, Victoria found herself standing in a waiting area with an empty desk. Behind the desk was a pale blue wall with a door leading into an inner office. Next to the door were two plastic chairs.

In one of the chairs sat Jack Hastings.

For a panicked second, Victoria wondered if he would know, just by looking at her, how much she'd been thinking about their conversation on Leonard Street; how she'd played it over and over in her mind until it was as tattered as a page of one of her favorite cookbooks.

For a long second, neither of them spoke. In the silence Victoria felt hyperconscious of everything—the cool breeze through her T-shirt, the loud click of the door as it shut, the hum of Dean Gordon's absent secretary's computer, how her bag dug into her shoulder from the weight of her books.

Jack looked up at her from under his bangs and said, "We've got to stop meeting like this."

Victoria couldn't have responded if her life depended on it.

"That was a joke," Jack said finally.

Victoria nodded.

He tried again. "So, you come here often?"

"No," Victoria said, relieved that her voice was working again.

"Well, by all means, have a look around." He spread his hands out to show her what she should check out.

Victoria stood by the door, looking at the office. There wasn't much to see—chairs, the unoccupied desk, a dispenser holding brightly colored pamphlets on which she could read the word *City*, a tired-looking plant in one corner. When she finished examining the room and arrived back at Jack, he was watching her. Victoria quickly dropped her eyes from his face and read the letters on his dark blue T-shirt. CBGB's. She wondered what it meant.

"So," he said seriously, "you're in trouble."

"I am?" Victoria asked anxiously, looking up.

Jack shook his head. "I don't know. Are you?"

Victoria felt stupid for having taken his joke seriously. "You sounded so . . . sure."

"Are you standing up because you're afraid to sit next to me or something?" He gestured at the empty chair next to him.

"Am I . . . what? No!" Her cheeks felt hot. She wished she could lean her face against the cool, cool wall behind her.

"I don't bite," he assured her.

"I know," she answered stupidly. Obviously he didn't *bite*.

She made her way across the tiny space and sat in the chair next to him, then crossed her legs. "How was the concert?" As soon as she'd spoken the words, she regretted them. He probably wouldn't even know which concert she was talking about.

If Jack thought it was weird that Victoria still remembered he'd been on his way to a concert when they ran into each other almost two weeks ago, he didn't indicate it. "Good," he said thoughtfully. "My dad was in it. He plays with the New York Philharmonic. Wait, did I tell you that already?"

The odds of Jack's having told Victoria a major detail about his family, and her having forgotten it, were pretty much nil, but all she said was, "I don't think so."

"Oh. Well, he's a cellist. Anyway, I think you would have liked it." She glanced at him and saw that he was looking at her.

She immediately looked away again, but as she was staring at the floor, she thought she heard him say something.

Victoria lifted her head. "What?"

"I didn't say anything," he answered.

Their eyes locked, and Victoria found herself speaking without deciding to speak. "Are *you* in trouble?" she asked quietly.

He nodded.

"What for?" Her voice was a near-whisper.

Jack waited. Then, his voice low also, he asked, "Are you a music lover? Because if you're a music lover you're going to feel completely sympathetic, and if you're not, you're going to think I'm some kind of delinquent."

Victoria couldn't think of another time when she'd whispered with a boy. It was intimate somehow, private. Like they were exchanging not just information but secrets.

"I mean, I like music," she told him.

Jack gave her a long stare. "Not a music lover."

She hesitated, then finally shook her head, feeling like she'd failed a test of some kind. "I guess not," she admitted, disappointed. Now he wasn't going to tell her why he was in Dean Gordon's office.

They sat without speaking for another minute before Jack turned to her, crossing one ankle over the opposite knee and leaning forward. "Okay. So if I tell you why I'm in trouble, you have to insert whatever it is you're passionate about for music. Like, if I tell you, oh, I don't know, that some friends and I used fake IDs to get into clubs and Dean Gordon found out about it and is trying to shake me down to find out who *made* the fake IDs, you replace music with something *you'd* break a law to see. Hypothetically," he added quickly. "That's, you know, a completely hypothetical scenario."

Victoria giggled. "Um, I don't think you have to break any laws to bake stuff."

Jack opened his eyes wide. "No way, you're a chef?"

"Not a chef," she corrected him. "A baker."

"Oh." He wrinkled his forehead. "What's the difference?"

No one had ever asked Victoria to explain the difference between cooking and baking before. Most guys her age probably wouldn't care.

"Well," she began slowly, "baking's all about precision." She realized for the first time just what it was she preferred about baking, and growing confident, she turned to him and tucked her foot under her leg. "You have to be very exact or cakes won't rise, and your chocolate will burn instead of melting. But cooking's more a little of this, a dash of that." She mimed tossing some ingredients into an invisible bowl, then shook her head. "It's too unpredictable."

He nodded his understanding. "So you like things to be predictable."

Suddenly she fell silent, feeling exposed. Was he making fun of her? "I . . ."

"Sorry," he said quickly. He touched her gently on the knee, then pulled his hand away. "Sorry," he said again, and Victoria didn't know if it was because of what he'd said or because he'd touched her. "I shouldn't have jumped to conclusions. I think it's cool that you like to bake." He fiddled with his camera briefly, nervously.

"Thanks," she said, but she was still thinking about his calling her *predictable*. Predictable. Was that like uptight? Or was it something good, like reliable?

Jack pressed a button and looked down at the viewfinder of his camera. "Hey, want to see something?" he asked. Victoria watched as he scrolled through the pictures too fast for her to see what they were. Finally he slowed down and then stopped. "Look."

She did. The picture in the viewfinder was of Ms. Kalman, their bio teacher, from the back. She was pulling a wedgie out of her butt. Jack paused, then switched to the next image. It was another teacher, a man, also from behind, and he had a piece of toilet paper sticking out of the waist of his pants.

"What . . . what are these?" asked Victoria. She had a crazy fear that the next photo would be of herself, maybe picking her nose or smiling with food in her teeth. But it was another teacher, a woman. She was standing on the street corner, frantically trying to lower her skirt, which was being lifted by the wind.

Jack chuckled. "We're thinking about doing a most-embarrassing-moments spread in the paper. What do you think?" He raised his eyes and looked at her.

Victoria hated the pictures so much it made her dizzy. "I . . ." She meant to say, "I don't think it's such a good idea"; to tell him how humiliated her mom felt when *Us Weekly* ran a photo of her in a baggy, unflattering suit on its Worst Dressed page; to confess that she'd had dreams in which Satan came up to her with proof that she'd done or said something awful, something guaranteed to lose her father the election. But instead, she just blurted out, "I think they're awful."

The smile disappeared from Jack's face as quickly as if she'd slapped him. "What?"

She wanted to explain, but just then the door to the inner office opened, and Dean Gordon stuck his head out, looking even more rumpled and pudgy than he usually did. He frowned at Jack and smiled at Victoria. "Jack, I'm going to ask you to wait a minute. Victoria, come on in and let's talk about that baking club you're interested in starting."

Victoria felt angry and uncomfortable. Why had Jack showed her those pictures? Why had he *taken* those pictures? How could she like someone who thought it was funny to embarrass people like that? Then again, maybe it *was* funny. In which case, maybe there was something wrong with *her*.

She managed to stand up in a vaguely dignified manner. "I guess I'll . . . see you around," she said lamely.

"Yeah," he said. "See ya."

How often had Victoria fantasized about this moment—she and Jack alone somewhere, talking privately. Whispering privately. *If only we could get to know each other better.*

Well, they'd gotten to know each other, all right.

And now she wished they hadn't.

Chapter Nineteen

THERE WERE FEW things in the world that Jane loved more than an empty theater. After school she entered the main auditorium at the Academy and took a deep breath, inhaling the smell of leather seats, velvet curtains, and the heat of the lights. Onstage, twenty or so students were lounging, many in clumps of two or three. There was no sign of Mr. Robbins or his producers, despite its being only seconds before two forty-five. As she walked down the dark aisle toward the front of the house, it seemed to Jane that every eye swiveled her way.

The theater door flew open, and Mr. Robbins entered, Wendy and Sharon in his wake. Jane took advantage of their distracting arrival to sit down by the edge of the stage floor. A few feet away from her, Fran Sherman was lying with her head in the lap of a guy who was rubbing her temples.

"My sincere apologies for my late arrival." Mr. Robbins's leather briefcase swung away from him as he turned to greet the group, then smacked him lightly in the side of his leg.

"We forgive you, Len. And don't worry—we still love you." Fran spoke from her prone position.

"I'm planning on taking that to the bank." Mr. Robbins's voice was teasing, as Fran's had been, and he was smiling. Sitting down alone by the edge of the stage, Jane watched their banter, noticing again how handsome Mr. Robbins was. He dropped his bag on the floor, pulled his sweater over his head, then dropped it on top of the bag.

"Welcome, all of you, to the magical world of *A Midsummer Night's Dream*." He spread his arms wide to include, it seemed to Jane, not just the cast but the play, Shakespeare, and, perhaps, theater in general. "We are all very privileged indeed to have the opportunity to work on this incredible play.

"I'm going to walk you through some of the nuts and bolts of our rehearsal schedule briefly, then I want to do some exercises, and then I'll let you go. Before you leave, you'll make sure to get a copy of the script from Wendy or Sharon."

Both girls looked up from their seats in the front row. Wendy waved first, then Sharon, and Jane was glad to finally be able to tell which was which.

"Our calendar is much tighter than I'd like it to be, which has to do with all kinds of irrelevant things like the fact that

Christmas vacation comes early this year and we're staging *Chicago* in this theater immediately after *Midsummer*. I decided *not* to move *Midsummer* to the black box. It belongs on the main stage because it is going to be an outrageous, enormous, over-the-top production, and I want lots of razzle-dazzle that we can only have if we stage it here. But it means our rehearsal schedule is going to be brutal, so tell your friends and your boyfriends and your girlfriends and your parents that you'll see them in November.

"That said, being in one of my shows is no excuse for not doing your homework, so if you can't rehearse until six every day and again on Saturday mornings *and* get all of your work done, now's the time to say 'Thanks, Len, but no thanks.'" He paused for a moment, but no one expected anyone to leave, and no one left. Still, when the cast stayed put, Mr. Robbins looked around like he was surprised and genuinely thrilled they'd all decided to stay. "Okay, let's get up and walk around." He raised his hands, and instantly, as if they were the puppets and he the puppeteer, everyone was on their feet.

"Take up the whole stage. Don't clump together." Groups formed and separated as Mr. Robbins had them walk double-time, in slow motion, taking huge steps, baby steps, acting as if they were at a circus, then at a funeral, then a national park.

Jane didn't know people's names, but it didn't take her long to figure out who the stars were (offstage, anyway). As Mr. Robbins barked out settings, the cast broke into supposedly spontaneous groups and pairs to admire the sights or comfort imaginary mourners or buy last-minute Christmas gifts at a crowded store; Jane watched the same people find each other again and again.

Fran was always walking along either with the boy who had been giving her a head rub earlier, with a short, slightly pudgy girl with equally short hair, or with an insanely hot African American guy who wasn't the underwear model.

Every once in a while, right at the moment Mr. Robbins instructed the cast to do something, Fran and her friends would be standing with or near another actor—"You're at a sweet sixteen and the music is *loud*!"—then they would seem to absorb the outsider, but soon the foursome would somehow drift away, and the person would be left alone. Jane wasn't sure if it was her imagination, but she got the sense that for the few seconds or minutes people were acting alongside the elite group, they were trying . . . harder somehow. Like this wasn't just a rehearsal, it was also an audition.

"Okay, everyone, find a partner!"

Jane and a tall Asian girl made eye contact; the girl nodded slightly when Jane raised her eyebrows, and they made their way toward each other.

"I'm Dahlia," the girl said. Jane remembered that Dahlia was playing Peaseblossom, one of the fairies.

"Jane," said Jane.

Dahlia nodded as if she already knew who Jane was, and Jane felt her chest swell with pride.

"Okay, let's get this started. One of you is A, one is B. When I say go, A starts moving and B starts mirroring A's movements. When I say switch, you switch."

"Want to be A?" asked Jane.

"Sure."

"And go!" announced Mr. Robbins.

Dahlia raised her right arm slowly. Jane raised her left arm at the same pace. Dahlia opened her mouth to form a wide O, and Jane did the same.

"Nice work, Willis." Mr. Robbins strolled through the pairs, pausing at each couple and observing them briefly before moving on. "Now, switch!"

Jane continued Dahlia's movement seamlessly; she was sure even someone watching closely wouldn't have been able to pinpoint the exact moment when Dahlia began following and Jane leading.

"Slow down a little, Josh," Mr. Robbins advised. "You're not letting Hugh follow you. Okay, switch."

Jane sensed Mr. Robbins coming closer. Matching Dahlia perfectly, she made her movements even slower and more fluid. Was it her imagination or did he linger by them for longer than he had the other pairs?

"Very nice, Dahlia. Good work, Jane." He watched them for another long minute before clapping his hands once.

"Okay, that's enough for today. Read through your scripts, start learning your lines, see you tomorrow, two forty-five."

"'Hooray for Hollywood,'" Fran sang, and Jane felt a tingle of envy when Mr. Robbins joined her and they sang the next line together, "'That screwy ballyhooey Hollywood.'"

The cast gathered up their things. As they made their way down the steps from the stage, Dahlia said, "So you're the freshman."

"Yup," said Jane. "That's me." Dahlia's reminding her that

she was *the* freshman in the play made her feel better about not being the person who sang show tunes and joked around with Mr. Robbins. After all, when she was a freshman, had Fran done those things?

"See you." Dahlia gave a little wave as she went over to get her stuff off a seat, and Jane headed to where Wendy and Sharon were sitting.

"Here you go," said Wendy, handing her a script as she approached.

"Thanks." The pale yellow book with its crisp pages would, she knew, soon be dog-eared and ratty. She loved the feel of a new script in her hand, but she loved a used one better.

The cast moved out of the theater in clusters of two's and three's, laughing and joking.

Jane made her way up the aisle, passing a boy telling a girl, "I *totally* thought I bombed. When I saw my name up there, I was like, *No way!*"

The girl nodded but didn't say anything. Jane smiled at the boy. "Me too," she said.

He winked at her in a way that made Jane think he knew who she was. "And here we are," he congratulated her.

"Here we are," she echoed.

Mr. Robbins was standing by the exit, just outside the auditorium, talking to a guy wearing a tool belt and carrying a stage light under one arm. As Jane walked by, Mr. Robbins called out to her.

"Jane?"

She spun around, feeling her hair fan out around her head

and then settle gently on her shoulders, like she was in a shampoo commercial. "You called?"

His smile was wide, his white teeth sparkling in the lobby, so bright after the dimly lit theater.

"Nice work today," he said.

It wasn't as good as singing a duet together, but it was the next best thing. She gave a slight bow, then walked (or, rather, floated) to the front door.

Standing on the front steps of the Academy, she felt so giddy she couldn't help laughing. She was the only freshman in the cast. She was the only freshman in the cast, and Mr. Robbins thought she'd done a good job. She'd been at The Academy for the Performing Arts for less than a month, and already people were talking about her.

She wished she could call Nana and tell her all about the rehearsal she'd just had. Thinking of how proud Nana would be, Jane's eyes fill with tears. *I did it, Nana,* she thought to herself. *I did it.*

Chapter Twenty

"NATALYA, I'D LIKE to speak with you after class."

"Sure, Dr. Clover," answered Natalya. She stopped packing her bag and settled back down on her lab stool.

"Good luck," Jordan whispered, shoving her textbook into her overstuffed bag. "Do you need a cross or some garlic or anything?"

"I think I'll be okay." Natalya laughed. "See you at lunch."

Since their one lunch together, Morgan hadn't invited Natalya to eat with her again, and most days she ate with Jordan and her friends. She liked them and they were easy to be with, but she often found her mind wandering to what Morgan, Sloane, and Katrina were saying in their secret room. Every night when she checked her e-mail, she clicked on the message Morgan had sent with the details of the party. If she hadn't received it, she might have thought she'd imagined ever talking to her.

Leaving the bio lab, Jordan gave Natalya a supportive smile that Natalya appreciated but—perhaps foolishly—didn't feel that she needed. Natalya genuinely *liked* Dr. Clover. It wasn't as if Ms. MacFadden had asked her to stay after class in order to learn which theater companies her parents were on the board of.

Now *that* would have been scary.

"I won't keep you long," Dr. Clover informed her, doing her strange walk/march over to Natalya's table. "I was just wondering if you've been enjoying the reserve reading you've done."

Wait, hadn't Dr. Clover said the reserve reading wouldn't earn them extra credit? "How do you know about that?" asked Natalya, proud but a little confused.

"I have my ways," Dr. Clover answered, not smiling.

"The librarian," Natalya realized, thinking out loud. "The librarian told you."

"An interesting hypothesis," Dr. Clover responded. Was it Natalya's imagination or was there just the hint of a smile at the edge of Dr. Clover's mouth? "But you haven't answered my question."

Natalya had read the articles Dr. Clover had put on reserve each week. "I really liked the one about how trends are viral. But the one about the politics of funding for science research and the one on the biosphere weren't as interesting to me." As she rated the articles for Dr. Clover, Natalya suddenly wondered if she'd liked the article about trends best because it was while she was photocopying it that Morgan had asked her to have lunch in order to invite her to the party.

"Yes, that author's work is influential." Dr. Clover nodded briefly. "Have you considered doing an experiment of your own?"

"I thought we're doing a research paper, not an experiment." Natalya remembered Sloane and Katrina talking about writing their reports on outer space. It wasn't as if they could decide to go live on the International Space Station.

Or could they?

Dr. Clover waved her comment away. "I want you to engage in a current scientific debate, that's all. And given your work in class and your willingness to go the extra mile in your reading . . ." She shrugged. "You have an impressive mind. I wouldn't want you to feel constrained by secondary sources if it is primary research that is really appealing to you." Without waiting for Natalya to respond, Dr. Clover made an abrupt pivot and headed to the back of the room. "Think about it, Natalya," she called. And then she disappeared into her office.

Natalya didn't walk to the cafeteria, she floated there. Dr. Clover had said she had an impressive mind. *An impressive mind.*

The lunchroom was crowded, but Jordan waved her over. "You survived!"

Natalya laughed at Jordan's relief. "Come on. Clover's not that bad."

Catherine shook her head in disbelief. "Please, that woman is S-C-A-R-Y."

Perry nodded in agreement. "I don't want to throw around

the word *soulless* lightly, but, you know . . ."

Now was probably not an ideal time for Natalya to announce that Dr. Clover was her favorite teacher in the world. Instead, she dropped her bag on an empty chair. "I'm going to get some food."

"Not the mac and cheese," Jordan reminded her. She held up her own sandwich. "Ham. It's the other white meat."

"Thanks." Natalya nodded and headed toward the food area. She couldn't believe it. The scariest teacher at Gainsford had complimented her mind. The most popular girl in the grade had e-mailed her an invitation to the party of the century. A group of totally nice girls saved her a seat at lunch and warned her away from the dangerous food offerings.

There was a spring in her step and a smile on her face as she crossed the cafeteria.

High school totally rocked.

Chapter
Twenty-one

FRIDAY NIGHT, JANE and Natalya arrived at Victoria's within seconds of each other. When Jane saw Natalya waiting for the elevator, her fingers clutching the handle of a suitcase on wheels, she laughed.

"How much did you *bring*?" Jane had a slim garment bag slung over one shoulder and a tiny tote over the other.

"Pretty much everything in my closet," Natalya confessed. "But I still don't think I have anything good."

"What's your new friend's name again?" Jane asked as the elevator door opened. "The one who's so much cooler than we are?"

"Ha-ha." Natalya stepped in next to Jane and watched the

numbers ascending. "Her name's Morgan Prewitt."

When they'd gone three floors without Natalya's speaking, Jane bumped her friend's shoulder lightly with her own. "Are you okay?" she asked. "You seem a little tense."

"I'm not tense," said Natalya, spinning her head in Jane's direction. "Why would you say I'm tense?"

Jane held her hands up as if to show there was no weapon in either. "Sor-*ry*," she said quickly.

Natalya sighed and returned to studying the numbers above the door. "No, I'm sorry. I'm just . . . Maybe I am a little nervous."

"Don't be," said Jane. "I mean, they obviously want to be friends with you or they wouldn't have invited you."

The door opened on Victoria's floor. "Sure," said Natalya, stepping out into the hallway. She took a deep breath. "I mean, yeah. Of course." Pulling the suitcase behind her, she walked down to Victoria's door just ahead of Jane and rang the bell.

A second later, as if she'd been standing with her hand on the knob, Victoria yanked open the door. "They're gone!" she whispered excitedly. "My dad's flight from Syracuse was delayed, and my mom said they weren't going to go, but then Satan went totally crazy on her. They were on the phone, and he was screaming, *We've got less than three weeks, Jennifer. We've got less than three weeks!* So they went."

"Oh my god." Natalya's eyes opened wide with fear. "I didn't even *consider* that."

Victoria nodded. "I *know*." She reached out and pulled Jane and Natalya into the foyer. "Come on, guys! Let's get gorgeous."

• • •

Forty-five minutes later, the three stood in Victoria's room, knee-deep in rejected outfits.

"It's like an issue of *Lucky* threw up in here," Jane observed, surveying the damage. She was wearing a strapless black dress and a pair of high heels, both of which her mom had lent her.

"Okay, what about this?" Natalya opened her arms for Jane and Victoria to see what she was wearing.

"That could work," Victoria chirped. She was wearing what she'd worn to their One Room graduation: a pale green sundress with a wide, puffy skirt.

Jane looked Natalya up and down, then shook her head sadly. "Sorry."

"No?" Natalya plucked at the shiny silver shirt she was wearing and spun around to show the slight flare of her short black skirt. "Doesn't it say party of the century?"

Still shaking her head, Jane told her, "It says Old Navy."

"That's bad, right?" asked Natalya, dropping to the floor in defeat.

"Well, it's better than Little Miss Muffet over here," said Jane, gesturing with her shoulder to Victoria.

"Hey!" Victoria objected, "I like this dress." But she was laughing.

"Guys," Jane explained, throwing her arms wide, "we're in *high school*. We're going to a *high school* party. You can't be all G-rated." She pointed at the tight bodice of her dress. "You need to be PG-13. At a *minimum*."

"This is a disaster," Natalya moaned. She flipped open the top of her suitcase, but it was empty. Not that it mattered. The tight silvery top was the most PG-13 thing she owned.

"Totally," agreed Victoria. She gnawed at her lower lip. "What are we going to do? I don't have anything like that." She indicated Jane's dress.

"What about your mom?" asked Jane.

"I mean . . ." Victoria did a quick mental scan of her mother's wardrobe. "She has some fancy stuff. But it's not, you know, sexy."

"This *sucks!*" Natalya wailed. She flopped onto Victoria's bed. "This totally *sucks!*"

"Okay, okay." Jane paced what little clear floor there was, her hands on her hips. "We need a plan. Option A, we don't go."

"No *way!*" Victoria said immediately.

Natalya rolled over and stared at her. So did Jane. "Listen to this one," Jane said, raising her eyebrows at Natalya and pointing her thumb at Victoria. "First she's all worried about getting caught; now suddenly she's a party girl."

"We're *going*," Victoria announced. "If I have to find a store that's open at"—she checked the time on her bedside clock—"nine thirty on a Friday night." Seeing how late it was made her panic. "Oh my god, we don't even have time to go shopping anywhere."

Suddenly, Jane, who had stopped pacing, jerked her head up and snapped her fingers. "That's it."

Natalya sat up. "Shopping? First of all, probably nothing's open. Plus, by the time we go shopping we'll have to turn around and come home."

"Not if we already *are* home," Jane observed.

"Okay, you're losing it," said Victoria. She looked down at Natalya. "She's lost it."

"Au contraire," Jane corrected. "I've found it." She paused dramatically. "We're going shopping in Emily's closet."

"Oh my god," whispered Victoria. Her eyes doubled in size. "That could be very, very bad."

"True," acknowledged Jane. There was a pause as Victoria and Natalya considered Jane's suggestion.

Finally, Victoria broke the silence. "Did I ever tell you guys what she called me a few weeks ago?"

"No," said Natalya.

"What?" asked Jane.

"Betty Crocker."

"She did *not!*" Natalya screeched.

"That *bitch!*" Jane agreed.

Victoria reached down and pulled Natalya to her feet. "Let's go raid that bitch's closet."

They crossed the hallway to Emily's room, but paused at the threshold.

"If you don't want to do this, we don't have to," Natalya whispered.

Without answering her, Victoria reached over and flipped the switch; immediately the room exploded with light.

Even though Emily was away at college, her room still felt as though someone lived in it. There was a jewelry box on the wooden dresser, and half a dozen throw pillows were strewn on the futon in the corner. The bulletin board next to the window was covered with certificates and honors Emily had won with the debate team and photos of her with friends from the soccer team, at her high school graduation, and shaking hands with President Obama. The bookshelves were piled with paperbacks and old textbooks, jumbled against one another in no particular order. There was a Princeton pennant tacked to the wall above the light switch, and on the opposite wall hung two posters. One was a photograph of a beach in Alaska where people in boots and raincoats were wiping oil off baby birds. Underneath, the caption said: *Never doubt that a small group of thoughtful, committed citizens can change the world. Indeed, it is the only thing that ever has. —Margaret Mead.* The other poster showed a girl on a motorcycle racing along a desert road. This one read: *Good girls go to heaven. Bad girls go everywhere.*

The posters were Emily in a nutshell.

Victoria crossed the room and pulled open the closet door. "God, I can't believe this is what she left behind." The closet was stuffed with clothes. They seemed to burst off the racks. Above the girls' heads, boxes of shoes were stacked almost to the ceiling.

"Seriously," Jane agreed. "It's like, how did she find the time to buy all these clothes *and* make dean's list?"

"Did she bring *anything* to Princeton?" asked Natalya.

Victoria turned from the treasures of the closet to look at her friends. "We rented a van to get all her crap up there."

"Can I just tell you something, darling?" Jane asked.

Victoria nodded.

"She is so not going to notice that we borrowed something."

Chapter Twenty-two

"WHAT FLOOR DOES Morgan live on?" asked Victoria. They were standing in front of number 65, a small apartment building, and Victoria's bare shoulders glowed in the soft light of the old-fashioned gas lamp beside the bright red door. She was wearing an ice blue strapless dress that Emily had worn to Morningside's spring formal her junior year.

Natalya shook her head. Emily's black dress, which was slightly too big on her, came up high in the front but plunged so low in the back that she'd made Jane and Victoria watch her walk all around the apartment to make sure her underwear wasn't showing. "She didn't give me an apartment number," Natalya said. "The invitation just said Sixty-five East Seventy-fourth."

Jane shrugged away the anxiety in Natalya's voice. "Don't worry. The doorman will know." There was a buzzer to the right of the front door, and Jane pressed it as Victoria rubbed her hands up and down her arms. "I'm freezing."

"You look amazing, though," said Natalya. "If Jack could see you now, he would *freak out.*"

Victoria looked away. "I don't really like him anymore."

"What?" asked Natalya, surprised.

"But he's so cute!" objected Jane. "What happened?"

Just then, the front door swung open.

Jane, Natalya, and Victoria stepped inside, toying with their necklaces without noticing they were doing it. They looked around the lobby for a doorman, then, simultaneously, they all realized the same thing.

This wasn't a lobby.

This wasn't an apartment building.

This was a house.

All thoughts of Jack were immediately forgotten.

"Oh. My. God." Victoria squeezed Natalya's fingers, and Natalya squeezed Jane's. They were standing in a large foyer with a white marble floor and an enormous winding staircase that slid up seemingly forever—in the shimmering light of hundreds of candles it was impossible to tell where it ended. Small recessed chambers lining the staircase held marble sculptures, and on the walls were gigantic oil paintings. Starting a few steps up, boys and girls were lounging on the stairs as if they were on sofas.

It was a good thing they had raided Emily's closet. One of

the girls sitting on the stairs was in a black dress, longer and tighter than the one Jane was wearing. Another had on what looked like pajamas, but they were pale bronze silk, nothing like the matching Old Navy pajamas Victoria and Jane had bought in June.

Still holding hands, Jane, Natalya, and Victoria began to climb the steps.

"Hey," Jane greeted a group of three people—two guys talking to a thin girl in a tight white dress.

"Hey," said one of the boys. He was wearing a pair of soft-looking beige pants, and he had a square, handsome jaw. As the girls passed the threesome, the guy said something about a regatta.

"What's a regatta?" Victoria whispered in Jane's ear.

"Maybe it's a dessert," Jane whispered back. They giggled as behind them someone said, "Cheese!" and there was a burst of light. A second later, a girl's voice squealed. "Oh my god, I look like *crap*. Delete that!"

Natalya stopped at the top of the flight of stairs they had just climbed, an enormous landing with archways opening up onto three of the biggest rooms any of the girls had ever seen outside of a school or a museum. They could see the corner of a grand piano. One of the rooms had a fireplace in which a fire was roaring. There were dozens of kids around, but no one was yelling or even talking loudly. If they'd been told everyone else in the house was ten years older than they were, Natalya, Jane, and Victoria would have believed it.

"We are so not in Kansas anymore, darling," Jane whispered into Natalya's ear.

Before Natalya could answer, someone called, "Hey, Natalya." They all looked to the room straight ahead of them. From a white sofa as big as a king-size bed, Morgan and Katrina waved, and the girls made their way into what would have been a living room except that once they were in it, they could see it opened onto another enormous room that *also* looked like a living room. There was a gigantic chandelier dripping glass teardrops that reflected the blaze of the fire like diamonds. The ceiling seemed to hover dozens of feet above their heads.

"Hi!" Natalya called back to Morgan. Taking Jane and Victoria by the hand, she pulled them to the sofa where Morgan and Katrina were sitting.

"I'm Morgan." Morgan stood up and embraced first Natalya, then Victoria, and then Jane. She was wearing a silver dress of a shimmery material that made Natalya think of the invisibility cloak in Harry Potter. It was tight through the hips and then fell gently into a skirt. Her hair was up in a sloppy bun. "And this is Katrina." Katrina, in a short, bright red dress, gave a little wave.

"It's so nice to meet you," said Morgan, linking her arm through Victoria's. "I'm really glad you could come."

Victoria smiled a slightly confused little smile.

Morgan opened her mouth to say something else, but Natalya interrupted her. "Where's the bathroom?" she asked abruptly.

Morgan pointed toward the landing, and Natalya skittered in the direction of Morgan's finger, not waiting to see if Jane or Victoria wanted to come.

Chapter
Twenty-three

NATALYA COULDN'T FIND the bathroom. There was a door under the stairs, but when she opened it she found herself looking at a wall of sporting equipment. Shutting the door, she turned around. She didn't have to pee that badly. She should just go back to her friends. But then she turned around and saw Morgan, arm through Victoria's, speaking seriously to her.

Was Morgan telling Victoria how her mother was obsessed with Andrew Harrison? Saying the only reason she'd wanted to be friends with Natalya was because of who Victoria's dad was? The thought made Natalya's hands grow damp. She was standing at the bottom of a second flight of stairs, and she climbed them, making her way over strangers' outstretched legs and past people pushing their faces together and saying "Cheese!" into the bright flash of the camera. She recognized a couple of girls from school, but they were busy talking, and she didn't stop to say hello.

Through an open door at the top of the stairs she saw a bathroom, and she shut and locked the door. It was enormous, as big as Natalya's kitchen, and tiled from floor to ceiling in tiny, pale blue tiles, like a swimming pool. She leaned back against the cool wall, closed her eyes, and breathed deeply. This party had been a major mistake. She should never have lied to Victoria. Friends didn't lie to friends. What she had to do was go downstairs, tell Victoria and Jane why Morgan had really invited her, and then they'd all go home.

Opening her eyes, she found herself looking at an extremely pretty girl. Natalya smiled, and the girl in the mirror smiled back. She stuck out her tongue, and so did her unfamiliar reflection. Jane had done her makeup, lining her eyes with a pale silver powder and putting a smoky color on the lids. Her eyes looked twice as big as they normally did—a dark, dark brown so deep it was almost black. She'd wanted to use Jane's bright red lipstick, but Jane had refused. *Your eyes are your best feature. You don't want to overpower them.* She'd been right. The pale coral she'd traced over Natalya's mouth—a shade not unlike the one Natalya had applied that day at lunch with Morgan, Sloane, and Katrina—was perfect.

It was weird to look at herself and see someone so . . . well, sexy. Natalya twirled in front of the enormous mirror. She stood with her back to it and checked one more time that her underwear didn't show. She turned and faced the mirror, still amazed to find someone so pretty staring back at her.

She knew it was time to go downstairs, but the thought of leaving the party made her sad. She wanted a chance to be sparkly for a night. Just one night. Then she'd tell Victoria everything, and never, ever put her in this position again.

Unless . . . What were Victoria and Morgan talking about? Was it already too late? Had her secret been revealed? Or . . . maybe everything was going fine. Maybe Morgan, Victoria, and Jane were even becoming friends.

Maybe she was crazy to worry.

She pushed open the door and looked around. Across the landing from her, in another enormous room, people were watching a movie she'd never seen. It was a black-and-white film, and the glow from the projection TV was the only light in the room. There was a room next to the movie room, but it was dark, and the door was only partially open; it was hard to tell what was inside.

So this was a mansion. She, Natalya Petrova, was standing in a mansion. Walking quickly, she made her way across the landing and pushed open the door to the mysterious room. The moon pouring through the high windows provided enough light for her to see the gigantic pool table that dominated the space. She walked over to it and gently touched the soft felt. As her eyes adjusted to the dim light, she made out a wooden rack lined with cues on the opposite wall.

A pool room. An actual pool room. Natalya had only seen rooms like this in the movies.

Suddenly she heard footsteps. A minute later, someone said,

"In here," flipped a switch, and the room was flooded with light pouring down from the low-hanging, green-glass-shaded lamps. At least seven guys swarmed into the room. Natalya steeled herself for a humiliating exchange. *What are you doing lurking in my family's private pool room?*

But no one seemed to find it even remotely odd that she was standing there. A couple of the boys said hi as they made their way to the wall and grabbed cues from the rack. One turned to her. "You want to play?"

She was so surprised she laughed. "Me? Oh, no thanks."

"You sure?" asked the guy, taking a cue.

Natalya just nodded. She couldn't believe she'd just been invited to play pool with a bunch of guys. Was it the dress? The party? Some combination of both? The night had a magical feel, like anything could happen.

"Solids," said someone.

"Whatever," said someone else, and then Natalya slipped out the nearest door and shut it behind her.

She was standing in a small hallway that led to a different staircase from the one she'd come up before. *Two staircases.* There were *two staircases* in this house. This one wasn't nearly as grand as the front one. Was it the servants' staircase? The house must have dated back to the days when people had servants. Or, wait. Maybe people still *had* servants.

If anyone had servants, it would be the Prewitt family.

Curious, she climbed the flight of stairs. At the top she pushed open a plain wooden door and found *another* flight. At the top of this flight was *another*.

How big was this house?

She kept climbing and, to her relief, didn't find another flight at the top of this one. She was standing at one end of a long hallway. It was completely silent up here—you would never have guessed there were any other people in the house. Far, far down the hall was a dimly lit room. Through the open doorway, Natalya could see an armchair and a reading lamp; there was a book open over the arm of the chair, but no one was sitting in it. Even though she knew it was rude to snoop around someone else's house, she found herself making her way down the long hallway.

At the threshold, she hesitated, looking into what was almost definitely a guy's room. Above a bed with a plaid bedspread was a poster of the solar system. The desk was under a window, and on it was a computer with a screen dear to Natalya's heart.

It was a chessboard.

Natalya couldn't resist. Moving silently, she crossed the thick blue carpet and studied the board. It was a tight game. Black had the advantage, but only slightly. She leaned her hands on the desk and put her face closer to the computer screen. Maybe he should . . .

"Can I help you?"

Even though Natalya was the intruder, the male voice made her yelp in terror. She spun around, heart thudding. "I'm sorry. I think . . . I think I'm in the wrong place." This was so stupid. What if the person complained about her to Morgan? The dim light made it hard to see who'd discovered her, but his voice was deep enough to tell her he wasn't a little kid.

Could she have invaded one of the servants' rooms?

"I'm really sorry," she said again. She started to make her way toward the door. As she did, the stranger did something to the light, and suddenly it was bright as an operating room. Natalya blinked and shaded her eyes.

"Oh," he said quickly. "My bad. I didn't mean to blind you." He adjusted a dial, and this time the light was more normal.

Natalya's eyes were still swimming, but even so, she could tell the boy was about her age. Unlike the boys from the party, he was wearing jeans and a T-shirt, but like theirs, his hair was cut short and neat. He was slightly taller than she was, and he stood staring down at her, his look a question.

"I . . . Sorry," Natalya said again. She was about to explain that she hadn't been able to resist looking at his chess game, but that would have revealed she was a snoop *and* a dork. Better to just have been trespassing.

The boy kept studying her. "You were checking out my game."

"No I wasn't," Natalya lied.

The boy laughed. "Yes you were. I saw you. Do you know about chess?"

Natalya didn't say anything, and the boy looked at her for another moment before he shrugged, walked past her, and sat down at his computer. Natalya noticed he was carrying a can of soda, and she wondered if he'd left his game to get it.

Without turning back to look at her, the boy said, "Never mind." He ran his hand back and forth over his head a couple of times and seemed to be speaking more to himself than to

Natalya. "I don't seriously expect some random girl who accidentally stumbles into my room during a party to be able to save my ass in a chess game I've been losing for the past several hours."

Natalya waited a second, then realized feigning ignorance was lame. Obviously this boy played chess. Why would he think someone *else* who played was a dork?

"You opened with the dragon," she announced abruptly. It was something of a guess, but given where the board was now, there were a limited number of possibilities.

There was a pause, and then the boy said, "Okay, so it turns out that the random girl who accidentally stumbled into my room during a party just *might* be able to save my ass in the chess game I've been losing for the past several hours."

Natalya took a step back toward the desk, then examined the screen for a long time. The boy let her; he didn't ask her any questions or tell her anything about what he'd been planning to do. Finally, she said, "Rook to D-four." She took a step closer, then reached forward and lightly touched the screen, tracing the move she'd just suggested. "If you do that," she said, "I bet he'll . . ." and she drew a line from the boy's opponent's queen to a square near the edge of the board.

"Wow." He shook his head in amazement, and she got a whiff of a sweet, pleasant-smelling soap or shampoo.

Suddenly Natalya realized something. This boy lived here. She stepped away from the desk. "You're Morgan's brother." Her question came out sounding more like an accusation.

"Um, okay, you got me." His hair was the same rich blond

as Morgan's, and his eyes, also like Morgan's, were so dark a blue they were almost purple. His nose was straight and long, the male version of Morgan's. "I guess I'll plead guilty," he added.

He extended a hand toward Natalya, and she took it, feeling a little funny to be shaking hands with someone who wasn't a friend of her parents.

"I'm Natalya," she said.

"Nice to meet you, Natalya. I'm Colin."

Colin? Who was Colin? "Wait, I thought your name was Grant." Natalya tried to remember if Morgan had mentioned her brother Colin, but she drew a blank. Still, they'd only talked that one day at lunch, and Grant had only come up because of Katrina's crush on him. For all Natalya knew, Morgan had twenty brothers and sisters.

Colin shook his head and put his lips together in mock regret. "Sorry." He pretended to check his watch. "It's ten thirty on a Friday night, which means Grant's the one with a bottle of beer in one hand and a girl's butt in the other."

Natalya laughed, and Colin added. "I'm the other brother."

"The other brother?" Natalya repeated.

"You know, the funny one who plays a mean game of chess."

"Mmmm, not *that* mean," Natalya said.

Colin clutched at his heart. "Ouch."

"Sorry," said Natalya quickly, worried for a second that what she'd meant to sound funny just made her seem mean.

"Don't be," Colin said, smiling to show he meant it. "I was kidding."

Natalya had just enough time to realize she was smiling back at him before her phone buzzed, and she glanced down at the screen. *Where r u? We r in the library.* It was Jane. Had something happened with Morgan and Victoria?

"I should probably go."

"Okay," said Colin. "Party hardy."

"Um, where's the library?" Natalya asked, trying not to sound disappointed that he didn't seem to care that she was leaving.

Still facing the screen, Colin said, "Out the door, staircase to your right, go down two flights, through the kitchen, up half a flight, make a left."

"Out the door, staircase to my right, go down two flights, um, kitchen . . ." Natalya hesitated.

Instead of speaking, Colin spun his chair around so he was facing her. "What are we going to do with you?" he asked, shaking his head in mock disappointment. He grabbed a pen from a container next to the computer and rolled close to where she was standing. "Hand," he commanded.

Without asking why he wanted it, she held out her hand. He took it lightly in his own and started drawing something on the back. His fingers, as they held her palm, were warm, and she noticed the nails were clean and short but not bitten. A minute later, still not having spoken a word since *hand*, he rolled away, leaving, along with a tingly sensation that had traveled up her arm to settle in her chest, a small map on the back of her hand.

"So you won't get lost," he said.

To her embarrassment, Natalya realized she was slightly breathless. "Right."

Again, Colin turned back to his computer. "See you later."

I sincerely hope so.

Natalya wished she were cool enough to say something like that. Instead, she stepped backward, then turned and walked out the door, pulling it closed behind her.

Chapter
Twenty-four

COLIN'S MAP WAS FLAWLESS: Natalya made her way back downstairs and through the gigantic kitchen with the wall of glass doors leading out to a garden where a small pond shimmered in the light of another gas lamp. The house was more crowded than it had been when she went upstairs. She headed back up the main stairs but turned at a landing half a flight up.

This room was not quite as big as the living room, but it was still pretty big. The dark green walls were lined with hundreds and hundreds, maybe thousands of books.

Jane was sitting at the end of a small, dark green love seat. Across from her, on another love seat, sat Victoria. On a third love seat sat Morgan, Katrina, and Sloane.

As Natalya entered the room, Morgan looked up and beckoned her over eagerly. "We were just talking about you. Victoria says you guys aren't going to the costume gala at the Metropolitan Museum!"

"Um," Natalya began. She looked at Victoria. Costume gala? Museum?

Victoria laughed and shrugged at Natalya's unasked question. "I didn't even know about it."

"Me either," Natalya admitted. Hearing Victoria laugh, Natalya felt a sense of relief so great she could have cried. It was okay. Everything was okay.

Just to be sure, she sat down on the sofa next to Victoria and whispered into Victoria's ear. "Are you having fun? Really?"

Victoria gave Natalya a puzzled look as Jane asked Natalya from across the space between them, "Where were you?" Her voice sounded ever so slightly accusatory, though maybe Natalya was imagining it.

Natalya turned. She wished she could tell her friends about Colin, but there was no way to do that in front of everyone. "I got a little lost."

"Hel-*lo*!" Morgan sang toward the sofa Natalya and Victoria were sitting on. "What are we wearing to the gala? You are totally coming as my guests." Still amazed at how unnecessary all of her worries had turned out to be, Natalya finally let herself relax against the back of the couch.

"I still say we should go as movie stars," said Sloane.

"Dibs on Audrey Hepburn," said Jane, leaning forward. "From *Breakfast at Tiffany's*."

"Oh my god, I *love* that movie," said Katrina.

"Jane's made us watch it about ten million times," said Natalya, laughing. Her cheeks felt flushed.

"I didn't *make* you watch it," Jane corrected.

A tall guy appeared in the archway of the room and looked around. He was chubby, with short black hair, and he was wearing a black T-shirt and the same khaki pants as all the other boys at the party.

"Hey, George!" Morgan waved and beckoned for him to come over.

"Where's Grant?" Katrina called. Then she giggled and buried her face in her hands.

Morgan pushed at Katrina's shoulder. "You have *got* to stop." Katrina just giggled harder, and Morgan rolled her eyes at Natalya. For the first time, Natalya felt as though it was okay for her to roll her eyes back at Morgan; they grinned at each other.

George came over, and Morgan gestured around the circle. "George, this is Natalya Petrova. She goes to Gainsford with me."

"Hi, George," said Natalya.

"Hey, Natalya," he said back.

"And this is Victoria Harrison, and this is Jane . . ."

"Jane Sterling," supplied Jane.

George gave a little wave, then sat on the love seat next to Jane.

"Where's Grant?" asked Katrina again.

"He's getting the booze," said George, shaking his head at Katrina. At the word *booze*, a small flicker of anxiety crossed Victoria's face. Natalya squeezed her hand. Maybe Grant was hours away. Maybe he'd get caught trying to buy alcohol with a fake ID, and he and the booze would never arrive.

"It's not like asking me a million times is going to make him get here any faster," George added. He looked at Natalya. *"Petrova.* Are you Russian?"

Natalya nodded. "I'm sooo Russian."

"Oh my god!" Morgan squealed. "George is Russian too." Morgan pointed one index finger at Natalya and the other at George. "Quick, say something in Russian to each other."

"Privet. Kak dela?" Now that she knew he was Russian, Natalya was surprised she hadn't been able to tell right away. With his high cheekbones and round face, George looked a little like the boys in her neighborhood.

"Horosho," replied George.

"That sounded so cool," observed Sloane, shaking her head in amazement.

"Guys," George said, laughing, "we just said hello to each other. It's not that big a deal."

Natalya laughed also. At home, everyone spoke Russian— and usually way better than she did. Here her ability to speak it made people think there was something special about her.

How crazy is my life, she thought, giggling.

"Where's Grant?" Katrina repeated.

Natalya's phone buzzed in her bag, and she took it out. But the text wasn't from one of her parents, magically sensing that she was speaking Russian. It was from Jane. R u drunk?

"George, will you please tell Katrina here that there is nothing sexy about desperation?" Morgan said.

Why would Jane think that? Natalya looked over at her, a

shocked expression on her face. Shaking her head, she mouthed, *Why?*

A second later, Natalya's screen read u r acting weird.

"Katrina, there is nothing sexy about desperation," George parroted.

Really? typed Natalya. She raised her eyes to look at Jane, who nodded back at her and mouthed, *Really.*

Natalya couldn't help being annoyed with Jane. Here this night was going perfectly—PERFECTLY—and Jane was criticizing her. No one else seemed to mind how she was acting.

What was Jane's problem?

But it wasn't like she was going to get into all of that in a text. Instead, Natalya just typed, I m having fun. U?

Jane shrugged. I m ok.

"Natalya," George said. He leaned forward and tapped her knee. "Natalya," he repeated.

"What?" She turned her phone to silent and slipped it back into her purse. She didn't feel like reading any more criticism from Jane right now. "Sorry."

He laughed. "I just asked what 'sooo Russian' means."

Natalya tried to explain. "You don't live in Brighton Beach by any chance, do you?"

George shook his head. "I've been there a couple of times. I think I know what you're getting at."

Natalya giggled.

Victoria leaned toward her. "Why are you giggling?" she whispered. In response, Natalya giggled more, which made Victoria giggle.

"I don't know," Natalya answered between giggles. "I'm just having fun." She took Victoria's hand. "Are you *sure* you're having fun?"

"Yeah," answered Victoria. She smiled at Natalya, and Natalya hugged her. "I'm having so much fun." Victoria lowered her voice. "While you were gone, this boy came over and he quoted *Shakespeare* to me."

"No!" Natalya couldn't believe it. She *and* Victoria had both met amazing guys.

Victoria nodded. "But Morgan made him go away. She said he's a shark who smelled fresh blood." She laughed at the memory.

So much for their both meeting amazing guys. "Still, it's cool that he recited Shakespeare," Natalya pointed out.

Victoria nodded, a dreamy look on her face. "It was. And Morgan's really nice."

"I'm so glad you guys like each other," Natalya whispered into her friend's shoulder. She felt like she might explode with happiness.

A handsome blond guy came over to where the girls were sitting. George stood up, and Katrina suddenly looked vaguely nervous. "Hey," said George. "Where've you been?"

"It just took forever to get back from Jersey," said the boy.

"Hi, Grant," said Katrina, smiling and lifting a finger in the newcomer's direction.

"Hey, Kat," said Grant. He turned back to George. "Paul's parked outside. Can you help me unload the car?"

George stood up. "Sure," he said. He turned back to Natalya. "Nice meeting you."

"You too," she said as the boys walked out of the room.

Katrina leaped up. "We can help," she offered. She turned and pulled at Morgan's and Sloane's hands. "Come on."

"No way," said Morgan. "Here's what I'm not doing. Carrying heavy boxes in *this*." She gestured at her beautiful dress.

"Don't be such a princess," Katrina said.

"Don't be so obvious," said Morgan. She got up. "I'm going to the bathroom. Anyone want to come?"

"I'll come." Sloane stood up, too, and then Victoria, Jane, and Natalya were sitting alone on the couches.

"Okay, *what* is up with you?" asked Jane, moving to where Morgan had been sitting. "You are being *so* weird."

Choosing to ignore the irritation in her friend's tone, Natalya directed her answer to Victoria. She spoke in a whisper. "I feel really sparkly." She laughed. "Don't you guys feel sparkly?"

Jane didn't say anything, but Victoria nodded. "Now that you mention it, I *do* feel a little sparkly." She looked around the room at the party surrounding them. "This is fun."

"*See?*" said Natalya, still amazed by how perfectly everything was going. "Aren't you glad you came?" Then she pulled Victoria and Jane close to her and said, "I met a really cute boy."

"You *did?*" asked Jane.

Victoria squeezed her hand. "Oh, Nat, that is so cool. Who is it?"

"It's Morgan's *brother*."

As if on cue, Grant's voice called out from the landing. "It's the moment you've all been waiting for, folks. Come aboard and let the booze cruise begin."

"Him?" asked Jane, shocked.

"No, no," Natalya corrected her quickly. "Her *other* brother. He's upstairs."

People started filing out of the room, and Victoria turned to her friends sadly. "Guys, I don't think I should stay if there's drinking."

Natalya's eyes widened. Was this Victoria's way of saying the party was over? "But . . . I mean, *we* won't drink anything."

Victoria stood up. "I'm really sorry, Nat," she said. Then she added, "If you guys want to stay, you can stay. Just meet me at my house before midnight."

"Don't be crazy," Jane said. "Of course we're not staying without you."

"Yeah," said Natalya quickly. "Right. We're not staying without you." But she was nervous. Would Morgan think it was weird if they left early? And what if Colin came looking for her?

Jane put her arm around Natalya's shoulders. "If we go now, he'll look for you all night. He'll be *obsessed.*"

Natalya laughed at how easily Jane had read her mind. "Do you really think so?"

"Definitely," Jane promised. "Exhibit A: Cinderella."

Natalya thought for a second. "Should I leave one of my shoes?"

"Um, negative," said Victoria, holding a finger up to correct Natalya. "My sister would *kill* me if we lost one of her shoes."

"Besides," Jane pointed out. "Imagine if Morgan's brother searched the whole of New York City for you and wound up with Emily instead."

Victoria shook her head sadly. "Poor guy. That would really suck."

"Seriously," said Jane. "Now, say good night."

"Can we come up with an excuse?" asked Natalya. "So they don't think we're lame for leaving."

"Sure," said Jane. "We'll make up something totally glam."

Morgan had apparently gone off to some distant wing of the house, but Jane, Victoria, and Natalya found Katrina at the bottom of the stairs. Jane explained that they had another party to go to, and Katrina looked genuinely sad to see them go. She promised to relay their good-byes to Morgan.

"Tell her thanks for having us," said Victoria.

"Yeah, thank you," said Natalya.

"Of course," said Katrina. "See you guys around."

"This is cool," Victoria said when they were finally in the foyer. "Sneaking out like this."

Natalya touched the pearl at her throat. "It is."

"This is having a real *life!*" Victoria snapped her fingers and spun around like a flamenco dancer.

"Easy, tiger," said Jane, laughing. She looked at her friends. "You're both sure you didn't have anything to drink?"

Natalya shook her head and leaned against Jane. "We're drunk on life, darling."

And with that, they stepped out into the cool night.

Chapter
Twenty-five

IT WASN'T AS IF Jane always had to be the center of attention, but she couldn't help thinking it was weird how *totally* Natalya's new friends had ignored her. Saturday morning, when Jane, Natalya, and Victoria went on Facebook, Morgan had already sent Victoria and Natalya friend requests, and later she invited them to look at her photos from the party. Natalya and Victoria were so busy being relieved about there being no pictures of Victoria in Morgan's photo album (*Oh my god, the campaign people would kill me!*) that they hadn't even noticed Jane's being excluded from the friend invitation.

Was she being paranoid? Had Morgan and her friends not liked her for some reason? Had she done something? But the energy they'd focused on Victoria—that had been there from the second the three of them walked in the front door. It was almost as if they were . . . waiting for Victoria to get there. There was no way Jane could have imagined that. Could she?

"So, Jane, tell me about Hippolyta."

Jane jerked her head up. The cast was sitting on the stage in a circle, and Mr. Robbins had just announced that they were going to talk about their characters before blocking the next act. She'd been only half paying attention, assuming he'd start by asking about Hermia or Lysander or maybe Puck or Oberon— one of the major characters in the play. But now that everyone had quieted down, he'd turned to her.

Tell me about Hippolyta.

Jane took a deep breath. Her job was to focus on *A Midsummer Night's Dream*, not the party she'd been to Friday night. She thought about Hippolyta.

"Well . . . she's the queen of the Amazons. And she's going to be a bride," Jane said. The play started with Theseus and Hippolyta talking about how they were about to get married, so her statement was pretty incontrovertible.

Mr. Robbins grinned as though Jane had just said something amusing. She found herself smiling back at him. "An Amazonian bride." He laughed, and so did several cast members. "Seems like an oxymoron, doesn't it?"

As she nodded, Jane silently thanked her fifth-grade English teacher for teaching them that an oxymoron was a contradiction in terms. "I'd be scared to marry an Amazon," she confessed.

Mr. Robbins laughed again. "Me too." He turned to Matt, who played Theseus. "How about you, Matt. You scared to marry this woman?" He gestured with his shoulder at Jane.

Jane tossed her head and raised her eyebrows at Matt, mock seductively. "You scared, Matt?"

"A little." Matt smiled down over at her, which made Jane feel cool. Matt was a senior; he wasn't one of the stars of the drama clan like Fran, Bethany, Hugh, and Daniel, who played the lovers. But he hung out with them sometimes, and at Friday's rehearsal, Jane had been talking to him when Fran and Bethany arrived, and Bethany had said, "Hey, Matt. Hey, Jane," and Fran had given them a little wave.

Mr. Robbins clapped his hands together to punctuate Matt's admission. "Okay, that's important. Matt, you see Theseus as scared. Remember, this guy is King of Athens. He took on the Minotour, for god's sake."

Vaguely, Jane remembered a story about the Minotour from a book of Greek myths that her dad had read to her when she was little. It was some kind of monster, she knew that. Wasn't it a man-eating bull? She shuddered. Talk about scary.

Matt leaped to his feet. "That's right, I kicked Minotour ass!" he announced, staring at Jane. "I'm not scared of you."

Jane and the rest of the cast laughed, but Mr. Robbins asked, straight-faced, "So he's not scared."

Matt dropped back down and shrugged. "I can go either way on this."

Now Mr. Robbins laughed, but then he turned serious. "See, this is what we're going to keep doing—together *and* individually. It's very important for everyone that we make concrete decisions about our characters. At any given moment, you"—he pointed at Josh, who played Oberon—"and you"—he pointed at Lysander—"and you"—he pointed at Fran—"need to know what you're feeling. What you're thinking." Now he turned to Jane. "Theseus conquered you, but has he *conquered* you?" Jane opened her mouth to answer, but Mr. Robbins held his hand up. "Don't answer yet, just think about it." Looking around the circle slowly, Mr. Robbins continued. "Your performance will be believable because *you* believe it. If you don't know why you're saying a line, if you have no idea what motivates you, it's simple trickery." He moved his hands around in the air. "Smoke and mirrors. Your audience will sense it, and they'll get bored. Your fellow cast members will know it, and they'll feel betrayed. Most important, *you'll* know it, and you'll feel empty. Because you'll be violating the sacred commandment of theater: Be truthful."

Jane felt herself shiver. No one had ever described being in a play to her this way. It was like acting was . . . holy or something.

There was silence in the theater, a silence Mr. Robbins allowed to grow for a moment before he interrupted it. "Okay, Lysander, tell me a little about yourself."

Jane listened, but it was hard for her to focus on what Daniel was saying about his motivation for running off with Hermia.

Mr. Robbins's speech was like a light turned on in a dark

room, a black-and-white movie that had suddenly dissolved into color. Friday night was completely eclipsed by the intensity of his words.

Jane stared at Mr. Robbins as he listened to Lysander describe how he felt about leaving Athens forever.

He was the most amazing man she had ever met.

Chapter
Twenty-six

NATALYA FELT LIKE she was living in a dream. A sparkly, beautiful dream. After English class, Morgan said, "Much to discuss at lunch," and she gave Natalya a knowing smile. That smile told her two things: One, that she was welcome (expected, even) in the secret library room at lunch. Two, that Colin had told Morgan about his conversation with Natalya.

Natalya had to stop herself from skipping to Math, then to Greek, then to Bio. She could completely picture the upcoming conversation. Morgan was going to say something like, *So my brother's* totally *in love with you.* Katrina would gasp, shocked, but then Natalya would turn to her, put her hand on Katrina's arm, and say, *Don't worry, Katrina. She's talking about Colin.* Katrina would think about it for a second, then she'd smile and so would Sloane. *Oh my god, of* course*! You guys are perfect for each other.* Sloane and Katrina would be totally at a loss to figure out why they hadn't thought of putting Natalya and Colin together in the first place. When lunch ended and it was time to go to class, Natalya would find a way to be alone with Katrina. *I promise,* she'd say, *now that I'm in with the Prewitts, I'll do everything I can to help you get with Grant.*

"So," said Jordan, dropping into her seat at the other end of their lab table. "I heard you were at Morgan's party this weekend."

Jordan's statement felt almost like an accusation; the tone wiped the daydreamy smile off Natalya's face. "For a little while."

"Oh," said Jordan, fussing for something in her bag. "Well, was it fun?"

"Um, yeah," said Natalya, unable to completely repress the smile that came back each time she thought about the party. As soon as she'd said it, a hurt look flitted across Jordan's face, and Natalya felt bad. But what should she have said? *No, it sucked.*

She was relieved when Dr. Clover walked to the front of the room and started class, though it was hard for her to focus on what their teacher was saying. All she could think about was lunch and Morgan's forthcoming announcement.

My brother is so into you.

A double period of Bio had never felt so long. There had to be something wrong with the clocks—by the time the bell rang, she was sure she'd been in the lab for over a year, not an hour and a half.

Lingering by their lab table, Jordan watched Natalya shove her textbook and notebook into her bag. As Natalya slid off her stool, neither one of them said anything.

"Are you coming to lunch?" asked Jordan.

"I have to go to the library," Natalya said quickly. It sounded like a lie, and Natalya almost added *Really*, but she knew that would only make it worse.

Jordan exhaled through her nose in an almost laugh. "Right."

"No, I do," Natalya said. But she was talking to Jordan's back. "I'll see you later." Why had she said that? She was going to spend the whole period with Morgan, Sloane, and Katrina. She wasn't planning to go to the cafeteria today.

If things went well, she wasn't planning to go to the cafeteria *ever again*.

But did that mean she couldn't be friends with Jordan? She liked Jordan. Jordan was smart and funny. Did she have to choose Morgan or Jordan?

Apparently she did. Without turning around, Jordan lifted her hand briefly over her head in a sort of wave. Natalya started to wave back, then realized Jordan couldn't see her.

For a second she felt guilty, but then she was running through the crowded hallways. By the time she arrived at the tiny room where Morgan, Katrina, and Sloane were already lounging, she'd forgotten all about Jordan.

"There you are!" Morgan announced. "Oh my god, I have *got*

to talk to you. You will not *believe* who asked about you."

Should she say? Or was it cooler if she let Morgan announce what Natalya already knew?

Before she could decide, Morgan had grabbed her iPhone off the table and was waving the screen toward Natalya.

"Read *this*! I got it this morning."

Natalya took the phone from Morgan and read the brief message. How's your friend Natalya?

Natalya felt triumphant. She could have picked up the sofa Morgan was sitting on and carried it around the room.

"Is it from—" she began.

"*Yes*," said Morgan, "it's from George."

"George?" Natalya had completely forgotten about meeting George.

Morgan took her confusion as pleasure and smiled. "I know. He's completely cute, isn't he? We just need to get him to go to the gym a little more, that's all." She leaned across the small table to reread George's text. "We'll wait to answer, of course." She tapped her phone knowingly. "Strategy."

"Meanwhile, did we decide on costumes? Because in case you've forgotten, it's a *costume* gala." Sloane took a spoonful of yogurt. "What's the final verdict on movie stars? I say yes."

George? He was totally nice. But he wasn't . . . She didn't like him. Just because they were both Russian didn't mean they had to like each other. *Like*-like each other.

"It's not as if we can *all* go as Audrey Hepburn. And anyway, you look nothing like her," said Katrina.

"Oh, and you do?" Sloane spluttered.

"At least I have the right coloring," Katrina pointed out, patting her thick, dark hair.

Natalya couldn't take it. She had to know if Colin had asked about her. Mentioned her. *Some friend of yours got lost and I gave her directions.* She had to know if he'd at least . . . noticed her.

Natalya cleared her throat. "Um, I think I met . . . I mean, I met your brother on Friday."

As Natalya had predicted, Katrina's head spun practically three hundred and sixty degrees so she could glare daggers at Natalya.

"Oh god," groaned Morgan. "Not another one with a crush on Grant."

"No," Natalya said quickly. "I didn't mean Grant. I meant . . . um, I think he said his name was Colin?"

Now all three girls groaned simultaneously. It was Morgan who spoke. "Natalya, I am so sorry. He is *such* a loser."

Suddenly there wasn't enough air in the room.

Katrina rolled her eyes and put her fingers up to her forehead in an L shape.

"Okay, well, *I'm* going as a movie star," Sloane announced. She twirled her spoon thoughtfully through the air. "Maybe Marilyn Monroe."

Morgan gave Natalya a sad little smile. "Sorry about Colin. He didn't try to talk to you or anything, did he?"

Oh my god. Oh my god. Oh my god. To Natalya's amazement, her malfunctioning brain managed to form language. "No, he . . . I mean we didn't . . . We didn't talk at all."

"Let me guess," Morgan continued. "He was playing chess."

Natalya spoke quickly. "I don't remember."

Morgan dropped her head against the back of the sofa. "And he was wearing a shirt that said 'Han Solo shot first.'"

"No he wasn't." Natalya answered immediately. Then she added, "I mean, I didn't notice."

"*Why* am I related to such a gigantic loser?" Morgan asked the ceiling.

"I don't have anything against the movie star thing," said Katrina. "But what about this—Playboy Bunnies." She ran her hands down her sides. "Tight, tight black top, fishnets, high heels, bunny ears."

"Um, slutty much?" Morgan said, and they laughed. Then Morgan turned to Natalya. "You and George are going to be a *super*-cute couple. We'll find out what he's going as and figure out something good for you to wear."

"I don't know." Natalya felt dizzy. "He might not even want to go with me." She had to be alone. She had to get out of there.

Morgan rolled her eyes. "He texted me about you. In guy-speak, that's basically a declaration of love. Plus, you two have that whole Russian thing going." She smacked her lips together to make a kissing sound.

Standing up, Natalya announced, "I have to go to the bathroom." Her voice was nearly a shout.

"Chill," said Morgan, making a face. "No one's stopping you. And when you get back . . ." She waved her phone in the air. "We will compose an appropriate reply. Oooh, maybe it should be in *Russian*."

"Sure," said Natalya. "Sure." She practically ran out of the room, but not before she heard Katrina speak.

"Colin," snorted Katrina. "How are you and Grant even related to that guy?"

"Please," said Morgan. "Don't remind me."

Chapter
Twenty-seven

ALL WEEKEND, VICTORIA had felt different somehow. She remembered Natalya's word: *sparkly*. That was it. She felt sparkly. She'd snuck out to a cool party at a swanky mansion and she hadn't gotten caught. Why?

Because she was so *sparkly*.

Lately she'd been feeling the opposite of sparkly. And it wasn't just because, with the election getting closer, her parents were tense and snappish. She'd told Jane and Natalya she didn't like Jack anymore, but it wasn't as simple as that. She still liked him. She still thought about him *a lot*. Only now, every time she thought about him, she thought about how he'd taken those pictures, and she felt awful. She hated how looking at Jack made her feel—as if she had something to be ashamed of, and as if that something was liking him.

Not that it even mattered. Ever since she'd blown up at him in Dean Gordon's office, he hadn't so much as glanced in her direction. They'd pass each other in the hall or on the way into or out of Bio, and neither of them would acknowledge the other.

But while she was getting dressed for school Monday morning, she hadn't even thought about Jack. She'd spied the FOXY LADY T-shirt at the bottom of her drawer and started singing *Fox-y La-dy* to herself. *Fox-y La-dy.*

"That's right," she whispered. "I'm a foxy lady."

And without thinking about what she was doing, she'd pulled the T-shirt out of the pile and slipped it over her head, still singing to herself as she strolled out of her apartment building and into the warm October day.

The sparkly feeling hadn't diminished as the day went on. In homeroom, Mr. Frank had announced the upcoming meeting of the Morningside Baking Club. Then he'd lifted his eyes and looked toward Victoria. "There she is, if anyone has any questions." A few people looked Victoria's way, which normally would have terrified her into a coma. But whether it was because of the T-shirt or the party, Victoria had just smiled and nodded.

When she got to French, Victoria saw Maeve sitting at the back of the room, an empty chair besides her. Had she really been afraid to talk to some random girl in her class?

Why would anyone be afraid to do that?

Victoria made her way to the back of the room, dropped her

bag over the back of the chair, and sat down. "Hi."

Maeve looked startled by Victoria's greeting. "Oh, hi." Her voice was quiet, and she didn't look at Victoria. There was a pause, during which Maeve toyed with the spiral binder of her notebook. "I heard about that baking club you're starting. I really like baking."

Victoria could see the blush on Maeve's cheeks.

"You should come," Victoria said. Her voice was confident. To her own ears she sounded like the kind of person who would have the courage to start a club.

Which, when you thought about it, was exactly what she was.

Maeve turned to face Victoria just as Madame Desbonnet walked into the room, clapping her hands to get their attention. *"Bonjour,* class! *Bonjour."*

"I think I will," said Maeve. She smiled at Victoria, and Victoria smiled back.

She and Maeve walked out of class together, and when they got to the hallway, Victoria turned and asked if Maeve wanted to meet at Rick's for lunch tomorrow.

"Um, sure," answered Maeve, and the happy smile she gave Victoria wasn't nearly as shy as her earlier ones had been. "Okay. Great."

Victoria was practically strutting as she walked along the hall, then headed toward the lobby and the main stairs to get to history. It was pretty cool, hearing her baking club announced, making a lunch plan with Maeve.

Halfway to the main stairs, she saw Jack, and all at once her sparkly feeling disappeared, as if she were a match that had been held under running water.

Jack high-fived the guy he'd been talking to, then turned and crossed the lobby in Victoria's general direction. She stood stock still. Was he coming toward her? Or was he simply crossing the lobby? It wasn't like he *couldn't* cross the lobby just because she happened to be standing in the middle of it.

Right as she decided either he hadn't seen her or he was purposely *pretending* he hadn't seen her, Jack shook the hair off his forehead and stared straight into her eyes. Then he changed his course slightly so he was headed right for her.

Victoria could feel her heart stop beating.

"Can I talk to you?" he asked, arriving next to the spot where she was standing.

Victoria was sure she'd misheard him. "Me?"

He frowned slightly as he tried to make out the writing on her chest. "Foxy Lady." As soon as he'd read the words out loud, he looked away, like he was embarrassed to have deciphered them. Then he shifted his weight uneasily from one foot to the other, finally raising his eyes to meet hers. "I just wanted to tell you. I'm not running the photos."

He wasn't . . . "Wait, what?"

"I'm not running the pictures," he repeated. "Because . . . well . . ." He took a deep breath and spoke the rest of his sentence in a rush. "Because this girl I know told me it was really uncool."

"Seriously?" she asked, amazed. "Just because *I* told you not to run the photos, you didn't?" The sparkly feeling she'd had all morning came back a million times stronger than ever. She could practically *hear* herself bursting into glorious flame.

Jack hesitated, then admitted, "It wasn't *just* you. It was kind of a combination of you and my mom." He laughed.

"Your mom?" Victoria found herself laughing too.

He nodded and spread his hands wide as if to say, *What can you do?* "Well, it's like this. After you made it clear you thought I was the meanest person who ever—"

"Hey! I never said—" Victoria objected.

"—*lived*," he finished. "I took your opinion under advisement, as I *said* I would. When I told my mom about it, she said you were right." He moved his backpack to his other shoulder. "So. I couldn't, you know, fight you *and* my mom."

Suddenly Victoria felt lighter than air. Jack wasn't a mean person. Jack was a nice person. Jack was a nice person who didn't think she was a humorless drip. He was a nice person who didn't think she was a humorless drip, and who she—

"Condoms, get your free condoms!"

Both Victoria and Jack jerked their heads in the direction of the voice. She'd been so focused on their conversation that she hadn't noticed that the lobby where they were standing was ground zero for Safe Sex Week. Looking up, Victoria was greeted by a wall of Technicolor, homemade signs. SAFE SEX=GOOD SEX! NO PROTECTION? NO THANKS!

Noticing where she was looking, Jack read the signs, then looked back at her.

"Look, Victoria, we hardly know each other, okay? I'm really not ready for a step like that."

Instead of being embarrassed, Victoria found herself laughing.

Across the lobby, a guy who was holding a banana gave the thumbs-up to his friend, and a second later, there was the flash of a camera.

A girl Victoria didn't know approached her and Jack. In one hand she had a condom package, in the other a banana. She held the banana out to Victoria. "It's very important that teens know how to use condoms. Used correctly, they can prevent the spread of pregnancy and STDs, including AIDS." From the girl's matter-of-fact tone, she could have been discussing the importance of a liberal arts education or higher literacy rates in the third world. She placed the banana in Victoria's hand. "There's really nothing to it."

Okay, it was one thing to sneak out to a party with your friends or to wear a T-shirt that said you were foxy. But this? "I . . ."

Jack put his hand on Victoria's shoulder. "I think Victoria's going to take a pass," he told the girl.

Jack had just touched her.

"Um, I think *she* can speak for herself." The girl put a condom in Victoria's hand and gave her a significant look. Then she lowered her voice. "You should never let your boyfriend pressure you to do anything you don't want to do. You know that, right?"

This girl thought Jack was her *boyfriend*? Did they look like a couple?

"Speaking of pressure . . ." Jack began to interrupt.

"No means no!" the girl said firmly. "Look, there's nothing to it."

Victoria and Jack stood watching silently as the girl expertly opened the condom wrapper and slipped the condom out. Then she slid it onto the banana, placed the condom-clad banana in Victoria's hand, and stepped back to admire her work.

"Now, wasn't that easy?" The pride she took in the lesson she'd given Victoria was evident. "Now you try it!" She slipped the condom off the banana and dropped it into a baggy safety-pinned to her waist.

Victoria knew she was going to pass out. Literally. She was going to lose consciousness, fall to the floor, and die of a concussion.

At least, she hoped she was.

"Here," said Jack, reaching for the banana with one hand and the condom with the other. He handed the banana to Victoria, whose fingers automatically closed around it. Then he began wrestling with the condom wrapper. A long minute passed during which he seemed to be making little or no progress.

Once again it was impossible not to laugh. "Here," said Victoria. "You hold this." She handed him the banana, then took the condom from him. The package was small and slippery, and she immediately dropped it.

"Nice," Jack said. "Very nice."

The girl sighed impatiently and handed Victoria another condom. "Here."

Jack slipped the banana under his arm and held the condom package. "You rip. I'll hold."

Victoria knew she should be embarrassed. She was standing with her crush, trying to tear the condom package that he was holding for her while Attila the Hun scowled at them. But she didn't feel embarrassed. She felt excited. She felt . . . *exhilarated*.

She was here with Jack and he was so cute and he'd changed his mind about running the photos because of something she'd said. Life was so impossibly good.

How could she *not* laugh?

"I'm glad you think this is funny," Jack said, but he was laughing too.

When she felt the small preformed tear in the condom package split across the entire top, Victoria was pretty sure she'd never been so relieved in her life.

"We did it!" she shouted excitedly.

"You did it," Jack corrected. He handed the banana to Victoria, then took the slippery condom from her and rolled it on. "Voilà!"

Jack gave her a thumbs-up, and together they held the banana out toward the girl. Victoria realized she was grinning from ear to ear, and when the girl took the banana from their hands, she turned to Jack and held up her hand. "High five!" she said.

He slapped her palm with his. "High five."

They stood there smiling at each other, as if they'd just accomplished something monumental. The warning bell rang.

Jack looked down at her and grinned knowingly. "And here I thought all you did was bake." With that, he gave her a wink. "Later, foxy lady."

She nodded, then watched him sail out of the lobby and down the stairs. She loved him. She loved him. SHE LOVED HIM!!! She was still watching the spot where he'd been when her phone buzzed urgently. She took it out of her bag and read the text from Natalya.

I have 2 talk 2 u guys right after school. Emergency!

Chapter
Twenty-eight

"DID THIS WORK? Are you there?" asked Natalya. She was sitting at her desk in her room, her back so rigid it didn't even touch the chair she was on,

"I'm here," answered Victoria. She tucked the phone more firmly under her chin and whisked together dry ingredients that would become the cake batter. She was considering making angel food cake at her first meeting with the baking club.

"Me too," said Jane, sitting cross-legged on her bed. "I'm sorry I couldn't talk before. I was at rehearsal. What's the emergency?"

Natalya took a deep breath. "Okay, remember how I said I like Morgan's brother?"

"Oh my god, he likes you too!" In her excitement, Victoria dropped the whisk. "We're both in—"

"No!" Natalya yelled. "No. He doesn't like me. And I don't like him."

"You don't?" asked Jane. "I thought you did."

"I was wrong." Natalya's voice was emphatic.

"You were *wrong*?" Jane repeated.

"Did something happen?" asked Victoria, digging the whisk out of the bowl.

Natalya closed her eyes and leaned back against the chair. "He's a total dork."

"He *is*?" Victoria was confused. "How do you know?

Natalya hesitated for a second, then admitted simply, "Morgan told me."

The words were hardly out of Natalya's mouth before Jane snapped, "*Morgan* told you?"

"Will you stop repeating everything I say?" Natalya demanded, leaping to her feet indignantly. "Yes, Morgan told me, okay?"

"How does Morgan know?" asked Jane, and it was possible to hear in her voice the sound of her eyebrows rising.

"She lives with him, Jane." Natalya's voice was impatient. "Of course she knows."

No one spoke. Finally Victoria announced, "Well, if you don't like him, you don't like him."

Jane cut in. "I can't believe I'm hearing this. Nat likes him, Vicks. She just doesn't want to do anything to make Princess Morgan mad."

"Hey!" snapped Natalya.

"Jane," warned Victoria. There was another silence. Victoria wiped her hands on her apron.

"I should go," said Natalya, sitting back down and staring at her assignment pad without really seeing it. "I've got a ton of work."

"No, wait!" Victoria pleaded. "Guys, don't fight about this."

"No one's fighting," insisted Jane.

There was a long silence, and finally Victoria said, "Well, apparently no one's *talking* either."

"We've all got a lot of work, Vicks," Jane assured her. "That's all. I'll call you guys later, okay?"

"Jane . . ." Victoria began.

"It's true," Natalya agreed. "I have to go too."

A second later, Victoria still had her phone pressed to her ear, but no one else was on the line.

Chapter
Twenty-nine

MR. ROBBINS HADN'T BEEN kidding when he'd said their rehearsal schedule was going to be insane. As opening night drew closer, Jane barely had time to do her homework and go to class, much less call her dad every few days and grab an occasional quick sushi dinner with her mom. She was being honest when she told Victoria and Natalya that she was crazy busy, but she wasn't telling the whole truth.

All the two of them ever wanted to talk about was the upcoming costume gala and how exciting it was going to be and what they were going to wear. They thought she was bored by their conversations because the party was at the same time as the *Midsummer* dress rehearsal, and so she couldn't go. But that wasn't the reason. She was *glad* she couldn't go to the party. And not just because Natalya's new friends had totally ignored her.

Natalya was being so . . . different lately. Pretending not to like some guy she really liked just because Morgan Prewitt said he was a dork. She'd practically made Jane and Victoria swear a blood oath never to utter the word *Colin*. In eighth grade history class, their teacher had been obsessed with how fascist regimes erased and rewrote historical events. *They can make it as if history never happened.*

Maybe she was exaggerating, but Jane felt as though Natalya were totally being that way.

Victoria, too. All she seemed to care about was being "sparkly." It was so weird and boring. They acted like Jane should be heartbroken because she had to go to rehearsal and couldn't go to some stupid party, when really she'd much rather spend a Saturday night working. Theater was what she loved. Theater was going to be her life.

Mr. Robbins had helped her to see that if you wanted to be an actor, you had to be serious. When people were late or missed rehearsal or hadn't memorized their lines or goofed off instead of focusing, he always asked them the same question: *Are you serious about acting or aren't you?*

Jane was serious.

The Wednesday before Saturday's dress rehearsal, Jane's last-period class was canceled, and she headed across the street to Starbucks to grab a coffee, thinking about Mr. Robbins. Lately she thought about him a lot.

"Will that be all?" asked the barista.

And Jane found herself saying, "No, actually. Make it *two* coffees."

When she got back to the building, there were still a few minutes before last period ended; Jane pushed open the door of the theater and walked inside. The auditorium was empty, but the stage was crowded with flats and furniture, the nearly completed scrim that would be dropped at the beginning of the forest scenes partially lowered. Jane stood in the middle of the stage in the light from a single row of lamps. She looked out at the empty seats that stretched before her like an ocean.

Was there any place in the world more wonderful than center stage?

She began speaking her first lines. "'Four days will quickly steep themselves in night. Four nights will dream away the time. And then the moon, like to a silver bow new-bent in heaven, shall behold the night of our solemnities.'" The words rang out in the empty space, and Jane reveled in the silence almost as much as she had the speech.

From the wings she heard the sound of a single person clapping, and she whipped around.

"Well done." Mr. Robbins stepped out of the shadows, his familiar leather bag over his shoulder, his shirt coming untucked from his jeans. The dim lighting and his casual outfit made him seem even younger than usual.

"Thanks." She tossed her head in appreciation of his compliment. Gesturing at the two cups of coffee at her feet, she added, "I brought you a coffee, Mr. Robbins."

Nodding appreciatively, he came over to where she was standing. "Starbucks. Fancy. But I think if you're bringing me coffee, you can call me Len."

"I don't know. I think I'll stick with Mr. Robbins." She'd called him Len at her audition, but now she liked being the only one in the cast who called him Mr. Robbins; it was almost like a private nickname.

"Suit yourself," he said, picking up one of the cups.

"I wasn't sure how you like your coffee," she said, watching him drink.

Raising an eyebrow, he said simply, "Caffeinated," then drank some and nodded his approval. "And hot." He took another swig, then dropped to the floor and looked up at Jane standing a few feet in front of him. "Let's take it from the top."

Jane felt a pleasurable warmth come over her at his attention. "Okay." She began the speech again, but this time Mr. Robbins stopped her when she was halfway through.

"Wait a sec. Can you hear the natural rhythm of the words?"

Jane wasn't sure what he meant, but she didn't admit it. "The rhythm?" she repeated.

He put down his cup. "Listen. 'Four *days* will *quick*-ly *steep* them*selves* in *night*. Four *nights* will *quick*-ly *dream* a-*way* the *time*.'" He clapped on every other syllable. "What do you call that?"

Jane smiled at him. "Clapping?"

He laughed a deep, full laugh that made Jane feel as if she were the funniest person on the planet. "It's iambs. The speech is made up of iambs." He repeated the opening lines, again, emphasizing every other syllable.

"Wow," said Jane. "I never noticed that."

"That's why they pay me the big bucks." Mr. Robbins jumped to his feet and crossed his arms. "Try it again, only this time, feel the rhythm of the language."

Jane spoke the opening line, but it sounded weirdly singsongy. "Can I say it again?" She remembered her botched audition.

"Of course. It's going to take a while." He stepped back to where he'd dropped his bag. "You want the rhythm there . . . but not there."

"Okay, that's impossible," said Jane.

Crouched over his bag, he looked up at her. "Of course it is," he said, smiling.

Jane said her lines, trying to emphasize the iambs without emphasizing them. To her ears, the words sounded stilted and awkward. "Again!" Mr. Robbins called, digging in his bag.

She repeated herself. It was a little better, but still pretty bad. "Again," he said.

Once more, she launched into the speech. She could feel the rhythm, how each word flowed into the next, like water finding a path through rocks.

"Better," he said. "Again." He was looking up at her, a folder in his hands.

She repeated the lines. Halfway through, without telling her to stop, he said, "Remember, the end has to be triumphant." She continued speaking, and so did he. "It's like you can't believe it. The very meter of your speech is trumped by the announcement you're making." They spoke the last line of the speech together, nearly shouting it. "'Behold the night of our solemnities!'"

Jane was panting slightly. "That was great!"

"That was better," he corrected. They grinned at each other as he crossed to where she was standing and opened the folder he was holding. "Look at these."

Jane found herself looking at drawings of two dresses, one with blue at the waist and neck, one red where the other was blue. *Hermia/Helena*, it said in the lower left-hand corner. He turned to the next page, and Jane was surprised to be looking at a drawing marked *Hippolyta*. The dress had a silver bodice and long sleeves; the wrists were thick, gold cuffs.

"Wow," said Jane. "Did you design these?"

"I came up with the guiding principle, but Alona really gets the credit. Do you like? You'll get to see the real thing at dress rehearsal Saturday."

"They're amazing." Her dress was feminine but somehow strong; different not just in color but in kind from the ones for Helena and Hermia. Theirs were girly, feminine. Even though it was fitted through the waist, there was something almost military about the dress for Hippolyta.

"Sexy, right?" He nodded at the drawing. "This girl is one sexy Amazon."

Jane felt the air in her lungs freeze. Her heart seemed to stop beating, then to start up again at double its normal pace.

Had Mr. Robbins just called her . . . sexy?

The rear door of the auditorium burst open. Jane was flooded with annoyance. She glared over her shoulder at whoever it was that had just barged in on her private moment with Mr. Robbins.

"Hey, Len!" called Dahlia. "Hey, Jane."

Jane had happily eaten lunch with Dahlia less than three hours ago, yet now Dahlia felt like a mortal enemy. Jane wanted to be alone with Mr. Robbins, to see if he'd follow up on his observation that she was sexy. Or even better—she wanted Fran or Bethany or Hugh or Daniel to walk in, to see her talking privately with him.

Dahlia didn't notice that Jane didn't say hello. "Whatcha lookin' at?" she asked, coming to stand between Jane and Mr. Robbins.

"Costumes," Mr. Robbins answered.

Was it Jane's imagination, or was Mr. Robbins as irritated as she was at Dahlia? Jane glanced past Dahlia to look at him, but Mr. Robbins appeared engrossed in the sketches.

"Cool!" Dahlia announced.

Jane stared daggers at the back of Dahlia head.

Okay, he had *totally* called her sexy. *This girl is one sexy Amazon.* Those were his exact words. And *this girl* was Jane. That meant he had basically said, *Jane is one sexy Amazon.* Or maybe, *Jane, you are one sexy Amazon.*

The next afternoon in the auditorium, she watched him from across the aisle, their exchange playing over and over in her head like a beautiful performance. What did it mean? Could he be thinking about her as much as she was thinking about him? Was she crazy to think that a teacher liked her? But why was that crazy? Her mom knew two teachers who had married former students. Okay, one had been a graduate student and one had been in medical school. But still. It clearly happened.

Why shouldn't it happen to her?

Besides, it wasn't like Mr. Robbins was *old*. He'd made a comment recently about how his ten-year college reunion was coming up even though he felt like he'd just graduated. Ten years. That meant he wasn't much more than thirty.

Lots of couples had age differences that were *way* bigger than theirs.

But how could she know? How could she know for sure that she wasn't misreading what he'd said?

"Jay, you've got your back to the audience!" Mr. Robbins called out. He stood up.

Jay turned around from center stage and winked at Mr. Robbins. "You mean you're not interested in Bottom's bottom?" The cast—both onstage and off—cracked up, but Mr. Robbins just gave a tight smile. Jay was a really funny Bottom, but sometimes it was as if he was *too* funny. To get a laugh he'd change his blocking and acting, which threw off the rest of the actors, even though—and sometimes because—he was hilarious.

Wanting to be by herself to analyze yesterday's exchange with Mr. Robbins, Jane had avoided Dahlia and the other girls she usually sat with. Now she looked casually around the auditorium, and she noticed that everywhere people were in groups of two's or three's, giving each other back rubs, braiding each other's hair.

The sight gave her an idea. Should she just offer to give Mr. Robbins a back rub? She imagined taking his shoulders in her hands, telling him he felt tense. Could she do it? Or was that too—

"Hippolyta!"

She snapped to attention. Mr. Robbins and most of the cast were staring at her.

"Sorry." She stood up.

"We're taking it from 'I was with Hercules and Cadmus once,'" said Mr. Robbins, his voice frustrated.

"Sure." How long had he been calling for her? She made her way to the front of the auditorium as quickly as she could, taking Matt's hand as he reached down to pull her onto the stage. What seemed like an instant later, she was walking with Matt's arm through hers, reminiscing about her days spent hunting in Crete.

Mr. Robbins watched from the edge of the stage, his hand wrapped around his chin. Almost as soon as Matt started his speech praising his hunting dogs, Mr. Robbins interrupted. "One second." He crossed to where Jane and Matt stood surrounded by members of their court.

"Excuse me," he said to Matt, taking him by the shoulders and moving him slightly away from Jane. A second later Mr. Robbins had his arm linked through Jane's and he looked down into her eyes. "You need to woo her here. You're talking about the dogs, but you're not talking about the dogs. You're telling her she isn't going to regret marrying you, but you're telling her by praising your amazing hunting dogs."

"Come on, Len. We know all about Theseus's incredible dog," Jay shouted up at the stage.

Most of the cast laughed, but Mr. Robbins ignored them. He continued to stare at Jane, then spoke Shakespeare's words quietly, gently, looking into her eyes the entire time. "'My hounds

211

are bred out of the Spartan kind, so flew'd, so sanded, and their heads are hung with ears that sweep away the morning dew.'" He touched Jane's cheek gently, tracing his finger along the edge of her face almost to her neck. "Got it?" he asked.

He was staring at her so intently that Jane thought she was supposed to answer, until Matt said, "Check, Chief."

But Mr. Robbins didn't move. There was no reason for him to be standing next to her anymore, no reason he hadn't told Matt to come take her arm and try the scene again. No reason for him to still be staring at her.

No reason at all . . . unless there was.

Chapter
Thirty

AS SOON AS she finished her Greek homework, Natalya headed into the living room and switched on the computer. When Safari opened, she navigated to her Facebook page and read her wall posts and messages. Morgan had posted more pictures from the party. There was one of Morgan sitting with Katrina and Sloane on either side of her, all of them laughing for the camera. There was a shot of Morgan standing on the first-floor landing, talking to a boy Natalya hadn't met. He was cute, but not as cute as Grant.

Not as cute as Colin.

She shook her head, as though thoughts of Colin were an

irritating bug she wanted to get rid of. Tonight she was going to be good. She was going to stop. She wasn't going to keep doing what she'd secretly been doing for the last several nights. It was over. She'd been stupid and careless and she had to stop.

She made herself stare more intently at Morgan's pictures. There was a photo of Morgan on the love seat in the library, which she'd been sitting on when she was talking to Jane, Natalya, and Victoria. In the foreground was a small lump of black that looked like it might be a knee. Was it Natalya's knee? She tried to picture where she'd been sitting when she was talking to Morgan. She hoped it was her knee. That made being at the party more real somehow—if her knee had been there, so had the rest of her.

She clicked away from the pictures. George had sent her a quiz: "What mixed drink are you?" Since he'd texted Morgan about Natalya, he'd sent Natalya a bunch of groups to join and people to become fans of. So far he hadn't sent her an actual message, and she was kind of relieved. As long as the only evidence of his liking her was Morgan's saying he did, she didn't have to decide how she felt about him.

She took the quiz, skewing her answers in the hopes of finding out she was a virgin piña colada. But in the end, she was something called a daiquiri, which she'd never heard of.

When she was done, she sent Victoria the quiz and a message about Morgan's new pictures, but she just sent Jane the quiz. She knew Jane wouldn't want to see the pictures, but she didn't get why. What did Jane have against Morgan? And why did she care that Natalya didn't want anyone to know she'd thought Colin was cute? So Natalya had decided she wanted to be friends with Morgan more than she wanted to pursue a crush on some random guy she'd met for like, five seconds. Did that make her a criminal?

Starting to think about Colin made it hard for Natalya to stop thinking about Colin. She remembered his smile, how it had felt when he'd said "Hand," and pulled her hand toward him so he could draw the map on it. He was so cool. So confident. How could he possibly be a geek?

And before she could stop herself, she was clicking onto the Web site, breaking the vow she'd made (and broken) every night this week.

It had started innocently enough—Sunday afternoon when she finished her homework, she'd wanted to play some chess, but her dad was working. Her mom and brother didn't play. She wasn't supposed to play online with strangers, but it wasn't like she'd be dumb enough to give her name or her age or anything to some creepy nut job she met online. Still, just to be safe, she'd started by searching Web sites connected to schools, where hardened criminals doing life in prison for violent crimes probably *weren't*.

Which was how she'd stumbled onto the New York City Independent School's consortium. It was a clearinghouse Web site for the private high schools in the city, and all you needed to gain access was an e-mail address from one of the member schools. Natalya logged on with her school account and started to make her way through the site. Most of it wasn't especially interesting—you could list your contact information if you wanted to be part of a babysitting service, participate in a peer tutoring center, recommend summer camps and after-school activities (did that many kids at New York City private schools really ride horses? Apparently so). And then she discovered it.

Games.

Natalya had scrolled past Scrabble, Dungeons & Dragons, and virtual baseball. She'd clicked on the "chess" link, then casually read down the list of current players, telling herself she wasn't looking for anyone in particular, she was just looking. Just looking to see if she recognized any names. Just looking to see if . . .

And there he was: cbprewitt@thompson.edu.

Colin B. Prewitt. What did the *B* stand for?

Did she care? She was crazy to care. She was crazy to do this. It was like sacrificing your queen.

It was like sacrificing yourself.

Still, she'd found the mouse moving closer and closer to his name as she played a game of chicken with herself.

Finally, she clicked. A window opened up. Would you like to challenge cbprewitt@thompson.org to a game?

She'd closed the window immediately, then opened it, then closed it. This was so stupid. Morgan, Katrina, and Sloane were her friends. They thought she was cool. They were taking her to a huge costume gala at the Metropolitan Museum of Art in less than a week. Nobody, *nobody* knew about her conversation with Colin, about the fact that he was still on her mind.

She opened the window. Would you like to challenge Colin Prewitt to a game?

Yes.

Heart pounding, she waited as the little beach ball spun around for half a minute.

Colin is not online at the moment. Would you like to make the first move in a game he will be invited to join when he logs on?

Would she like to make the first move? Would she like to make the first move in a game Colin would be invited to join?

Her hand was shaking so much that she had trouble moving the mouse to the box she wanted to click on. Or thought she wanted to click on. Or couldn't not click on.

Yes. Yes, she wanted to make the first move.

A chessboard opened on her screen. She moved her pawn to D4, and before she could change her mind, she hit SEND.

It was an opening move, all right. The only question was: What game was she playing?

Now, several nights and as many moves later, she was like an addict. The first thing she thought about when she woke up was whether Colin was sitting in his room, studying the board. So far they'd never been online at the same time; she made a move, then sent it into the cybersphere, and when she logged on, he'd always made a counter move.

Tonight, when the game came up on her screen, she could see he had her in a tight place. It seemed impossible to avoid losing her rook. She stared at the pieces, studying her options, so consumed by the game that she forgot about Colin, Morgan, even herself. There was nothing but the moves she could make, the moves she couldn't, nothing but the board.

It took her a long time to decide what to do, but when she finally slid her bishop to E6, she was feeling pretty proud of herself. It was a good move. If he fell into her trap, his rook was in danger and so was his bishop. She leaned back in her chair and folded her arms across her chest, realizing, to her amusement, that she was sitting exactly how her father sat whenever he'd made a move he was pleased with.

"Chess is like life, Natalya," she said out loud, mimicking her father's accent. Then she laughed to herself.

The computer emitted a tiny ping, and a window popped up on the lower left-hand corner of her screen.

cbprewitt@thompson: Of all the chess games in all the world, she walks into mine.

Natalya's heart started to pound. He was there. He was writing to her. He wasn't just a nameless, faceless player. He was Colin. He was Morgan's dork brother.

Should she say something back? Should she say nothing back? Should she log off, pretending she hadn't even seen his message?

npetrova@gainsford: I

"Hello? Anyone home? Natalya? Alex?" It was her mom.

npetrova@gainsford: I have to go.

Without waiting to see if he typed a response, she frantically exited and shut the computer down.

"Hi, Mom." Even though she hadn't been doing anything wrong, Natalya leaped out of her chair and headed to the front door to meet her mom, as though she'd been making out with Colin, not playing online chess with him.

"Hello, sweetheart." Her mother pulled Natalya into a gentle hug and kissed her lightly on the cheek. Her skin was soft and unwrinkled, which she said had more to do with good genetic luck than any of the expensive products sold at the spa. "How was your day?"

Natalya followed her mother into the kitchen. "It was okay. The Greek quiz was harder than I thought it would be." So much of Natalya's life at Gainsford was about nonacademic things, it was strange to find herself discussing class work and tests with her parents, as if that was what her school day was comprised of.

"Did you do well?" asked her mom, taking out a pot and filling it with water.

"I think so." Her mother was still wearing her work whites, and Natalya realized she was trying to avoid looking at them, like if she focused really, really hard on her face and hair, she could pretend her mom wasn't in a white polyester jacket/shirt and pants.

Unbuttoning the top button of her jacket, her mother said, "I should change before I start cooking. Will you take the broccoli out and wash it?"

"Sure." Natalya crossed to the refrigerator and pulled out the vegetable drawer.

On her way to the bedroom, her mother patted Natalya lightly on the head. "And when I'm changed, we can have a real talk and you can catch me up on everything that's happening in your life."

"Okay." Natalya thought about how she was pretending to Morgan that she was into George, how she'd lied to Victoria, but then Victoria had seemed happy to be at the party, so she'd never told her the truth. How Jane seemed angry about her new friends. Her secret online chess game with Colin.

Was she really going to tell her mother everything? Impossible. But equally impossible was the idea of trying to tell her mom one thing without explaining how it tied into everything else.

Washing the stalks of broccoli, Natalya decided that when her mom came back, she'd talk about her classes. To her mother, school meant school*work*. For tonight, Natalya would pretend that was also what it meant to her.

Chapter
Thirty-one

AT 2:59 ON FRIDAY AFTERNOON, Victoria placed the last mixing spoon next to the last mixing bowl, for a total of five cooking stations. There was a bowl for her and one for Maeve. Yesterday a girl named Sheniqua had come up to her after math and asked if there was any room left in the baking club for her and her friend. Victoria had almost laughed at the idea that the club would be full. "Totally," she'd promised. So she'd put out a bowl for Sheniqua and one for her unnamed friend. If twenty people came, it was going to be a problem, but if only Maeve showed, having a few extra bowls out (as opposed to a few dozen) wouldn't be completely humiliating.

For just a second, she let herself imagine what it would be like if Jack walked through the swinging doors and into the kitchen, then felt embarrassed for even having had the thought. Why would Jack come? He'd never expressed even the slightest interest in baking.

Ever since their team condom moment (she blushed even redder thinking about *that*), they'd gone back to saying hey to each other in the hallway or if they arrived simultaneously at the door to the bio lab. But they hadn't had a conversation. Still, sometimes lately when Ms. Kalman stood behind Victoria and Jack was facing the back of the room, Victoria was pretty sure he really *was* looking at her. But she was never *totally* sure. And it wasn't as if he'd ever spoken to her. It wasn't as if he'd come up to her after class and said, *So, about that extra ticket I mentioned . . .*

Three o'clock. She could hear the building quieting now that classes were over, and she started to get worried. What if *nobody* came? What if everyone was talking about the lame club Victoria Harrison had tried to start? What if . . .

The door to the kitchen opened, and Maeve peeked cautiously into the kitchen. She hesitated a few feet away from the table, as though she wasn't sure if it was okay to approach.

Victoria gestured her over just as Sheniqua and another girl barreled through the door.

"Sorry we're late," Sheniqua said. "Julia here only took ten years to get her stuff out of her locker."

"That's okay," Victoria assured them. "We haven't started yet."

A second later the door opened again, and two girls, one of whom was Grace, Chloe's friend who Victoria had had lunch with that first day of school, stepped into the kitchen. Before the door could swing closed, another girl came racing in, slightly out of breath. "Am I late?" she asked. Her cheeks were bright red. "My practice just got canceled and I thought I'd try to make it."

"You made it," Sheniqua assured her.

By ten after three, there were nine people in the room. Victoria was so busy rustling up extra bowls, measuring cups, and spoons, she forgot to be nervous. When she'd finally found enough equipment for five pairs of bakers, she took a deep breath and surveyed the room. Every eye was on her.

"Hi." Her voice was shaky and she could feel her cheeks growing warm. She felt the same panic she'd felt that morning when she'd entered the dining room and her father's entire campaign staff had stared up at her. Realizing her hands were clutched together in front of her, almost as if she were praying, she yanked them apart so hard, her right hand slapped against a whisk, nearly sending it flying off the table. Automatically, her fingers wrapped around the handle, and the familiar feeling of the cool metal against her palm gave her confidence.

"Welcome to the first meeting of the Morningside Baking Club." She sounded better. Still nervous but better. She took a deep breath. "I was going to teach you how to make an angel food cake, but that needs a long time to cool, and I didn't know how late everyone could stay."

"Can we make it next time?" asked one of the two girls who had come in at the very last minute and whose names Victoria had forgotten to ask. One had straight brown hair, the other had hair the exact same color but crazy curly, as if they were a before and after picture of someone who'd stuck her finger into an electric socket.

Next time? They were already planning on a next time? Their enthusiasm gave Victoria confidence. "Sure, if you want. So, today, let's make lemon meringue tarts. They're a little bit tricky, but anyone you make them for will be totally impressed."

"Hear that? Justin's going to be *impressed*," Sheniqua whispered to the girl whose practice had been canceled. Both girls laughed, and Victoria realized that everyone in the room was happy, giggly. None of them thought she was lame for baking, or wished she'd joined the debate team or model UN. If she were a member of one of those clubs, there'd be no one to teach them how to bake.

"Okay. The first thing we have to do is separate eggs. So, take an egg and gently crack it against one of the small glass bowls you each have."

An hour and a half later, she stood in an empty kitchen.

She felt triumphant.

Okay, Sheniqua's meringue had never really gotten stiff, and Julia's lemon filling had been kind of bitter. But ultimately all the tarts had come out edible.

As she carried a dirty mixing bowl over to the sink, she remembered Maeve beating her egg whites. "Is this what you mean by 'stiff peak'?"

Victoria had been helping the curly-haired girl, and she walked over to get a look at Maeve's bowl. She shook her head. "Keep beating it. They'll get stiffer."

Julia looked over at Maeve's bowl, too, as Maeve began

mixing again. "Really? How do you know?"

Victoria thought for a second, then laughed briefly, a little embarrassed. "I don't know." She shook her head. "I mean, I don't know how I know."

"Oh!" Maeve's voice was excited. "You were right. Look." They all peered into Maeve's bowl, studying the mountains of fluffy egg whites in it.

"Perfect," Victoria announced.

"I can't believe you know all this stuff," said Georgia, the girl with the straight hair. "I want to start my own business, you know?"

"Doing what?" asked Victoria. Then she said to the group, "If you're happy with your egg whites, you can measure out your dry ingredients. Start with the flour. Sorry," she turned back to Georgia. "Tell me about your business idea."

"Okay." Georgia pushed her long brown hair out of her eyes and turned to Victoria, her face animated. "You remember how when you were little, your mom would bake cupcakes and cookies or whatever for your birthday at school?"

Victoria's mother had never baked in her life; every birthday cake her family had eaten, either her father or Victoria had baked or her mother had purchased. Still, she knew what Georgia meant. "Yeah?" she asked. Julia turned her bowl so Victoria could see her egg whites, and Victoria gave her a thumbs-up.

Georgia continued. "Well, a few years ago my mom was all, 'This is it. You're going into middle school and you're old enough to use the stove. If you want cupcakes at school for your birthday, you make them yourself.'" Georgia rolled her eyes. "Nice, right?"

"My mom would never in a million *years* make me cupcakes for my birthday," Sheniqua said. "She's obsessed with childhood obesity."

"Hmm . . . okay, that could be a problem." Georgia paused to consider what Sheniqua had said. "Well, I can always make sugar-free ones."

"Sugar-free what?" asked Julia.

Beating her egg whites, Georgia explained. "I'm starting a business making stuff for peoples' birthdays at school. It's going to be called *Happy Birthday to You,* and I'll make cupcakes, cookies, or regular cakes." Her beater ran up the side of the bowl and spattered her with raw egg and sugar. She wiped the mixture off her cheek. "I just have to learn to bake first." Then she nodded meaningfully at Victoria. "Which is where you come in."

As Georgia described her business and Sheniqua complained about her mother's new rule to combat juvenile diabetes (*No sweets in the house unless you make them*), Victoria started to get an idea. She thought about all the times her dad had critiqued how little money there was for preventative health care in the United States. *Just a little education, just a little monitoring, and half the people who end up in the hospital wouldn't be there.*

By the time she shut the oven door, Victoria's thoughts had started to coalesce into a plan. And while they waited for the tarts to bake, Victoria broached the subject.

"How much of a profit do you need to make from your business, Georgia?"

Georgia looked up from the text she was reading and shrugged. "I don't know. My friend Olivia's going to be my business partner.

She's the one who has to deal with all the finances."

"Because I was thinking . . . what if we combined your idea and Sheniqua's idea and did some kind of outreach, teaching people how to bake healthy desserts?"

"Healthy desserts?" Georgia sounded suspicious.

Sheniqua clapped her phone shut. "Like sugar-free stuff?"

"Sure." Victoria considered their options. "Or just . . . I mean, a homemade cake is automatically healthier than a store-bought cake. It has fewer preservatives. You can include fresh fruit, nuts, all kinds of healthy stuff."

Sheniqua thought for a second, then snapped her fingers. "We could do it at the community center where my mom volunteers. She's *always* trying to get me to go over there with her."

Maeve had been listening to their conversation. Now she said in her whispery voice, "There's a community service requirement to graduate, did you guys know that?"

Victoria, Sheniqua, and Georgia shook their heads. "No *wonder* my sister did all that volunteer work," Victoria mused.

Maeve seemed to know just what Victoria meant. "Yours too?" she asked. They gave each other knowing looks.

"It's not like it's *bad* because we'd get credit for it," Sheniqua pointed out. "Teaching people how to make their kids a healthy birthday cake is automatically a good deed."

Georgia grinned. "It's definitely a good *transcript* deed."

They all laughed; as if on cue, the timer dinged.

"To be continued," said Victoria, and she made her way over to the stove to check the tarts.

• • •

Now, alone in the kitchen, Victoria felt like doing a victory dance. She'd done it. She'd been really, really scared to do it, and she'd done it anyway. Nana would be so proud of her. And her parents—she imagined their response when she told them she and some girls from school were going to volunteer at a community center. *See, Emily? Baking* can *be an act of civic good.*

Before leaving, everyone had asked if they could help wash the few dirty dishes that were left, but Victoria said she didn't mind doing them herself, which was true. There weren't that many, and she liked washing dishes, the sense of accomplishment that came from seeing a pile of dirty stuff become a pile of clean stuff.

Outside the kitchen window she heard a group of girls laughing, and when she looked, she saw the soccer team making their way back to the locker room. For a split second she was jealous of the girls walking with their arms around each other, giggling together. It made her think of Jane and Natalya and how they were never again going to be able to just take it for granted that they'd see each other every day, hang out at lunch, between classes, after school. Not have to *make plans*, like they did now. Over the past few weeks it seemed as though she was always talking to Jane *or* Natalya, not both of them. She knew Jane was mad about Natalya's new friends, but she wished Jane would get over it. It was so exciting that Morgan had invited them to the big party at the Met tomorrow night. Why couldn't Jane be happy that Natalya had new friends and that her new friends were kind of becoming Victoria's and Jane's new friends, too?

Jane. Natalya. She had to call them and tell them how the baking club had gone. Flipping open her phone, she saw that she'd been so absorbed in the class she'd missed three texts from them. She started to write back. U will not believe how awe—

"Hey," said a male voice from behind her.

She spun around. Standing in the kitchen, the door swinging quietly behind him, was Jack Hastings.

The text evaporated from her mind.

"Hello," he said. There was something serious about his voice, as if he'd come on business or a mission.

"Hey," she said, her heart racing. He was here. He was really here. She wasn't imagining it.

"I didn't just come to snag sweets," he assured her. He lifted his camera away from his neck, where it hung like Victoria's pearl. "I was hoping to get some shots of the club for *The Scoop.*"

Oh. The Scoop. Her heart sank. "It's over," she said. "They're all gone."

He pointed to the single lemon meringue tart that sat on an aluminum table in the middle of the room. "That's yours."

She nodded and forced herself to smile. Her new club was going to be featured in the school paper. That was a good thing. She should be *psyched* Jack had come to photograph her baking.

So why wasn't she?

Jack squinted at the tart, then at her, then back at the tart. "It's beautiful," he said finally. "Any objection to my taking a picture of it?"

"No. I mean, yes. I mean . . ." They both laughed, and she shook her head and gestured at the tart. "Go for it."

Jack squatted down, getting his eye to counter level, and

started shooting pictures. Victoria watched him. He seemed to have completely forgotten she was in the room, and as he slid the pastry around on the counter to get a better angle, then made his way over to the sink to get a shot of the dirty dishes, it was as if he'd entered another dimension. She wondered if that was what she was like when she was baking.

Her phone buzzed in her pocket and she automatically answered it. "Hello?"

It was Natalya. "Hey, sorry to interrupt your cooking thing. Are we meeting at Jane's when you're done? It's Operation Desperation for costume ideas."

Right. The costume gala. Two minutes in Jack's presence and she'd completely spaced on a party she'd been looking forward to for weeks.

"I have to go to that dinner with my parents tonight." Victoria glanced over at Jack; he had his back to her, one hand in the back pocket of his jeans. She realized she was literally staring at his butt and shifted her gaze to the wall beyond him. "But we could get together tomorrow morning. Early."

"We're cutting it *really* close," Natalya said.

Jack turned around. He was looking at her.

No way could Victoria focus on this conversation with Jack's eyes on her like that.

"Let me . . . I'll call you after, okay?"

"Yeah, sorry," Natalya apologized. "I totally didn't mean to interrupt. How's it going?"

"It's . . . I'll call you. Okay? As soon as it's done."

"Yeah, sure. Bye."

Jack was still watching her. Nervous, she walked over to the sink.

"That's a lot of dishes," Jack observed.

"Not that many, really. We did most of them while the tarts were baking."

He didn't say anything as she turned on the water and started washing a bowl, but when she placed it, clean, on the counter, he picked it up and began drying it.

They worked that way for a few minutes, Victoria washing and Jack drying. The silence between them grew until Victoria wondered if it was weird that neither of them was saying anything.

"You really don't have to stay," she said.

Jack just held out his hand for the plate she'd rinsed, took it, and dried it off. Victoria felt herself ever so slightly relaxing. There was something nice about standing next to each other, washing dishes, not talking. It was so domestic, almost like they were married. The thought made Victoria laugh.

"What?" asked Jack. He bumped her gently with his hip.

"I . . . nothing," she said. Imagining telling him that she'd been laughing because she'd pictured their being married made her laugh again.

"Okay, am I doing something wrong?" asked Jack. He held the bowl out in front of him so she could see how he was drying it. "Is this not how you dry a dish?"

"No," she said, smiling at his profile. "You're perfect." Suddenly she realized what she'd just said, and quickly added, "I mean, *it's* perfect. It's . . . How you're drying the dishes is . . . It's great."

"Oh, you're just saying that," he joked, turning to look at her.

Their eyes met, and they stood staring at each other for what seemed like ages.

"I . . ." she began, but couldn't think of anything to follow. She could feel Jack standing just a few inches away from her; she could see the dark gray of his eyes, the pale red of his cheeks. Jack leaned toward her. He moved so slowly it was almost as if he were standing still, but then his soft lips were pressing gently against hers, and she was closing her eyes and kissing him back. It was the most delicious feeling she'd ever experienced, but almost as soon as he'd started, he'd stopped.

Her eyes flew open. Why was he stopping? Had she done something wrong? She looked at him, and when he stayed where he was, not speaking, not moving away from her, not making a move to kiss her more, she realized his light kiss had been a question.

Is this okay?

She couldn't find the words to answer, but she knew she didn't need words. Instead, she dropped the measuring cup she'd been washing and raised herself up on her tiptoes. She heard the cup hit the bottom of the sink and had a second to be grateful that it was metal and not glass, and then her lips met his, and they were pressed against each other, his arms around her waist, her hands on the back of his neck, the bowl he'd been drying clattering against the kitchen floor.

Yes, said their kisses. *Yes. Yes. Yes.*

Chapter
Thirty-two

"WHAT TIME IS IT?" asked Jane. "Maybe Victoria has an idea." She glanced over her shoulder to check the clock. It was just after five thirty.

"She said she'd call me back as soon as she finished." Natalya lay on the floor of Jane's room, studying the ceiling, where, despite the early evening light streaming through the big open window, it was still possible to make out a few of the nearly invisible, glow-in-the-dark stars Jane's mother had stuck to the ceiling years ago. "Anything?"

Jane stared at the screen on her phone. "I guess her baking club still isn't over." She typed a text. Call as soon as u r done.

"I wish she didn't have to go to that dinner with her parents tonight."

Rolling onto her stomach, Natalya agreed, then added, "I wish I had something to wear tomorrow."

Jane was sitting at her desk—a massive Victorian rolltop with dozens of cubbies, drawers, and shelves—spinning back and forth on her rolling wooden chair. When they were little, the girls had loved to play jewelry store, putting Nana's collection of costume jewelry into the different spaces, then taking turns admiring the pieces as if they were customers who might be interested in purchasing them. Now both the jewelry and the desk belonged to Jane.

"What about Marie Curie?" Jane offered, spinning to a stop. "*She's* a scientist, *you're* a scientist." Lately it seemed as if she and Natalya were always a little uncomfortable talking to each other without Victoria; Jane hated the weirdness between them. Even though, as far as she was concerned, Natalya cared way too much about this party *and* her new friends, Jane wanted to help her figure out something good to wear. Maybe if she helped Nat solve her costume crisis, everything between them would go back to normal.

Natalya groaned and raised herself up on her elbows just enough to look at Jane. "Have ya *seen* Marie Curie?" When Jane shook her head, Natalya dropped back down. "Let's just say she probably didn't drive the guys in her lab wild with desire."

Jane didn't say anything, and for a long minute the only sound was the noise of the chair's wheels rolling back and forth on the ancient Persian carpet.

"Any ideas?" asked Nat.

"I'm thinking," answered Jane. It was true. She was thinking. But not about Natalya's costume. There was only one thing on her mind these days.

"I know!" Natalya sat up with excitement. "What if we go as cats. Just . . . black tights, black noses. It's simple. It's classic." When Jane didn't answer, Natalya sighed and lay back down. "I know, it's totally middle school."

Jane had to tell someone. She'd considered telling her mom, but cool as her mother was, she would *not* be psyched to hear about Mr. Robbins and her. Maybe if Jane were in college and he were her professor, her mother would accept a relationship between them. But not now.

Would Natalya understand? Victoria would absolutely freak. But maybe Nat wouldn't. Hesitantly, her voice little more than a whisper, Jane said, "Nat?"

Natalya had her chin on her hands and was studying the worn weave of the ancient rug. "Mmmm?"

"Can I tell you something?" She was almost as frightened as she'd been at her audition.

"Mmmhmm."

"I think I like Mr. Robbins." As soon as the words were out, she felt simultaneously relieved and even more terrified than she'd been before. What if Nat laughed?

Natalya sat up and looked at Jane, a puzzled expression on her face. "What do you mean?"

"I mean . . ." Jane sighed. Did she really have to explain? "What do you mean what do I mean? I mean I like Mr. Robbins."

She threw her hands out to the sides, to show the magnitude of what she was trying to express.

For a second, Natalya didn't say anything. And then, "Like, *like* like him?"

Jane nodded but didn't speak. With her eyes, she pleaded with Natalya to understand what she meant.

"Jane, he's a *grown-up*." Natalya spoke slowly and carefully, as though a great deal depended on Jane's understanding the words she chose.

"Aaaand . . ."

On her butt, Natalya scooted toward Jane's chair. "And he's not just a grown-up, he's your *teacher*."

Jane gave a little wail of frustration and spun all the way around in her chair. Why was Natalya *torturing* her? "Could you please tell me something I don't already know?"

Natalya hesitated. "I just mean . . . I'm not saying you can't have a crush on him, or—"

Was *that* what Natalya thought she was describing? A *crush*? "It's not a *crush*." Jane practically spat out the word.

"Sorry!" Natalya held out her hand as if Jane were a wild animal she needed to pacify. "I just. I mean, are you . . . You're not going to . . . You're not going to *do* anything, are you?"

Jane shrugged and looked off into the distance, as though she were seeing a place or a time somewhere other than the moment and the room they were sitting in. "I don't know." She wanted to add, *I don't know what to do*, but she didn't.

Natalya studied her friend for a long minute. "Jane."

"Yeah?"

Natalya looked down and traced the grain in the arm of the chair. "Remember when I tried to teach you chess?"

Jane did. She'd been a hopeless player—every time Natalya explained why something Jane did would cost her a piece just a few moves in the future, Jane would shake her head, amazed. *How can anyone* think *that far ahead? I just deal with things as they come up.*

Natalya raised her eyes and watched until it was clear from her friend's expression that Jane remembered what she was talking about. Then she spoke. "I think this is like that. I think . . . I think you need to think a few moves ahead."

Jane pushed herself out of her chair and walked over to her closet.

Natalya didn't understand.

No one could understand.

"I must have *something* in here that you can wear," Jane declared.

"Jane . . ." Natalya began.

Jane opened her closet door. "What?" Her voice was distracted. There was no point in talking about it anymore. She should have known better than to bring the whole thing up in the first place.

Natalya didn't say anything for a minute, then her eyes glanced down at her silent phone. "That cooking class is really taking forever," she observed.

Jane nodded, not sure if she was relieved or disappointed that her attempt to change the subject had worked. "I guess they're making something really delicious."

Chapter
Thirty-three

HAD HER FEET touched the ground once since she'd left the Morningside kitchen? Victoria's hand still felt warm from where Jack had squeezed it good-bye as they'd parted ways at Amsterdam Avenue, he to head south, she to head north.

"You aren't by any chance free to go hear some music tonight?" he'd asked. "Because Pony is playing a late set at the Pea Bar. They don't start until midnight, but it's going to be great."

She laughed, partly because she couldn't believe Jack had just asked her to go out with him, partly at the idea of telling her parents she'd be going out at midnight. "Um, I think I have to take a rain check."

He nodded and squeezed her fingers. "Well, I won't take it personally."

She squeezed his in return. "Don't," she said, then sailed across Seventy-ninth Street with the light.

When she turned onto her block, her face was still plastered with a smile. Did she look deranged? She might look deranged, walking along and smiling at nothing. She tried to make the corners of her mouth turn down, but it was impossible. She felt like that character in *Brigadoon*, the musical she and Natalya had gone to with Jane and Nana for Jane's tenth birthday. *It's almost like being in love.*

From the corner she saw a crowd gathered around her building's awning, and her smile dimmed slightly. The election was a week from Tuesday, and Satan was obsessed with keeping her parents in the public eye. Those were the words he used, *In the public eye.* The phrase grossed Victoria out—every time he said it, she imagined having something in her eye. But Satan couldn't get enough. Her mom had done a photo shoot for this week's *New York* magazine, and tomorrow she had to go to a nursing home with her parents so they could be seen chatting with the old people. Plus there was tonight's dinner, the last fund-raiser before the election. Ugh. Whenever she said hello to people at one of her dad's fund-raisers, she felt them evaluating her worth, trying to decide if her family were something they wanted to buy.

Her phone buzzed and she looked down. It was from Jack. Just so u know, I m thinking about u. If u rnt thinking about me, I feel v lame. Laughing, she texted back, u r not lame. She saw she'd missed three texts from Natalya and Jane. And she'd missed a bunch of calls, probably from them, too. They were going to *freak* when she told them about Jack.

Victoria was two doors down from her building, still reading the texts from Jack and Natalya and Jane, when a voice shouted, "There she is!" Glancing up, she saw that the crowd outside her building was looking her way. She heard the now-familiar whirr of a camera taking multiple shots.

Okay, this was really weird. The campaign released her parents' schedule every morning, so she'd figured these photographers had wanted a shot of her mom and dad all glammed up for an evening out, but now they were turning their cameras on her? Talk about a slow news cycle. She kept walking toward her door, but suddenly the crowd surged, and what felt like dozens of people were shoving their cameras in her face, calling her name.

"Victoria! Over here! Victoria!"

Within seconds, the whole pack had taken up the cry, and Victoria felt the crowd close around her, pushing her. She couldn't breathe, they were swarming her, she was going to fall.

Suddenly she felt a strong hand under her elbow, and she was being guided toward the door of her building as a voice said, "Coming through. Get back. Get back behind the barriers." For a second she thought it was her dad, but then she looked up into the familiar face of Frank, the doorman. He pushed his way through the crowd and into the lobby. As soon as the door had closed on the bright flashes and loud voices, he turned to her.

"You okay, honey?"

Victoria realized she was shaking. Someone had pulled at the sleeve of her sweater hard enough to rip it. Her stomach was in knots. Could something horrible have happened to her father? Sometimes she heard her parents discussing a threat that had been made against him or the family. When she asked, they'd always brushed away her concerns, assuring her the family was completely safe. But what if . . .

Her mouth was dry, and she barely managed to whisper, "Is my dad—"

Frank smiled and patted her arm reassuringly. "They're all upstairs. I'll buzz and tell them you're on your way."

Victoria wanted to ask what was going on, but Frank nudged her toward the elevator, so she crossed the lobby, tucking her hair behind her ears. The lurch in her stomach as the elevator ascended had, she knew, nothing to do with its climb.

Before she could even put her key in the lock, the door flew open to reveal her mother wearing a long green dress, an unfamiliar, frightened expression on her face. Behind her mom, her father stood at the dining room table, the bow tie of his tuxedo untied, his arms crossed. On his right sat Julie, the communications director. The tiny, tense smile she gave Victoria was a faded replica of the huge grin with which she normally greeted her. On her father's other side stood Satan, who stared at Victoria as though he wished she were dead.

"Victoria, what is going on? Why didn't you return our calls?" her father yelled across the space between them. "Where have you been?"

"I was at baking club!" Victoria was so eager to prove her innocence she practically tripped over the words. "I told you about it!" Had they found out who she'd been at the class *with*?

Could someone know what she and Jack had been doing in the kitchen less than an hour ago? Satan's warning boomed in her brain. *Anything you say or do will be held against your father.*

What had she been thinking? How could she have been so stupid as to make out with a boy in the kitchen of her *school*?

Her father's tight-lipped expression didn't change, but even from the foyer, Victoria could see a flicker of what looked like relief pass over his features.

"Victoria," her mother began, putting her hand on her daughter's wrist, "we need to ask you about something, and we need you to be scrupulously honest about it. Do you understand?"

Victoria could feel herself beginning to freak out. Were her parents having her *followed*? *No one* had been in the kitchen with Jack and her—she was sure of that. Had someone seen them walking out of the building together holding hands?

She followed her mother into the dining room. Her dad, Julie, and Satan looked at her as she approached, and something about the way their eyes raked her up and down made her feel as if she were naked.

"Victoria, do you have an explanation for this?" Her father's face was red, the anger in his voice barely contained. As he spoke he held something in her direction.

The top page was a fax cover sheet with a hastily scrawled message on it. *J— FYI, you're going to need to do some damage control on this one. Also, you owe me BIG-time. If it gets out who you got this from, I'm toast. —FS*

J could be Julie, but Victoria had no idea who *FS* was or how this fax had anything to do with her. She flipped to the next page and gasped. It was a copy of a photograph of her and Jack. They were both smiling, and Jack was giving a thumbs-up. Victoria was wearing her FOXY LADY T-shirt, and in her hands was a condom-clad banana.

Victoria felt the lemon meringue she'd sampled all afternoon rising in her throat, and she worked hard to swallow it down. "Oh my god," she whispered. Then she looked up at the ring of faces bearing down on her. "What is this?"

Was it a flyer someone had put up at school? Could it possibly have been slipped under their apartment door?

It was Satan who spoke. "It's the cover of tomorrow's *New York Mirror*," he said.

"What?" Victoria swayed slightly, then put her hands on the table to steady herself.

Steven crossed his arms and nailed Victoria with a vicious stare. "Were you at a party recently? A party where no parents were present and there was drinking?"

Oh my god. Oh my god. Oh my god.

"I . . ."

"Because guests posted photos of you on Facebook, and those are going to be in the *Mirror* too."

Before she could respond, her father said, "I don't understand, Victoria. Are you sneaking out and going to parties? With this boy?"

"No. Daddy, I—"

Her father cut her off. "When Julie told me about this, I honestly thought it was some kind of joke. I would never, *never* have expected this from you. You lied to us?!"

"I never lied to you!"

"You never . . . Victoria, you went to a party without our permission. Do you seriously think that isn't lying?"

It had all seemed so clear when she was talking to Jane and Victoria about it in her kitchen. They'd definitely used the word "lying," but somehow they'd agreed it *wasn't* lying. Or it was, only it wasn't the bad kind of lying. But now, with her father and her mother and Satan staring at her, it was impossible to re-create the train of logic that had made it okay to go to the party.

Satan's cell phone rang. "Steven Mack here," he barked. He listened briefly, then said more gently, "Oh hi, Tim, thanks for getting back to me." He placed his hand over the phone and whispered, "It's the *Times*." Julie and both her parents nodded, and Satan walked toward the kitchen, "Mmmhmm. Mmmmhmmm." He laughed. "Well, not ideal *is* one way of putting it."

Victoria started to cry. "I'm sorry, Daddy."

"Look at this shirt." Her father pointed at the photo and turned to his wife. "How could you let her out of the house in this?"

Her mother put her hands up. "Don't blame me! I didn't see her wearing it."

"How could you even *buy* a shirt like this?" her father demanded.

"I didn't buy it," Victoria said quickly. "It was a present. Jane gave it to me. As a joke."

"Fine, okay, it was a joke," her mother allowed. "So you wear it at home, not out in public."

"I just thought . . ."

Her father ran his fingers through his hair, then gave it a

frustrated yank. "Were you and your friends drinking at this girl's party?"

Victoria shook her head violently. "No. No! I swear."

He snorted. "You can't seriously expect me to believe that."

"It's true!" Victoria leaped to her feet. She looked pleadingly at Julie, but Julie was reading something on her BlackBerry.

"Andrew," her mother said quietly.

He spun to face his wife. "What? She's experimenting with condoms and wearing outrageous clothing. She lied to us. She and her friends got all dolled up and went to some party. And we're supposed to believe she wasn't *drinking*?" He glared at her. "Please, Victoria. Don't insult my intelligence."

By now Victoria was completely hysterical. "It's true, Daddy. As soon as people started drinking, we left. I swear."

Her father shook his head slowly. "I'm just so disappointed, Victoria. What on earth could possibly have led you to have such bad judgment?" He looked back down at the fax in his hand. "Whose party was it?"

"She goes to Gainsford," Victoria managed to choke out, "with Natalya."

"Natalya!" For the first time in the conversation, her mother sounded genuinely shocked. "This was a party with *Natalya's* friends?"

Her father hadn't taken his eyes off the picture he was holding. "Whose idea was it that you go to this party? Was it Natalya's?"

Still sobbing, Victoria nodded. Her father shook his head. "So Jane bought you this outrageous T-shirt, and Natalya convinced you to go to a party with a bunch of drunk rich kids. Very nice." His voice was sharp with sarcasm. "That's really what you want in friends."

"Drew," her mother said softly. "Don't blame Natalya and Jane. This is Victoria's fault." Her mother looked at her. "Am I wrong to say that, Victoria? Did they pressure you into going?"

Now Victoria was crying too hard to answer, and her mom reached over and took her hand. "Victoria, you are such a sweet, innocent person. Those are two of your best qualities. But you're old enough now to know—we thought you *did* know—that the world is not as sweet and innocent as you are."

Her mother's words hung in the air. The only sound was Victoria's quiet sobbing. Then Satan surged back into the room. "That was Tim Williams at the *Times*. He's going to cover the nursing home visit. A nice, wholesome family outing. And it will run next Sunday—seventy-two hours before the polls open." He rubbed his hands together greedily.

Victoria inhaled a deep, ragged breath.

"Why don't you go splash some cold water on your face," suggested her mother.

Her father pressed his index finger into the table so hard the tip turned white. "Except for school and campaign events, you are grounded, young lady. We expect you home immediately after school every day, and you are not going out on the weekends." He turned to her mother. "We'll see if Emily can come up next weekend to watch her. We have to be upstate."

Victoria couldn't believe she'd heard right. "*Emily?!* Emily's going to *babysit* me?"

Her father's head snapped around, and he glared at her. "That's right. When you show the judgment of a child, you get treated like a child."

"But—" *Emily? Emily?!* Victoria remembered how she'd considered telling Emily about the party, how she'd imagined Emily's finally seeing her as an equal.

But instead the party had turned Emily into her *babysitter*?!

"Go to your room, Victoria," her father commanded. "I have nothing left to say on this subject."

Victoria turned and left the room, glad her back was to her parents and they couldn't see that she'd started to cry again. Why was this happening to her? She never did *anything* wrong, and the one time she did, she got caught. And not just caught but put on the *cover of the newspaper*. Everyone would see that picture— her teachers, the kids at school.

And what would Jack think? Clearly that he should never, ever have spoken to her, much less kissed her. She could practically hear the voice mail message he'd leave her tomorrow. *Um, hey, it's Jack. I'm into* taking *pictures for newspapers, not* being in *them. So, if it's all the same to you, can we just pretend that whole "thing" in the kitchen never happened. Actually, I'm already pretending that. Who are you? Why am I leaving you this message? Whatever. Bye.*

Her phone buzzed and she grabbed it out of her bag. It was another text from Natalya and Jane.

V???? Where r u???

Rather than responding, she scrolled through their other texts from earlier.

Do u want 2 b sexy scientists?

R u still cooking?

R u alive? Call us!!!!

There they were, laughing and joking together while she was locked in her room like some kind of criminal. And it wasn't as if Jane would even get in trouble if Victoria's parents called her mother—hadn't Jane already told her mom she was going to the party? And no one would be posting pictures of Natalya in the *Mirror*. She could go on with her life like nothing had even happened.

It was so unfair. Victoria thought about what her mother had said. *Did they pressure you into going?* Holding her phone to her chest, she flopped onto her bed. *Had* they pressured her? She couldn't remember the exact conversation, but she had *definitely* said they shouldn't go to the party. *And* that they shouldn't lie to their parents. And then . . . hadn't she said Jane and Natalya should go without her? And hadn't they said they wouldn't go if she didn't go? That she basically *had* to go? And wasn't that when she'd finally said, *Okay, I'll go.*

And now she was the one who was under house arrest, and *they* were having fun planning costumes to wear to the awesome gala that *Victoria couldn't go to because she was grounded.* Grounded for going to a party she hadn't wanted to go to in the first place.

The more she thought about how unfair it was, the angrier she got. She stood up and shoved her phone back into her bag, then lay down on her stomach on her bed in the darkening room.

Why should she bother to call them back?

Chapter
Thirty-four

SATURDAY MORNING, JANE rolled over and looked down from her bed at Natalya, who'd slept on an air mattress on the floor. "What if you go as a table and Victoria goes as a chair?"

Natalya, who had her phone pressed to her ear, laughed. "What if you bag your dress rehearsal and you and I go as hydrogen atoms and Victoria goes as an oxygen atom and we each carry an empty glass?" She was laughing so hard she was almost choking.

Jane laughed too. "I'm laughing, but I have no idea what you're talking about."

"Water," Natalya gasped. "We'd be a water molecule."

Jane laughed so hard she literally rolled off the bed. "That is so incredibly stupid, I almost can't believe it."

"I know," Natalya agreed, still laughing. For what felt like the millionth time, Victoria's recorded voice played in her ear. Natalya shook her head in frustration. "I can't leave *another* message."

"Leave another message," Jane ordered, climbing back onto her bed.

". . . *after the beep*," Victoria's outgoing message concluded.

"Hey, it's us again." Natalya said. "Where *are* you?"

"Tell her we're going to be forced to call her on a landline."

"We're going to call you on a landline," Natalya informed her phone. When it didn't respond, she added, "So, yeah, think about that. And just . . . you know, call us back." She hung up. "I think that'll definitely scare her into calling."

"This is so weird." Jane checked the time on her alarm clock. Ten fifteen. "Could she still be asleep?"

Natalya considered Victoria's evening. "Maybe she got home late from the baking thing, had to rush really fast to get dressed to go out with her parents, got home late, and she's not up yet."

Jane stared at her. "But she would have texted? Or . . . *something*."

"Phone's dead?" Natalya offered. When Jane kept staring, Natalya shrugged. "Well, *I* don't know."

Jane checked her clock again. "I have to be at dress rehearsal at one."

Natalya opened her eyes wide with mock hopefulness and smiled at Jane. "I know! You can snag me and Vicks costumes!"

In lieu of an answer, Jane chucked a pillow at Natalya's head.

"Hey!" Natalya objected, just as there was a knock at the door.

"Come in," they both called. A second later, Jane's mom was standing on the threshold in a pair of black yoga pants and a white T-shirt, her hair held off her face by a pair of small silver clips. She was carrying a shopping bag in one hand and a folded-up newspaper in the other. Her face was pale.

"Hi, Mom," said Jane. Sometimes she and her mom did yoga together on Saturday mornings, but not when her mom got up to hit the eight a.m. class.

Her mother sat on the edge of Jane's bed and looked from Jane to Natalya. "Has either of you spoken to Victoria this morning?"

Both girls bolted upright.

"Something happened to her dad!" Jane cried.

"Oh my god!" gasped Natalya.

"No," Jane's mother said quickly. "It's nothing like that. It's . . ." She sighed, then slowly unfolded the paper.

Jane grabbed it. As soon as her eyes saw the cover photo, she cried out as if in pain.

Natalya lurched toward the bed and huddled on her knees next to Jane, staring at the paper. *"Nooo!"* she wailed.

"The poor thing," said Jane's mother. She pressed her fingers to her eyelids and shook her head sadly. "Of all the people for this to happen to."

"That's why she hasn't called," Natalya whispered. She studied the cover. "Wait, isn't that *Jack*?"

With shaking hands, Jane turned to the spread on pages four and five, where the article was. There were pictures of Victoria that they'd seen before—a family portrait that had been taken in

June; a shot of Victoria and Emily from the weekend the family had dropped Emily off at Princeton; a few "candid" snaps from campaign events—and then there were unfamiliar ones: Victoria and Jack high-fiving and holding the condom-ed banana; a picture from Morgan's party of Victoria and Morgan walking arm in arm; one of Victoria alone on the love seat in the library, her head thrown back in what could easily have been drunken laughter.

"That bitch," Jane muttered.

"What?" asked Natalya, skimming the text. "*. . . a party earlier this month at an Upper Eastside mansion . . . other Facebook photos that show attendees drinking. . . . The candidate's daughter, who clearly enjoys a good time, undoubtedly shares her father's liberal values. . . .* Wait," said Natalya, "who's a bitch?"

Jane stared at Natalya as if she'd never encountered such stupidity in her life. "Isn't it obvious? Morgan posted these pictures of Victoria."

"No she didn't," Natalya protested. "She wouldn't do that. She wouldn't do something to make Victoria look bad. She and her parents are big Andrew Harrison supporters."

There was a moment of silence, and then both Jane and Natalya realized the significance of what Natalya had just said.

"Oh. My. God." Jane spoke the words slowly, staring at Natalya.

"What?" asked Natalya, not meeting Jane's eyes.

Jane continued to stare, then slowly shook her head back and forth in amazement. "*That's* why Morgan invited you to the party. Because of Victoria. I *knew* there was something that didn't make sense."

Natalya jumped backward off the bed and stared down at Jane. "What, Morgan couldn't just like me? She couldn't just like me for me?"

"Girls," said Jane's mother. She reached out and put a hand on each of their arms. Her voice was low and serious. "Whatever issues you two might have about this Morgan girl, now isn't the time. You have to think of Victoria. You have to help her." She took a deep breath that ended in her making a small clucking noise at the back of her throat. "Think of how awful this must be for her."

Jane pressed her palm to her forehead. "I'm sorry," she said quietly.

"Me too," said Natalya.

"My mom's right," said Jane. She stood up, crossed the room, and grabbed a pair of jeans from the floor.

"What are you doing?" asked Natalya, staring at her.

"Get dressed." Jane was digging around in her dresser for a shirt.

"What do you mean, 'get dressed'?"

Jane snapped her head in Natalya's direction. "We're going over there."

Chapter
Thirty-five

IT WAS CREEPY how there was a police barricade around the entrance to Victoria's building, and a cop car with its lights flashing parked right out front. Across the street a crowd of photographers waited, their cameras at the ready. Natalya and Jane hesitated before entering the small walkway between the blue barriers marked POLICE LINE, DO NOT CROSS, but then the doorman recognized them. He waved them through, and they walked under the awning and entered the building.

"Hello, girls." He beckoned. "Come in. Come in." He was a gray-haired man who'd worked as a doorman in the Harrisons' building since before Natalya and Jane had known Victoria. He smiled at them, almost as if he were Victoria's uncle or an old family friend, and quickly turned to dial Victoria's apartment on the intercom. "I'm sure Victoria will be very happy to see the two of you," he said, pressing the button for her apartment.

But despite his repeated buzzing, there was no answer.

"Did she go out somewhere?" asked Jane finally.

The doorman shook his head and buzzed again. "Mr. and Mrs. Harrison left, but she wasn't with them." He held up a finger to indicate that something was happening. "Ah! Hello, Victoria. I have your friends here to see you." He listened for a minute before nodding and hanging up. "She'll see you."

"Thanks," said Jane, and she and Natalya sprinted to the elevator.

Victoria came to the door wearing a pair of gray sweatpants and an oversized T-shirt, her hair in a sloppy ponytail. Natalya reached out to embrace her.

"Hi." Victoria's voice was as limp as her hair, and she endured Natalya's embrace more than she returned it.

Jane put her arms around Victoria, too. "Are you okay?"

Victoria didn't answer, just stood with her hand on the door-knob, almost like she was trying to block their entrance to the apartment. "Look, guys, my parents are going to be really mad if they find you here. They're coming back any minute, and I still have to take a shower and get dressed. We have to go to this thing at a nursing home."

"What happened?" asked Natalya.

"What'd they say?" asked Jane. "Are you grounded?"

Victoria dropped her eyes to the floor and nodded.

Natalya put her hand on Victoria's shoulder. "Oh no!"

"That sucks," Jane agreed. "Okay, what we need to do is come up with a way to explain what happened. You know, spin it so it doesn't look so bad. . . ." She squinted up at the ceiling as though there might be a reasonable explanation for what they'd done hidden there.

"No thanks," Victoria said quickly, her voice sharp.

Jane heard something in her tone that made her study Victoria's face. Victoria met her stare for a minute, then looked away.

"Vicks?" Jane asked.

"Look, I told you, I'm grounded, okay? You can't be here." Neither Jane nor Natalya had ever heard her sound quite so angry.

There was silence, and then Natalya cleared her throat. "Are you . . . are you mad at us or something?"

Victoria shrugged. Natalya and Jane waited for her to say, *No, of course not! Why would I be mad at you?*—but instead, the silence between them grew.

"Are you?" Jane repeated after a long pause.

Still not meeting their eyes, Victoria said, "I said you need to go. Why aren't you listening to me?" She slapped her forehead. "Oh, wait, why am I surprised? You *never* listen to me."

Victoria, Jane, and Natalya had been friends for ten years. In all that time, Jane and Natalya had never once heard Victoria be sarcastic.

Until now.

Completely bewildered, Jane asked, "Vicks, what are you *talking* about?"

Victoria met Jane's confused eyes with a cold stare. "I *said* we shouldn't go to the party. I *said* it was a bad idea to lie to our parents. But did you listen to me? *Nooo*. Because you *never* listen to me." She turned slightly as if she were someone else addressing herself. "*'Oh, Victoria, I bought this shirt for you.'*" Then she turned back and faced the other direction. "*'I can't wear a shirt that says FOXY LADY, Jane.' 'You are wearing it, Victoria. If we can wear it, you can wear it.' 'Oh, wait! But your dads aren't running for national office.'*"

"Vicks, that's not what—" Jane tried to interrupt, but Victoria ignored her, continuing to act out a drama in which she played both roles.

"*'I don't think we should go to this party, guys.' 'Of course we should go. You want to face your fears, don't you? You don't want to be some Goody Two-shoes for the rest of your life, do you?'*"

"I'd *never* call you a Goody Two-shoes!" Natalya objected.

"Vicks, come on," Jane said. "Don't paint it like that. Nobody meant for you to get in trouble."

But Victoria was crying. "You mean nobody *cared* about my getting in trouble. You guys just wanted what you wanted. *'Let's go to this awesome party! Let's get funny T-shirts! Victoria, why are you being so lame?'*"

"Oh my god," Jane burst out, suddenly angry. "You're rewriting *history*! That's not what happened."

"Jane's right, Vicks," Nat said quietly. "You have to admit it wasn't like that."

Still crying, Victoria looked from Jane to Natalya. "Why am I so not surprised that you both think you know more than I do?"

"Please." Natalya's voice was low and pleading. "Don't do this."

"I'm not doing anything," Victoria said. Slowly, she began shutting the door between her and her friends. "It's already done."

Chapter
Thirty-six

THE VAST EMPTINESS they always encountered at Ga Ga Noodle was normally what made the restaurant feel as though it was their special place, but today the room just felt lonely. Out of habit, Jane and Natalya made their way over to their usual table, then sat there, not talking, as Tom came over with menus.

"Where's your friend?" he asked.

Both girls winced slightly at his question, but he didn't seem to notice, just stood there patiently, waiting for them to answer.

"She's not coming," Jane said finally.

He smiled and nodded, then slipped two menus onto the table and stepped away.

"What do we do now?" Jane asked.

In lieu of an answer, Natalya shook her head slowly.

"We did pressure her to go to the party," Jane stated flatly. "It's true."

Natalya nodded. "I thought . . . I mean, I never thought she would get into this kind of trouble."

"You mean, we never *thought*"—Jane corrected her—"period."

There was a pause. "Thanks for not telling her about Morgan," Natalya blurted out. "I mean, about her asking us to the party because of Victoria."

Jane shrugged. "Sure. Whatever."

"I feel terrible," Natalya said. She pressed against her eyes with the heels of her hands. "I'm so sorry," she whispered, though Victoria wasn't there to hear it.

They continued to sit in silence. Tom reappeared with two virgin piña coladas that neither of them wanted and placed one in front of Jane, one in front of Natalya. "Are you ready to order?" He put down a straw beside each drink.

The girls looked at each other, both nauseated at the thought of eating.

"I think we need another minute," said Jane.

"Okay," said Tom, taking a backward step away from the table. "Take your time."

As soon as he was gone, Natalya's phone buzzed, and she and Jane both jumped. Natalya checked the screen and shook her head in response to Jane's unasked question. "It's not Victoria. It's Morgan. She wants to know what I'm wearing tonight."

Jane snorted, and Natalya looked up. "What?"

"Nothing," said Jane, but the expression on her face said she *hadn't* meant nothing.

"What?" Natalya repeated.

Jane shrugged slightly. "Just . . . Does she want to know what *you're* wearing or what *Victoria's* wearing?"

"What's your point?" asked Natalya, hurt.

"Well, I mean, is she even going to want you there now that Victoria's not coming?"

Natalya put her phone back in her bag without responding to Morgan's text. "We're *friends*, Jane. Morgan and I are friends, okay?"

"You're *friends*? That's why you begged Victoria and me not to reveal that you like Morgan's brother? Because you and she are such good *friends*?"

Natalya stared at the tablecloth. "That was weeks ago, Jane. Can you let it go already?" She looked up. "And anyway, I don't like him, okay? I met him *once*. I don't even *know* him."

"*Now* who's rewriting history?" asked Jane, leaning across the table. "You did *so* like him. You're just too chicken to admit it to his oh-so-popular sister."

Natalya's eyes snapped fire. "Fine, Jane. I liked him. I did. But you know what? That doesn't mean I have to give up everything *else* I like to get with him, okay? Some of us have something called *impulse control*. It's a concept you might want to familiarize yourself with."

"What are you saying?" Jane's eyes were as angry as her friend's.

Natalya crossed her arms on the table and leaned forward

over them. "My *point*, Jane, is that some of the things you call brave, i.e. contemplating an affair with your *teacher*, are what some people would call *stupid*. Did it ever occur to you that some things are taboo because they're *gross*?" Natalya jabbed out the last word with her index finger.

"What's *gross*, if you want to know, is being so scared of your so-called new friend that you pretend to be someone you're not. And what's gross*er* is *becoming* something you're not so you can be friends with someone. You have *completely* changed, Natalya." Jane leaned back in her chair and glared at Natalya.

"*I've* completely changed? *I've* completely changed?" Natalya threw her hands up, outraged. "You're just jealous that I'm making new friends."

"Jealous? Jealous?" Jane's repetition of the word and the laugh that accompanied it were slightly hysterical. "Like I'd ever be jealous of you. Like there even *is* a you. You're so busy being someone else that there isn't even anyone to be jealous *of*."

Natalya's phone buzzed again. Instead of checking to see who was calling, she stood up. "I have to go."

Jane snorted and rolled her eyes. "Oh yeah, go meet your bitchy new friends."

"They are *not*," Natalya half shouted. "You're—"

Suddenly she stopped herself. If Victoria were here, this fight would never, never have gotten so far. Somehow Victoria always knew just what to say when Jane and Natalya were about to go after each other—how to calm them down, keep them from going for the jugular.

Jane's mother's words from when she and Jane had been

bickering earlier came back to her.

You need to think of Victoria.

Could that sentence have a double meaning? Did they need to think of Victoria not just because she needed their help but because they needed to remember what she would be saying to them if she were here?

Before Natalya could try to imagine how Victoria might stop them from hurting each other, Jane was standing up also, demanding, "I'm *what*, Natalya. What am I?"

But thinking of Victoria—of how she was the glue that held them together, how without her, Natalya and Jane were two magnets whose similar charge repelled them from each other— made Natalya frightened. Because Victoria was mad. Really mad.

And Victoria was never mad.

She stared at Jane for a long minute, then reached down and took her bag off the back of the chair.

"Nothing," she whispered. She slipped her shoulder strap on and marched toward the door.

"Just say it, Natalya!" Jane called as Natalya walked out into the sunny afternoon that seemed to mock the fight they were having.

Natalya ignored her and kept on walking. Because even if Victoria wasn't there, there were some things she couldn't bring herself to say to Jane.

And one of them was on the tip of her tongue right now.

They're *not bitches, Jane.*

You're *the bitch.*

Chapter
Thirty-seven

JANE HAD COMPLETELY saved Natalya's *butt*, and this was the thanks she got? Getting called "gross"? Getting told she had no impulse control?

Natalya had so *clearly* chosen her new friends over Jane, that much was obvious. Well, fine. If Natalya's new idea of a good time was hanging out with a bunch of rich snobs from the Upper East Side, she was welcome to them. Jane had things to do, things other than going to stupid parties and pretending not to like guys she liked.

She paid for their untouched drinks and headed over to school for dress rehearsal, trying to put everything that had happened with Natalya and Victoria out of her mind. This was an important day. A serious actress couldn't afford to be distracted by the crazy accusations her so-called best friends were in the mood to hurl at her.

When Jane arrived, the theater was bustling with cast members moving between coatracks overflowing with the riotous rainbow of color and fabric that was their costumes. The stagehands were setting Act One, and a person in the lighting booth was brightening and dimming the lights as someone standing center stage called out numbers to him.

It was like stepping into the middle of a three-ring circus.

"Okay, Hippolyta." Wendy looked down her list and then sent Jane over to Sharon, who moved her fingers along the rack of hangers for almost a full minute before saying, "Ah-ha!" She wedged her hand into the densely packed forest of fabric, and slowly, an inch at a time, worked out Jane's costume. When it hung free in front of her, Jane could only stare.

"Wow," she said finally.

Wendy nodded. "Seriously. Somebody up there wants you sexy." She held the costume in its clear plastic cover out to Jane, and Jane draped it over her arm. Jane knew that Wendy meant the costume shop, but she also knew that Mr. Robbins was the one who had come up with the . . . what did he call it? *The guiding principle for each costume.* The guiding principle.

In this case, SEXY.

The dress was a sheath of heavy silver velvet, high in the front and low cut in the back. The sleeves were also silver, but they were made of an almost transparent silk that had a tattered effect, as if the fabric had been ripped in battle. Even though Jane knew Hippolyta wasn't supposed to be wearing the very dress in which Theseus had kidnapped her, the nod to her warrior past was cool. Jane imagined Mr. Robbins talking to the costume teacher about how he wanted Jane to look. Picturing Mr. Robbins picturing her made Jane a little dizzy.

"Have you seen the dressing rooms yet?" asked Wendy.

Jane shook her head.

Wendy grinned. "You're going to freak out."

Considering the ideas floating through her mind, Jane was already kind of freaking out, but when she pushed open the door to the girls' dressing room, she saw what Wendy meant.

A graduate Jane had never heard of, someone who apparently had never made it as an actor but had married the heir to a dot-com fortune, had donated tens of thousands of dollars to the Academy to modernize the dressing rooms and backstage areas. The floors were a rich, dark wood. On the walls hung huge mirrors framed by rows of big, bright lights; the makeup tables were highly polished marble, and the changing areas were spacious rooms with full-length mirrors and thick blue curtains that dropped down for privacy. Jane remembered the dusty linoleum floors of the dressing rooms at One Room, the communal changing areas, how she and the other girls had to practically elbow each other out of the way if they wanted a chance to see their reflections in the minuscule, stained mirrors. She wanted to send Natalya and Victoria pictures. She wanted them to see what she was seeing.

Except they wouldn't want to see it.

Her stomach hurt, and she barely focused on her dress as she slipped into it. Was it possible her friends weren't going to be there opening night? She'd never done a show without them and Nana in the audience. During her curtain call, Jane always looked for her mother, Nana, Natalya, and Victoria. Now Nana was gone.

Were Natalya and Victoria gone too?

Okay, she *had* to stop thinking about them. She was here at school, and she had a rehearsal to participate in. The cast was counting on her. Mr. Robbins was counting on her.

It was time to be serious.

She pushed aside the curtain of a changing room and thoughts of Victoria and Natalya with it. Her costume hugged her body, the fabric soft as butter, like something she'd been born to wear. As she walked into the hallway that connected the changing space with the makeup room, she ran into Dahlia, who raised her eyebrows in appreciation of how Jane looked.

"Can you *believe* this place?" Dahlia, in a green silky costume with beautiful gossamer wings, grabbed Jane by the arms and squeezed. "You look a-*mazing*, by the way."

"You too," Jane agreed.

"Okay, guys," called Wendy, coming through the dressing room. "Mr. Robbins wants everyone onstage for a minute."

Jane followed the stream of female cast members toward the stage. As she looked around her, she saw performers transformed by their costumes: Theseus walked with a powerful, confident stride, and the way he surveyed the theater, it was as if he were studying an Athens of which he really was king. Jane realized that she felt different too. The snug material of her dress made her feel strong and fearless. She hadn't even had a chance to check herself out in the mirror, but now she held her arm out in front of her then placed her hand firmly on her hip. The light, shimmery sleeves made even this casual gesture dramatic. She felt indestructible, as though putting on this dress had somehow turned her into another person.

She was Hippolyta: Queen of the Amazons.

Mr. Robbins stood at the front of the stage, surveying the cast as they entered. When Jane had stepped out from the wings just ahead of Dahlia, she saw him see her, and it seemed he was watching her. She let Dahlia walk past her, feeling the strength of her character in her solitude. She didn't need Natalya and Victoria. She didn't need anyone. She rotated slowly, surveying the familiar cast members suddenly made strange by their new costumes. Her circle complete, she turned her eyes in the direction of Mr. Robbins. She wasn't surprised when she found him still watching her, but his gaze made her feel shivery.

Mr. Robbins looked the group over, then nodded his satisfaction that they were all there. "Okay, guys, I'm looking forward to a very exciting afternoon. I'd like to thank our incredible costume crew. They've been working day and night like magic elves to do the impossible and get your costumes finished on time." The cast broke into applause, and the crew looked around, a bit embarrassed.

Mr. Robbins clapped too, then continued. "Now, we have a lot of work to do this afternoon. Remember—a bad dress rehearsal means a great performance, so we're all prepared for some bumps in the road. If there's a problem with your costume, if it doesn't fit or if you can't move around in it the way you want to—that's especially true for you, fairies—don't panic. Alona's here, the costume crew is here, and we *will* fix whatever is wrong." Everyone applauded again, but this time it felt more as if they were clapping out of excitement than appreciation for the costume crew's hard work.

Jane glanced around the stage. Hermia and Helena looked radiant in their near-matching dresses, the fabric flowing gently out from the tight waists, the transparent silk of the sleeves making their arms seem almost like fairy's wings. She felt the fabric of her own dress hugging her waist and hips and felt confident that nobody was going to have a problem with the costumes.

"Okay, I think that's all I have to say. We'll take it from the top in fifteen minutes." Mr. Robbins turned to leave the stage, then turned back.

"Hey!"

In an instant there was complete silence. The entire cast looked at the director, whose face was split in an ear-to-ear grin.

"Break a leg, everybody." There were loud cheers as people began streaming off the stage, and then Jane heard her name being called.

She turned around. Mr. Robbins was standing in the same spot from which he'd addressed the group, and he was staring at her.

"You called?" Jane knew she looked better than she'd ever looked in her life. Better even than she'd looked that night at Morgan's party. And the way Mr. Robbins was looking at her made it clear that he knew it too.

He gave her a knowing grin. "Just wanted to check in."

Yeah, right. She spun around so he could admire her from every angle. "You like?" she asked flirtatiously.

He nodded, still smiling, but when he spoke, his voice was serious. "You're going to be dazzling."

She winked at him, then headed offstage to join the rest of the cast. She felt both like she was standing outside of her body, watching herself, and also like she had never been more who she was than at that moment.

Mr. Robbins's lips had said, *You're going to be dazzling.*

But what his eyes had said was, *I'm dazzled.*

Chapter
Thirty-eight

NATALYA FELT SICK.

If only she'd told Victoria the real reason they'd been invited. Then Victoria could have said she wouldn't go to a party she'd been invited to just because of who her dad was, and she, Natalya, and Jane could have stayed home that Friday night, eating brownies and watching *Breakfast at Tiffany's*.

She remembered Sloane's plan to write her science research paper on outer space, and suddenly that sounded like an excellent idea. Maybe Natalya could research the time-space continuum and find a way to travel back to the night of Morgan's party and decide at the last minute not to go. Or maybe she could go further back, to Morgan's invitation, which she could decline.

Or maybe she could go even *further* back, to her parents' decision to have a baby. She could change their minds.

She could never be born.

If only she'd never been born.

She heard the front door open and shut, and then her mother called, "Hello? Anybody home? Alex? Natalya?"

From her prone position on her bed, Natalya called, "I'm in my room."

A minute later, her mother appeared at the door. She raised an eyebrow at Natalya, lying in the dark room in her pajamas as if it were four in the morning, not four in the afternoon.

"Don't you have a party tonight?" her mother asked.

Natalya rolled over onto her stomach. "I'm not going."

"Oh." Her mother didn't say anything else, just turned as if to go back down the hallway. But before walking away, she asked, "Did you tell your father?" Her parents had agreed that Natalya's dad would drive her to the Met and pick her up later, since he had to be on the Upper East Side that evening anyway.

Without moving any other part of her body, Natalya reached her arm down and felt around on the floor for her phone. "I'll text him."

Her mom took a step into the room. "What about Victoria?" she asked, before Natalya had a chance to dial her dad's number.

Natalya turned her head sharply and gave her mother a long look. Had her mom seen the *Mirror*? Her father usually read the Russian papers, and her mother listened to NPR. They both thought the *Mirror* was complete trash, but that didn't mean they never checked out a headline or a photo. Could her mom have seen the picture of Victoria, read the article, put two and two together, and realized that the party had been thrown by a girl from Gainsford, which meant Natalya must have been there also?

But her mother's face was perfectly composed, and she returned Natalya's stare with her own calm gaze. For a second, instead of relief, Natalya felt scared. Her life was literally on the front page of the paper and her parents had no idea. It wasn't as if she normally told them everything—she and her mom weren't like Jane and her mom, who talked about crushes and parties and stuff. But it seemed to Natalya that until just a few weeks ago her mother had had at least *some* idea of what was happening in her life.

"What *about* Victoria?" asked Natalya carefully.

Her mother shrugged and took another step forward. "Won't she be disappointed if you leave her to go on her own?"

Natalya rolled onto her back. Her mom didn't know anything.

"She's not going." At the thought of why Victoria wasn't going to the party, Natalya felt the lump grow in her throat.

"That's too bad." Her mom came to sit cautiously on the edge of the bed. "What about your other friends? Aren't they expecting you?"

Jane's words rang in Natalya's ears.

Don't you mean what Victoria's *wearing?*

Is she even going to want you there now that Victoria's not going?

Natalya stared up at the ceiling. "They won't care." Her voice was completely without inflection, but there was nothing she could do about the fact that as soon as she'd spoken, she started to cry.

Her mom nodded. "I understand," she whispered quietly, looking down at her hands.

Natalya shot to a sitting position and shook her head violently. "You *don't* understand, Mom. I really messed up." She was sobbing now.

"Shhh. Shhh," whispered her mother. "I know. I know." Sliding her arm around her daughter, she rocked her gently back and forth, as if Natalya were a little baby again. Natalya sobbed into her mother's neck for what seemed like hours. She was crying about everything—about Victoria and Jane, about Morgan and George, about Colin. She was crying for herself because she'd never been to Troy or seen the pyramids or gone to a patron's cocktail party with famous actors, and she was crying because she even *cared* about doing any of those things.

Finally, she took a deep, shuddering breath.

"It's hard, isn't it?" Her mother smoothed Natalya's matted hair off her hot, damp forehead.

Natalya tilted her head so she could look at her mother. There was a small, sad smile on her lips that made Natalya think maybe she understood a little of what Natalya was crying about.

Natalya's mom sighed. "You know, when you got that scholarship, your father and I weren't one hundred percent sure it was such a good idea for you to go to Gainsford."

Amazement stopped Natalya's tears. "What?" She swiped at her dripping nose with the back of her hand. "But you were so excited. You said you were so proud of me." She remembered sitting with her family at dinner the night her acceptance letter had arrived, her father raising his glass and saying, *To Natalya!* and then her mother and brother repeating, *To Natalya!* like she was the most amazing, brilliant person they'd ever met.

"We *were* proud of you," her mother said. "We *are* proud of you. Such a big scholarship. Such an impressive school." She shook her head slowly and bit her lip. "Remember that first day when I said you were going so far away?"

Natalya did remember, actually. "And I said I wasn't."

Her mother took a neatly folded tissue out of her pocket and handed it to Natalya. "Well, this was what I was talking about." She didn't explain what she meant by "this," but she didn't have to.

Natalya blew her nose. "These girls don't really want to be my friends. They just want to be friends with me because I'm friends with Victoria."

"Oh." Her mother considered Natalya's words, then asked, "They told you that?"

"More like *Jane* told me that." Natalya dabbed at her eyes with the tissue and gave a half laugh.

Her mother took Natalya's damp tissue and exchanged it for a clean one. "And Jane is friends with them also?"

Natalya snorted. "Hardly."

"Well," said her mom. And then, "Well," again.

"Well what?" asked Natalya, blowing her nose.

"Well . . ." Her mother hesitated, then said, "Maybe you should let the girls speak for themselves about whether they want to be friends with you." She stared Natalya in the eye to make sure she got the point.

"I don't know," said Natalya doubtfully, but she thought about what her mother was getting at. It wasn't like Morgan and Sloane and Katrina kept asking her about Victoria all the time. In fact, they hadn't mentioned her once since that first lunch.

Still, even if they *did* want to be friends with her—with *her*—there was one enormous hurdle standing between her and the party tonight.

"It's a costume party, Mom. A really fancy costume party. And I don't have *any* costume, much less a fancy one."

Her mother laughed and squeezed her shoulders. "It would be nice if Gainsford gave its students Halloween uniforms too, wouldn't it?"

"Yeah." Natalya sighed. "I could definitely use a uniform right about now."

"Well, that's good news." Her mom's voice was full of enthusiasm, and Natalya gave her a puzzled look in return.

"Why is that good?"

Her mom stood up. "Because," she answered, "we have one."

The Metropolitan Museum of Art was as decked out as the throngs of people filling its cavernous lobby. Dramatic orange-and-black banners draped the archways and ceiling, and millions of votive candles and tiny Christmas lights twinkled everywhere. Waiters in black, wearing harlequin masks, slid their way through a swirling crowd of knights, popes, robots, and Elvises. Spanish dancers chatted with Superman.

Despite the swelling she could still feel around her eyes from all the crying she'd done earlier, Natalya couldn't help feeling a little tingly about being at such a glamorous party. Making her way through the crowd and up the wide central steps to the balcony, where Morgan had said they'd be meeting, she passed people speaking French and German, elegant men and women dressed as kings and queens and presidents, some of them wearing clothes and jewelry that might actually have *belonged* to the royalty they were impersonating.

For a minute when Natalya got to the top of the stairs, the huge oil portraits in the gallery made her think of the paintings she and Victoria and Jane had been so amazed by at Morgan's house. Here it was, less than a month later, and she was going to another of Morgan's parties, only she was all by herself. It didn't seem possible.

She took a deep breath and turned along the walkway toward the balcony. Despite how crowded it was, she had no problem spotting Morgan, who was dressed as Cleopatra, in a long gold gown and a thick jewel-encrusted necklace and headdress. She was talking to Sloane, who, in a blue dress and dazzling tiara, looked exactly like Lady Diana. Katrina had her back to Natalya, but from her white tail, black satin top, and tall pink ears, Natalya could tell she'd decided to go with her Playboy Bunny plan.

Even in this crowd of glamorous, beautiful people, Morgan and her friends sparkled.

Natalya wished she sparkled too, but she knew she didn't. Wearing her mother's white jacket over a black turtleneck and a black skirt, and peering through a pair of glasses, she was afraid she didn't really look like a sexy scientist. She barely even looked like a regular scientist. She had the feeling she looked just like what she was—a scholarship girl trying to run with the beautiful people.

Sloane turned slightly and spotted Natalya. Her jaw dropped, and she whispered something in Morgan's ear. Morgan must have said something to Katrina, who whipped around to face the direction Natalya was coming from.

"Oh my god." Morgan mouthed.

Oh my god? Natalya knew her costume was bad, but she hadn't thought it was *Oh my god!* bad.

And then, just as she was about to turn and run down the steps and out the front door of the museum, Morgan started to clap. A second later, so did Sloane and Katrina. As if in a trance, Natalya made her way forward, and by the time Natalya was within shouting distance of them, Sloane had let loose with an ear-piercing whistle of appreciation.

"How did you *think* of that?" Morgan demanded.

"You're way too hot to be her, though," said Sloane. "You know that, right?"

"What?" asked Natalya, smiling nervously. There were so many people around; between that and the jazz combo playing nearby, it was hard to hear.

Sloane reached out her hand and pulled Natalya into the group. "I said," she yelled, "that you're way too hot to be Clover."

Dr. Clover?! They thought she was Dr. Clover?!

"No, I . . ."

But Morgan cut her off. "Where's Victoria?" She was looking in the direction from which Natalya had come.

Natalya felt her heart start to beat faster. Okay, her lame

costume had miraculously been mistaken for something clever. But there was no way out of this one.

"She couldn't come," confessed Natalya.

As soon as the words were out of her mouth, she regretted them. She should have said Victoria would come later. Or at least that she *might* come. Now that Morgan knew Victoria definitely wasn't going to show, would she tell Natalya to leave? Had Jane been right along?

It seemed to Natalya that a year passed before Morgan lazily shrugged one shoulder. "Oh," she said simply, "that's too bad. When you see her, tell her I'm sorry about those pictures in the *Mirror*, okay? I don't know what idiot posted them, but it wasn't me." The undercurrent of disgust in Morgan's voice at whichever guest had broken her unstated rule of hospitality made Natalya positive she was telling the truth.

"Um, sure," said Natalya, and to her embarrassment, she felt tears of relief welling up in her eyes. She blinked them back frantically before they could fall. Morgan *hadn't* posted those pictures of Victoria. Jane's theory that Natalya's new friend was diabolical was as crazy as Natalya had told her it was.

Morgan took a sip of champagne and gestured with her elbow. "If you want a drink, there's a bar over there." She said it as casually as if she'd been talking about grabbing a piece of candy or a handful of chips. *Have some candy corn. Take a pretzel. Oh, and would you care for a glass of champagne?*

"Then we'll meet the guys at the American Wing," said Morgan. "There's dancing."

"Oh. Okay." Still amazed that she'd been allowed to stay,

Natalya went around the corner to the bar, which was swarmed with people. As she waited in the massive crowd, she started to worry that she was taking too long, that by the time she got back to where she'd left everyone, they'd be gone. Maybe they liked her enough to hang out with her without Victoria, but that didn't mean they liked her enough to wait for hours while she got a drink.

The truth was, she didn't even want a drink. If her parents smelled alcohol on her breath, they'd murder her. But it wasn't like she could just say, *I don't want to drink anything.* She wished she didn't feel so . . . on probation with Morgan and her friends; that being with them was more like being with Jane and Victoria.

Really? You wish you were calling each other names and storming away from them at restaurants?

She didn't want to think about her fight with Jane and Victoria. She wanted to think about this amazing party, about what she could drink that wouldn't get her grounded for the rest of high school, about—

An arm slipped around her waist, and a voice whispered in her ear, "Don't panic, but I need you to come with me for five minutes."

And just like that, Colin whisked her away from the bar and down the stairs.

Chapter
Thirty-nine

VICTORIA SPENT SATURDAY afternoon campaigning with her parents at the Riverdale Nursing Home. It was, she was pretty sure, the most depressing place on earth, though that wasn't just because of how old everyone was and how bad everything smelled. The depressing nature of the facility was only background noise to the depressing way everyone treated her, as if she had cancer or a brain tumor or something.

"Aren't you a poor dear?" said an old woman with little fluffs of white hair, taking Victoria's hand in her papery one. "It's just terrible how that newspaper tried to embarrass you. Those people are *sick*."

Her mother put her arm around Victoria's shoulders. "Well, Victoria paid a high price for an important lesson, didn't you, honey?" Victoria nodded, and her mom gave her a little squeeze.

The old lady smiled sadly. As they walked away, her mother whispered, "No one thinks this is your fault, honey, okay? Julie just texted Steven. She's been monitoring the blogs all morning and people are up in arms about the press."

Victoria nodded but didn't say anything. As bad as it had been when her parents were yelling at her, she felt a little weird about how gentle everyone was being around her today. In the car on the way up to the nursing home, Tim, the *Times* reporter, had said, "I hate to dignify the *Mirror* with a question about that cover, but people are going to want to know how it all happened. I'd like to give you a chance to explain."

Satan had already told her that the reporter wasn't the *Times* political correspondent, the guy who usually traveled with the Harrison campaign. He was with the Styles section, and he was writing a sympathetic piece. That was the word Satan kept repeating, *sympathetic*. To Victoria, sympathetic sounded bad, like someone had died, but her parents and Satan seemed happy about his sympathy, so she didn't complain.

Sitting next to this sympathetic reporter in the back of the limo, she tried to think of something she could say that would make her deserving of sympathy. But before she could find the words to explain what had happened, her mother said, "Victoria is a very innocent and trusting young woman. She loves to bake, to be with her family. Innocent people are easily misled, and that's what happened here. I'm not excusing Victoria's behavior," she added quickly. "I'm just saying that when you trust your friends and they don't look out for you, well, sad things can happen."

Her mother's talking about her friends like that made Victoria want to defend them. She opened her mouth to say something, then closed it without anyone having seen. Wasn't her mom just saying to Tim what Victoria had said to Natalya and Jane when they'd come to see her? *Nobody cared about my getting into trouble. You guys just wanted what you wanted. "Let's go to this awesome party! Let's get funny T-shirts! Victoria, why are you being such a drag?"*

Tim was so sympathetic that he even nodded sympathetically as he wrote down every word Victoria's mother said. When he was done, he looked up at Victoria.

"Anything you'd like to add to that, Victoria?"

She thought of how she'd made out with Jack after cooking club. She remembered how exciting it had been to stand outside Morgan's door with Natalya and Jane, feeling sexy and grown up in Emily's dress. She felt the tingle in her hand after she and Jack had high-fived their successful condom work. Her mother had made her sound like some kind of innocent dupe, a girl who had never so much as had an impure impulse, much less acted on it.

Tim was waiting for her to speak, holding his pen over his notebook. Out of the corner of her eye, Natalya saw Satan glaring at her from under his thick eyebrows. When he caught her looking in his direction, he went back to typing something on his BlackBerry.

"Do you want to say anything else?" Tim repeated gently.

Victoria shook her head. "I think my mom said it really well."

"Thanks, honey," said her mother, patting Victoria on her leg.

For the rest of the ride, Victoria didn't say a word, just stared out the window. The sunny day had disappeared, and it had begun to rain. She watched the heavy drops hit the glass, then spread into long, thin streams that looked a lot like tears.

When they got home from Riverdale, Victoria went straight to her room, shut the door and the lights, climbed into bed, and fell into a deep, dreamless sleep. At some point during the afternoon she woke up to a buzzing sound. Drunk with sleep, she stumbled around her room until she located her phone, still in her bag. She took it out and checked the screen. Jack. She remembered their kiss, his smile as they parted.

She knew why he was calling now. *Victoria, I didn't exactly bargain for this when I made out with you yesterday. Um, can we forget it ever happened?* She couldn't deal with that. She couldn't deal with anything. She opened the middle drawer of her dresser and buried her phone under a pile of T-shirts, then crawled back into bed and lost consciousness again.

She didn't know if it was minutes, hours, or days later that she was awakened again, this time by Emily plopping herself down on the edge of her bed and flipping on her bedside lamp. "You totally got dirt all over the hem of my blue dress, you little tramp."

What time was it? What day was it? "I what . . . ?" Victoria opened her eyes and squinted against the bright light.

"You heard me." Emily was shaking her head with amazement. "I can't believe you had the balls to sneak out to a party. Little Miss Perfect."

"I'm not—" Victoria shot upright, completely awake.

"Oh, please." Emily waved away any defense Victoria was about to offer. "Spare me. You went to a party. You know how to put a condom on." Emily looked thoughtful for a second. "It sucks that you got caught." Then she shrugged. "But you're finally doing something besides *baking*. That's cool."

"There's nothing wrong with baking," Victoria snapped. "And it wasn't . . . I mean, I didn't even want to go to the party." She lay back down and gathered the edge of her comforter, making tiny folds with the fabric.

"What?" Emily looked bewildered.

"I kind of . . . I mean, it was Natalya's friend's thing, and she wanted to go."

"You've lost me." Emily leaned back, away from Victoria.

"I kind of couldn't say no, so I went." She lifted her eyes to look at her sister.

Emily was staring at her as if she were a complete stranger. Worse than that, as if she were a complete stranger with some horrible communicable disease. "You're saying they made you go."

Her parents had uttered almost that exact same sentence just yesterday, but coming from them, it had sounded like a statement of fact. Now it sounded like an accusation.

Victoria remained silent, holding her sister's stare. She wished Emily would just go already. Didn't she live in New Jersey now?

But Emily showed no sign of leaving. "Let me get this straight. Jane and Natalya *forced* you, against your will, to get dressed up in my clothes and go to a party that you did not want to attend?"

"Nobody said *forced*," Victoria corrected her quickly.

"Oh, I'm sorry, what was your word choice again?" Emily put her finger to her chin and mimed thinking deeply about something.

Victoria squirmed away from her and stepped off the bed. It was bad enough having her sister talk to her this way; she didn't have to take it lying down. "What's your point, Emily?"

Ignoring her, Emily continued. "And, correct me if I'm wrong, but I didn't think Natalya *or* Jane went to Morningside. Did they show up there one morning, *force* you to wear a really tacky T-shirt, then hold a gun to your head while you put a condom on a banana with your friend Mr. Sexy Bangs?"

Had Victoria just called Jack *sexy*? Victoria almost wanted to ask what she meant by *sexy bangs*. But the last thing she needed if she was going to win this argument was a distracting tangent. "I didn't say *gunpoint* and I didn't say *forced*," Victoria reminded Emily. "God, why do you have to be so dramatic?"

"I'm dramatic? *I'm dramatic?!*" Emily got to her feet. "Who's the one being all"—she made her voice high-pitched and whiny— *"Oh, Mommy, oh, Daddy, poor little me. I'm so helpless. I couldn't stop them. I'm just so sweet and nice and kind that people just walk all over me. I have no will of my own. I couldn't possibly be to blame."*

"I didn't say *any* of that, and I *don't* sound like that!" Victoria was screaming.

For a second, Emily didn't speak, just stood there glaring at her sister. "Do you realize that when I saw that paper I was actually proud of you?" She laughed briefly, then her voice grew serious again. "Well, I was sorry for you, too. It sucks that they printed that picture. But I mostly thought, *It's about time my sister became an actual* person." She shook her head slowly. "You always criticize me for talking too much, but at least I take responsibility for what I say, and at least I take responsibility when I screw up. You stand there in your apron, holding your little plate of cookies and being all innocent, and then when you finally *do* do something, instead of owning it, you pretend it's all someone else's fault."

Victoria was so shocked, she couldn't think of anything to say. She opened her mouth, but no words came out.

Emily waited a second, then said, "I came home because I wanted to offer you some support." She snorted at the absurdity of her plan, then spun around on one heel and walked across the room. "If I'd known you were such a coward, I would have stayed at Princeton."

With that, she stepped into the hallway and pulled the door shut behind her. Victoria stood where she was, staring at the empty space where her sister had just been, not even realizing her mouth was still open, as if she were just about to deliver a response.

Chapter Forty

JANE COULDN'T LOCATE the exact moment when her plan crystallized. All she knew was that one minute she was one hundred percent engaged in the dress rehearsal, feeling every missed line and cue as if it were her own, and the next she was only thinking about how, when rehearsal ended, it would be night, a Saturday night, and she and Mr. Robbins would both be in the auditorium.

And if she played her cards right, they would be in the auditorium *alone*.

It was a bad dress rehearsal. People botched lines. Fairy skirts split up the side. Props weren't where they were supposed to be. Lights dimmed and glowed randomly, casting bright sun over nighttime scenes and bathing the midday wedding of Hippolyta and Theseus in soft moonlight. Musical cues came and went with no relationship to the scenes being acted.

By the time the exhausted cast gathered onstage after the show, even Mr. Robbins couldn't seem to find the words to comfort them. He smiled ruefully at the group huddled on the floor around him.

"Well, that pretty much sucked," he said, and everyone managed a laugh. "Look, guys, I know you're all disappointed that tonight didn't go more smoothly. But I saw a lot of great stuff—you connected to each other, you spoke your words from a real and powerful place. And that's not nothing. Everything else, I'm not so worried about."

"Sure you are, Len," Fran called from the edge of the group.

He nodded and smiled again. "Okay, I'm a little worried." Another ripple of nervous laughter. "But I believe in this cast. I believe in you. So go home—and I mean it—don't go out partying with your friends. We're all counting on you to be healthy and well-rested come opening night.

"Call Monday is four o'clock for makeup and wardrobe. I'll give you my notes then. And you can be proud of the work you did tonight. All of you."

Jane barely registered the funereal quiet of the dressing room, the hushed conversations taking place around her. She watched grim-faced fairies, courtiers, and lovers hurry to get out of their costumes and into their street clothes, and she knew the expression on her face was nothing like the expressions on theirs. They were disappointed, despondent.

She was determined.

Everyone was moving so fast that no one had time to notice Jane moving so slowly. The advantage of having sat alone at rehearsals recently was that there was no one waiting for her tonight. Lots of people gave her a wave good-bye or said, 'Night, Jane, but they all left without her.

By the time she'd hung her costume on the rack, almost everyone was gone. Now Mr. Robbins was standing in the center aisle talking to Jay. Jane watched from the wings, biting her lip as Mr. Robbins clapped him on the back. "Don't worry so much. Get some shut-eye. See you Monday." Jay walked toward the exit, and Mr. Robbins came to the front of the auditorium and grabbed his bag. He didn't see Jane, and she watched him as he rubbed his forehead with his thumb and forefinger, looking more tired than Jane had ever seen anyone look before.

"Hey." She stepped into the light. Her heart was pounding—she was about to improvise the most important scene of her life.

"Oh hey. Hey, Jane." As soon as he saw her, his expression changed, as though he didn't want her to know how tired he'd been.

Or as though now that they were alone together, he wasn't tired anymore.

She walked to the edge of the stage and sat, legs hanging down. "You don't have to put on a happy face for me."

He made his lips into a deep frown, and they both laughed.

"No," he said. "It'll be okay. Dress rehearsals are always like this." He tapped her knee for emphasis.

It was like being struck by lightning. An electric current

surged up her leg from the spot where his fingers had touched her. Without letting herself think about what she was doing, she placed her hand on his.

He didn't take his hand away. They stayed like that for a long beat. The only thing in the world Jane was conscious of was how loud and fast her heart was pounding.

We're holding hands. We're holding hands. We're alone in the school and it's a Saturday night and we're holding hands.

And then Jane did what she was afraid to do.

"You could probably use a back rub," she said. She used her hand to pull him around gently, then rubbed his shoulders like all the other kids always did at rehearsals.

Only it wasn't like all the other kids at rehearsals. Because he wasn't a kid.

She rubbed his shoulders in silence for a minute, amazed that this was really happening. She was really here with him. She was really going to . . .

What? What was she really going to do?

Should she make the first move? Hadn't she kind of already made the first move by offering him a back rub? But what if he was afraid to say something definite, afraid that he'd misunderstood her cues, afraid that he would get fired. She rubbed the back of his neck, which was *really* tense.

It was definitely up to her to make it clear that they wanted the same thing.

She inhaled deeply. Do it. Do it. Do it *now*.

He turned around, gently taking her hands from his neck. "Jane, I hope you—"

But she was already speaking. "Do you want to go . . . I don't know, get a glass of wine somewhere?"

There was a moment while each one heard what the other had said.

A horrible moment.

The most horrible moment of her life.

Mr. Robbins was looking at her, his expression a mixture of pity and embarrassment. "Jane, you are such a talented actress and such an asset to this cast. I'm so sorry if I've misled you in some way." He was looking at her and smiling sadly.

"I . . ." Her voice was quivery. She tried to fake a laugh, like the sentence she'd just uttered had been a joke, but the sound froze in her throat.

"Here, I'll walk you out," Mr. Robbins offered. His voice was cool. Professional. "If you'd like, I can hail you a cab since it's so late."

Jane leaped to her feet. "No!" She hadn't meant to shout, hadn't realized her voice would even work. "I mean, I'm fine."

"Of course you are." He bent down to pick up his bag. "Why wouldn't you be?"

How was this possible? How was this happening? He'd said she was sexy. He'd given her that loving look the day he was directing Theseus. Earlier tonight he'd pulled her aside to talk to her. She hadn't imagined all of that. She hadn't!

Four years. She had to be at the Academy with Mr. Robbins for four years. Four years during which they would both know this conversation had taken place. Every time he looked at her, every time she looked at him, every time someone so much as mentioned his name, she would know she had made a complete and utter fool of herself after the dress rehearsal for *A Midsummer Night's Dream*.

He looked at her, waiting for her to say something. But what could she say?

"I'll see you Monday," she choked out.

And then she ran up the aisle of the theater, refusing to let herself look back.

Chapter
Forty-one

NATALYA AND COLIN sped along the balcony.

"Where are you taking me?" she asked, laughing. There was something exciting about racing through a museum at night, as if they were international art thieves or maybe detectives *pursuing* international art thieves.

"You'll see." He glanced back at her, his mackintosh and deerstalker cap making it clear that he was Sherlock Holmes. "Five minutes. I promise."

She wondered if she'd even be able to find her way back. As one gallery led to another, she sincerely doubted she'd remember that the Assyrian exhibit led to the back staircase that let out into the long hallway that led to the room with the enormous, wall-to-wall gold-and-iron gate. Besides, hadn't Morgan said something about how they were all going to head to the American Wing? She didn't have any idea where the American Wing was.

Colin finally pulled open a set of double glass doors and pulled her into a narrow room filled with knights, lances, horses covered in armor, and thick, rich tapestries. The room flickered in low light—it felt as if they were truly in a medieval castle.

A guy wearing a Dracula costume and holding a clipboard was talking to a girl dressed as an ice skater who had her hand on the arm of a guy who was wearing green scrubs. Dracula made a note on a piece of paper, then said, "Now you need to get an Elvis." The girl let go of the doctor and sped out through the doors Colin and Natalya had just entered.

"Oh!" Colin snapped his fingers and turned to her. "By the way, you're a—"

"Whatcha got, Sherlock?" Dracula called in their direction.

Colin pulled her close and whispered, "It's a scavenger hunt. I had to find someone dressed as a doctor."

"But I'm not—" Natalya protested, panicky.

"Dr. Petrova," said Colin to Dracula. He pushed Natalya gently toward the vampire.

Dracula looked Natalya up and down, lingering on her white coat. "You're a doctor?" His expression was one of extreme doubt.

She nodded, twice, but didn't speak.

As Colin came up beside her, Dracula said, "If you're a doctor, where's your stethoscope?"

Natalya could feel Colin tense. She reached her hand up to her neck and groped there.

"Oh my god, where's my stethoscope?" She whirled around in a fake panic. "I just had it!" She looked at Colin. "Do you think I could have dropped it when I tripped before?"

"You must have," Colin said quickly. "It's my fault. I'll take you back the way we came and you can check."

Natalya gave Dracula a pleading look. "Do you mind if I go now?" she asked.

Dracula hesitated, then made a mark on his clipboard and said to Colin what he'd said to the ice skater. "Go find an Elvis." A second later, the two of them were racing through the doors, laughing.

When they got to the enormous room with the stone floor and the towering metal gate, Colin finally slowed down. "Oh my god, you were amazing!" He imitated her feeling around her neck for the imaginary missing stethoscope, then shook his head. "Brilliant."

Natalya laughed. "Elementary, my dear Watson."

"I think I'm supposed to say that," Colin reminded her.

She nodded. "You're right."

Colin took off his hat and fanned himself with it briefly, then looked at Natalya. "You are awesome."

Natalya felt a surge of happiness run through her body. There was something about Colin that was just so . . . great. She laughed.

He put out his hand for her to take. "Come on, I'll bring you back where I found you."

She put her hand in his. She'd never walked somewhere holding hands with a boy before. It was really nice.

"So, where'd you learn to play chess like that?" They were swinging their arms slightly as they walked.

"My dad taught me. He's a great player."

"I'd like to play him sometime. Maybe he could teach me a thing or two."

Natalya liked the idea of her dad and Colin playing chess. Somehow she could imagine Colin coming over to her house and hanging out with her family more easily than she could see any of her other new friends doing that.

They were approaching the Great Hall, and the space around them grew increasingly crowded. The main stairs were jammed with people. Colin paused and frowned.

"I'm trying to think of the fastest way to return you to where I kidnapped you from," he explained.

For a second Natalya thought how nice it was that he was going to help her get back to her friends instead of just returning to his scavenger hunt, but then her stomach dropped sickeningly. If he took her back to where he'd found her, then Morgan would know they'd been together.

That could *not* happen.

"It's okay," she said quickly. "I can find my own way back. I don't want to take you away from your game."

He cocked his head to the side, then turned to look at her. "You know what? Let's just hang out, okay?"

Natalya felt a wave of terror wash over her. This was bad. This was so very, very bad.

"No!" she almost yelped. "I mean, that would be so . . . crazy. We'll hang out another time. We'll play chess." Realizing she was still holding his hand, Natalya quickly extracted her fingers from his.

Colin smiled. "Seriously, I don't care about the scavenger hunt."

Natalya was already shaking her head. "I don't think you'd like my friends. I mean, I know you wouldn't. I mean, I know you don't . . . like them."

"What, are you here with my sister or something?" Colin asked in a joking way, but when he saw Natalya's face, he stopped smiling. "Oh god, seriously?"

She nodded.

He sighed deeply, then reached for her hand. "Blow her off."

"I . . ." She didn't put her hand in his.

Laughing, Colin took a step toward her. "Come on. Just tell her you'll see her Monday."

Natalya still didn't take his hand, and after a second, he dropped it to his side. "What, you'd rather hang with my sister than with me?"

Natalya hesitated. She liked being with Colin so much. But what if Morgan found out?

"Natalya?" he asked.

There had to be some way she could avoid choosing between them. There just *had* to be.

"I . . ." She stared at him, helpless to finish the sentence.

Colin gave her a long look. "Whatever," he muttered. Then

he turned and headed toward the Great Hall.

She took a step forward and called his name. When he didn't stop, she added, "Wait!" But either he didn't hear, or he pretended he didn't hear. And before she could decide whether or not to follow him, he'd been swallowed up by the crowd.

Chapter
Forty-two

SUNDAY MORNING, VICTORIA was awakened by bright sunlight streaming through her window. She squinted against it, cursing herself for having forgotten to close the shade, then rolled over and pulled a pillow onto her head.

She *so* did not want to be awake. Being awake meant playing her fight with Natalya and Jane over and over in her head on some crazy loop of shame. It meant hearing Emily's accusations, seeing her sneer.

If I'd known you were such a coward, I would have stayed at Princeton.

Pursuing sleep was hopeless.

Emily was right. She was a coward.

But her parents had been so mad. They'd looked at her with such . . . disappointment. And Natalya and Jane *had* wanted her to go to the party. And she *had* hesitated about going.

But that wasn't the whole story, was it?

Victoria threw her covers and the pillow to the other side of the bed, then sat up and placed her feet firmly on the floor. She wished Jane or Natalya—she wished Jane *and* Natalya—had slept over and were there to help her with what she was about to do. But of course they weren't. Apparently that was what happened when you told your friends to get lost. You had to face the music all by yourself.

Sundays, her dad almost always went to give a speech at one church or another, so it didn't surprise her to see both of her parents wearing dark blue suits, her mother sitting at the table making notes on a printed document.

"I think it just reads better if you do the Medicare stuff before the spending cuts," her mom was saying. "Just reverse the order." She raised her eyes and smiled at Victoria. "Morning, sweetheart. You're up early."

"Good morning," said her dad.

Without giving herself time to chicken out, Victoria took the plunge. "Nobody made me go to that party. I wanted to go. I know you don't believe me about not drinking, but it's the truth. I *did* lie about the party, but I left when the alcohol arrived."

Her father leaned back in his chair, and her mother put the speech down in front of her very precisely, as if a great deal depended on the corners of the pages lining up. The only sound in the room was the *click* of the refrigerator cycling off.

Finally her dad said, "Well, I'm glad you weren't drinking, but I am extremely sorry to hear that you lied to us, both about the party and about your responsibility for going. I would have expected more from you. I'm disappointed." He lifted his cup and sipped at his coffee.

"Why didn't you just *ask* us?" Her mother was clearly angry, but she also seemed a little bewildered. "We might very well have said yes."

Victoria thought she might explode when her mom said that. "Are you *kidding*?" In her outrage she stomped her foot on the tile floor, not even caring how babyish a gesture of frustration it was. "You would *never* have said yes. Okay, *maybe* you would have, but then you would have just let Sat—Steven overrule you."

"Now, Victoria, that isn't fair. . . ." her father started. Annoyed, he put his mug down hard enough that some coffee slopped over the side.

But Victoria was mad too. "No, Dad, what isn't fair is that you never thought this running for senator thing through. *That's* what isn't fair. It's all a big . . . game or something." She took a step toward the table. "'Let's make a statement! We need to fight the good fight! I want to make sure these issues get the attention they deserve.'" As she spoke, she waved her arms in the air in an imitation of her father's early enthusiasm for his run. "You never thought about what might happen if you actually *won*. You never considered what it would mean for your family if we were suddenly put under a microscope."

"Victoria, I—"

But she cut him off. "What I did was wrong, Dad. I know that, and I'm sorry. But because you made the decision to run for national office—" She considered what she'd just said, then rephrased it. "No, actually you never *made* the decision to run for national office. So let's put it this way: Because you're suddenly a political rock star, *I'm* totally exposed." She saw before her the cover of the *Mirror*, imagined the voice mail message from Jack that was waiting for her, heard the fight she'd had with Natalya and Jane. Then she took a deep breath, fighting back tears. "I'm not saying this is your fault, okay? I said I'd take responsibility for my actions and I meant it. But if I were just some random teenage girl who'd worn a stupid T-shirt during Safe Sex Week or who'd gone to a party with a bunch of rich kids, I wouldn't have been on the cover of a New York City newspaper."

"But you're such a good *girl*, Victoria!" her father cried, placing his hands on the table. "That's what I don't understand. How could such a good girl *do* these things?'

Victoria opened her mouth to answer, but before she could speak, she heard a voice saying, "Oh, please, Dad. No one could possibly be as good as Victoria seemed."

Victoria, her mother, and her father turned to look at Emily, who was standing in the doorway of the kitchen, wearing a pair of plaid boxers and a tank top. She walked over to the coffee maker and poured herself a cup.

"Emily," said their mom, "I appreciate your trying to defend your sister, but this really doesn't concern you."

"Sure it does, Mom." Calmly, Emily crossed to the refrigerator and added some milk to her coffee, then went over to a drawer and took out a spoon. As she twirled it through her coffee, she explained. "There's a *really* good chance that Dad is going to win a major election in eight days. And if he does, Victoria and I are going to have to spend at least the next six years watching everything we do and say in public. And sometimes we're going to screw up. God knows I've done it before, and my guess is I'll do it again. I see this as a trial run, which means I have more than a passing interest in how you handle Victoria's little . . . malfeasance." Emily put her cup down on the counter, then hopped up to sit next to it, and calmly took a sip. "Well?" she said finally.

"I . . ." their mother began. But she didn't finish her sentence.

"I thought so," said Emily. Calmly, she turned to her father. "Dad?"

"We'll . . ." The corners of his mouth flirted with a smile. He glanced at his wife.

"We'll have to get back to you on that," their mother said firmly.

Emily raised her eyebrows. "Why am I so not surprised?"

"Don't push it, young lady," their dad warned, raising his eyebrows back at her. "You're not the only debater in this family."

Emily shrugged, then dropped lightly off the counter and picked up her mug. "No," she acknowledged. "But I am the best." And with that, she walked out of the kitchen and down the hall to her room.

All her life, Victoria had been jealous of Emily, how articulate she was, how determined, how fearless. Suddenly, for the first time, she realized one more thing about her sister.

She was on Victoria's team.

Amazed and thrilled by that fact, Victoria waved briefly to her parents and walked out of the room.

Why had she bought a black phone? Black equaled bad news. Black meant funerals. Black was voice mail messages in which boys broke up with you, and friends who didn't pick up when you called.

Next time, she was buying a pink phone.

Hands shaking, Victoria dialed Natalya's number. How many times had she heard Natalya's outgoing message? She could have recited it as it played. *"You've reached Natalya. I can't come to the phone. Please leave me a message."* Beep.

"Um, hi. Nat. It's me. It's Victoria." She took a deep breath. This was a million times harder than talking to her parents. "Please don't be mad, Nat. Please. I'm so sorry. Really. I just—" *Beep.*

It was over. It was over and she hadn't even gotten to explain. Should she call back? But how could she possibly tell Natalya everything in thirty-second increments? It would take a dozen phone calls. Twice that. Instead, she dialed Jane's number. *"This is Jane, and I sincerely hope you know what to do."* Before the beep, Victoria heard herself and Natalya laughing in the background. She remembered how they'd stood with Jane in the store the day she'd bought her phone, how they'd cracked up listening to her recite the suggestive outgoing message.

"Jane, it's me. I'm really, really sorry. Please call me, okay? I feel so bad." She hung up, scared she might start bawling right then.

There was one last thing she had to do. Calling her voice mail, she discovered she had not one missed call, but half a dozen. The first four were from Jane and Natalya. Victoria didn't know if she wanted to laugh or cry as she listened to them begging, threatening, demanding that she call them back. The last message they'd left was from Saturday morning. Saturday. And now it was Sunday. How had so much happened in just twenty-four hours?

And then she heard Jack's voice.

His tone was cold. "Hello, this is Jack. Would you call me? I just saw the paper and . . . we should definitely talk."

She swallowed hard. *We should definitely talk.*

That was never a good sentence to hear.

Before she could really process the implications of Jack's leaving her a message like that, the next message started to play.

"Hey," it began, and Victoria's heart pounded as she realized this was Jack calling, too. "Sorry, I just left you a really weird message." There was a pause. "Um, honestly, I guess I was a little freaked out, but I *meant* to ask if you're okay. So, this is me calling to see if you're okay. Also to tell you that I'm pretty sure in some cultures if you're on the cover of a newspaper with someone, you're technically married to that person. So, you know, yeah, I think I should probably walk you to school on Monday. Call me if you object. Or you know, just call me because you miss me. Um, yeah. That's about all I have to say. Except to point out that this picture is *kind* of out of focus. Which is, you know, just another reason that nobody with half a brain reads the *Mirror*. Nor does anybody with a full brain, for that matter. So. Yeah. My point is that their circulation is basically zero. I guess I'm rambling. Is this ever going to cut me off? Is it even still recording for that matter? Okay, I'm going now. Call me."

Oh my god. Oh my god. OH MY GOD!

Jack wasn't saying he never wanted to see her again. Jack was walking her to school on Monday. Jack was—

Beep. Beep.

Victoria looked at the screen. It was Natalya, calling her back. Heart in her throat, she took the call.

"Nat, I'm sorry!" she began before Natalya could say anything. "I'm such a bad friend."

As soon as the words were out of Victoria's mouth, Natalya started talking, speaking so fast, Victoria couldn't quite understand what she was saying. "Vicks, Morgan only invited me to that party because she knew we were friends. I should have told you. I wanted to tell you. But I was so scared that you wouldn't want to go."

It took her a minute to process what Natalya was telling her, and when she did, Victoria realized something.

She wasn't surprised.

In fact, she'd known it all along.

Natalya had been her best friend since preschool. There was no one Victoria loved more than her. But Morgan and her friends—they were more like college girls than high school girls. What did Natalya really have in common with them?

And when Victoria had gotten to the party, everyone had been so nice to her—hadn't she even thought at the time that it had almost been like they were *expecting* her?

Well, they had been.

"Vicks, are you there?" Natalya's voice was frantic. "Vicks, I'm so sorry. Please don't hate me. I don't blame you for hating me."

"I'm not mad," Victoria said. And she meant it. Natalya wasn't some girl trying to befriend Victoria because of her dad's fame. Natalya was Natalya. And how could she be mad at Natalya for not knowing how to handle something she herself had no idea how to handle? "Really. I'm not mad," she repeated.

"*What?*" Natalya sounded shocked. "Of course you're mad. I'd be *furious.*"

Victoria laughed. "Do you *want* me to be mad at you?"

"No!" Natalya said quickly. "Vicks, I'm so sorry I did that. I love you so much. I never meant for you to get in trouble."

"I know," Victoria assured her. "It's not your fault. I screwed up."

"*I* screwed up," Natalya corrected her.

"Can you come over?" Victoria was desperate to see her friends. "I just called Jane, but she didn't pick up."

Victoria heard Natalya take a deep breath. "Vicks, Jane and I had a really big fight yesterday."

Her stomach dropped. "A fight? About what?"

Natalya told her what had happened at Ga Ga Noodle. When she got to the part about storming out, Victoria gasped. Natalya had just . . . left? How was that possible? "And you didn't talk after that?" she asked.

Natalya's silence answered her question.

The thought of Natalya and Jane fighting made Victoria's chest tighten. At least when she was involved, there was something she could do. In the face of their being mad at each other, she felt totally hopeless. "Look, just . . . come over and we'll try and reach her, okay? This is insane."

"Vicks? I'm scared. . . ." Natalya's voice was quiet.

"Me too," admitted Victoria. Those things Jane and Natalya had said to each other, they sounded bad. Really bad.

"I'll be there as fast as I can," Natalya promised, and she hung up.

Victoria sat down on the floor, her back against her bed, her phone in her lap.

There was nothing to do now but wait.

Chapter
Forty-three

MONDAY MORNING, all through English class, Natalya watched Morgan. It was impossible not to be impressed by how elegant she was, how poised, how confident.

Natalya remembered for the millionth time how Colin had walked away from her at the Met. She could have chased after him and apologized. Instead she'd gone back to Morgan and Sloane and Katrina and spent the rest of her night pretending to have a great time. She'd spoken Russian when Morgan asked her to; she'd danced wildly to "Mamma Mia"; she'd accepted the glass of champagne George brought her. In the ladies' room with Morgan, she'd said she was totally bummed that George hadn't made a move on her, even though she was relieved.

She'd been wearing a costume. An *amazing* costume. Only it wasn't a sexy scientist costume. It wasn't even a Dr. Clover costume.

It was a Natalya Petrova costume. Natalya Petrova the good-time popular girl with a crush on George and a taste for sparkling wine. And for being sparkly. Picturing how she'd behaved Saturday night made Natalya cringe, and she heard once more the accusation Jane had hurled at her when they were at Ga Ga Noodle.

Like I'd ever be jealous of you. Like there even is a you. You're so busy being someone else that there isn't even anyone to be jealous of.

Her phone buzzed and she slipped her hand down and checked the screen. It was a text from Victoria.

Have u heard from J?

No, she typed back.

They'd called and texted Jane all day yesterday. They'd even gone to her apartment, but when the doorman rang the buzzer, nobody answered, and after almost an hour they finally left.

Jane really didn't want to deal with them.

Victoria's reply came immediately after Natalya hit send. We r going anyway. We r not missing opening night!!

Natalya typed the letter K, then dropped her phone back into her bag just as the bell rang and Ms. MacFadden said, "Well, I think we can leave it at that." She smiled around the room. "Read the next scene for tomorrow, and don't forget, your paraphrases are due Wednesday."

Natalya was too embarrassed to focus on what Ms. MacFadden

was saying. Jane was right. She *had* been busy being someone else. Someone *sparkly*! Someone *giggly*!

Well, she'd been so sparkly and giggly that now one of her best friends wasn't speaking to her.

Slowly she put *Othello* and her notebook into her bag and made her way to the door, walking out side by side with Morgan, who put her hand on Natalya's elbow as they started down the hallway.

"So," Morgan began, "I cannot figure out George's deal. We may have to go to plan B." Morgan's phone buzzed and she glanced at the screen, then scowled and put it back in her bag. "Katrina's got a stomach thing and she's apparently throwing her brains up or something." She shrugged. "I completely cannot deal with her right now."

Natalya took a deep breath and stopped walking. It was now or never. "I have to tell you something."

Morgan stopped walking, too. "What's up? You're being so serious."

For a long minute Natalya just thought about all the things she had to tell Morgan, all the ways in which she'd lied to or misled her so Morgan would think she was cool. She didn't like George. She did like Colin. She didn't drink. She wasn't even remotely considering becoming a vegetarian.

Natalya took a deep breath. "I think Dr. Clover is a really great teacher."

"What?" Morgan looked simultaneously shocked and bored.

Natalya didn't smile. "I think Dr. Clover is a really great teacher," she repeated. "I like her class."

"Ooookay," said Morgan slowly. "And you're telling me this because . . ."

And suddenly, maybe because of how nervous she was or because of how stupid the announcement sounded now that she'd made it, Natalya started to laugh. It began as a giggle, but soon she was bent over at the waist, hand covering her mouth, unable to catch her breath.

"Is this some kind of joke?" Morgan asked.

Natalya couldn't answer. She just waved her hands, trying to show the impossibility of speech.

"Are you okay?" demanded Morgan finally. "You're acting really weird."

The question and the statement that followed it echoed what Jane had said to her at Morgan's party, and the thought of Jane immediately sobered Natalya. "Sorry," she choked out, standing up.

Morgan shrugged. "Whatever." She turned and headed in the direction of the library. "Are you coming to eat?"

Natalya hesitated. She didn't want to eat lunch with Morgan. She wanted to find Jordan and talk to her. But could she say that? Could she tell Morgan she didn't want to eat with her today and still be able to eat with her tomorrow?

Looking back over their relationship, Natalya remembered all the times she'd told herself she shouldn't have to choose. Well, maybe she'd been right. Maybe she'd never had to make a choice at all. Maybe life could be Morgan *and*, not Morgan *or*.

Her voice steady, Natalya answered the question she knew Morgan had meant rhetorically. "I can't, actually."

Morgan stopped walking but didn't turn around all the way. Instead, she glanced over her shoulder. "What?"

"I've got some people I want to see," Natalya explained.

In the look on Morgan's face, Natalya had her answer: Yes, she had to make a choice.

It *was* Morgan or. Morgan or Jordan. Morgan or Colin. Morgan or Jane.

Morgan or Natalya.

Morgan wrinkled her perfect forehead. "Seriously?" her voice was incredulous.

Natalya nodded slowly. "Seriously."

And just like that a door slammed shut between them. Morgan rolled her eyes, then faced forward and headed down the corridor to the library, not even bothering to say good-bye. Natalya watched her go. Did Morgan hate her now? Were she, Sloane, and Katrina going to be mean to her for the next four years? Or was she less than a blip on their radar, someone they'd barely remember having hung out with, much less care to punish?

It was hard to know which was worse, and as she headed toward the cafeteria, Natalya forced herself not to think about it. She had more immediate concerns. She'd told Morgan she had some people she wanted to see.

The question was, did *they* want to see *her*?

Natalya crossed the threshold of the cafeteria and scanned the room for Jordan, Perry, and Catherine. They were sitting just across the aisle from the door, and almost the second she spotted

Jordan, Jordan glanced up and saw Natalya looking at her. Her eyebrows shot up in surprise.

Natalya pointed at herself, then pointed at the table. For a long beat, Jordan didn't respond. Natalya held her stare, and finally, Jordan smiled.

"Guess you missed us, huh?" she called.

Natalya laughed with happiness and relief. She *had* missed Jordan and her friends. As she crossed over to sit with them, she knew she was finally making the right choice.

Chapter
Forty-four

NORMALLY JANE LOVED the excitement of opening night. Everyone on edge, laughing for no reason, freaking out because they've suddenly forgotten their lines, the sizzle and buzz of dozens of people in one space all thinking about that magic moment when the curtain goes up and you're in free fall in front of an audience. By six o'clock, Fran was walking around in her bra and underwear singing "Give My Regards to Broadway" at the top of her lungs, and almost every girl in the dressing room was joining in.

Jane was quiet. She slipped into her costume without any help, and headed over to where Wendy and Sharon and some girls she'd never met before were making people up. As Wendy stroked foundation onto her cheek, Jane tried to get into character by conjuring the exercises Mr. Robbins had had them do the first day of rehearsal. But remembering their walks through imaginary forests, amusement parks, and sweet sixteens only reminded her of Mr. Robbins, and thinking of Mr. Robbins only reminded her of what she'd said to him after dress rehearsal.

And memories of what she'd said to him made her positive she couldn't walk onto that stage.

She hadn't been able to call Natalya or Victoria back. How could she tell them what had happened? Natalya was right. Victoria was right. She thought she knew everything, but really she knew nothing. She had no self-control. There was something seriously wrong with her. No one who knew what she had done would want to be her friend.

"Okay, can I have my cast, please?" Mr. Robbins called from the entrance to the girls' dressing rooms, and slowly everyone filed out to the communal space between the boys' and girls' rooms. He was wearing a sports jacket and a pair of khakis, and Jane's throat felt thick as she watched him and thought about how totally she'd misunderstood everything between them.

He hadn't said *Jane* was sexy, he'd said *Hippolyta* was sexy. And he'd given her that significant look during rehearsal because he was showing Matt how to look like someone in love; he was *acting* like he was in love. *Acting.* And he must have seen her walk out onstage before the dress rehearsal by herself, so he'd pulled her aside to be nice. He knew she was the only freshman in the cast, and he was probably worried that she'd gotten through the whole show without making any friends. Which she kind of had.

Because she'd been so busy trying to get with him.

The whole thing made perfect sense. Why hadn't she listened to Natalya? How could she have asked her teacher if he wanted to go out for a drink? Her *teacher*.

As the cast filled the room, Mr. Robbins looked from one actor to another, occasionally calling out instructions to the makeup people. "Can you give Lysander a little more color in his face?" he asked, and then, "Hermia needs more lip liner. Also, tone down the red cheeks." He glanced at Jane, but she looked away too quickly for him to comment on her makeup.

"Great!" he said, clapping his hands together once as he looked around the room. "I'll keep it short since I already gave you my notes. You guys know this play. I've never worked with a more dedicated, talented, capable cast. It's been an honor to direct you, and I know you'll do me and yourselves proud tonight. I'm going to be watching from the booth, and I'll be back here at intermission. Watch your pacing. Don't just act, *re*-act." There was a small group chuckle as he repeated the directions he'd uttered pretty much every day since they'd started rehearsing. "And what's that other one?" He tapped the side of his head, pretending to have forgotten.

"Have fun out there!" Fran shouted.

Grinning, he snapped his fingers. "Right! Have fun out there. Okay, everybody, break a leg." And with that, he was gone.

"Ten minutes, everyone," Wendy announced, and then, so quickly it seemed impossible for even a minute to have passed, Sharon walked through the room calling, "Places, everyone. Places for Act One, Scene One."

Jane's stomach was in knots. She'd always thought people who got stage fright were stupid amateurs. *You know why people get stage fright?* she'd once said to her mom. *Because they realize they suck.*

She couldn't do this. She couldn't do this. She couldn't do this.

Everyone who was in the first scene filed out through the doors and into the wings, no one seeming to notice that Jane wasn't with them.

She was having trouble breathing.

She was going to die. She couldn't get enough oxygen. She sat down and put her head between her legs. Tears burned at the corners of her eyes. Why was this happening? *How* was this happening? It was too late for them to get her understudy, who was already in her fairy costume. The play wasn't going to go on. She wouldn't be known as the girl who made a pass at Mr. Robbins. She'd be known as the girl who ruined the production of *A Midsummer Night's Dream.*

In the midst of her panic, she heard a voice from the hallway. "I'm telling you, you can't come backstage now. The play's about to start."

"You don't understand, you *have* to let us back there. It's an emergency!" The voice was familiar, but Jane couldn't place it through the roaring in her ears.

"There's no such thing as a theatrical emergency," corrected the first voice. "Emergencies are about blood and death. And I don't see any blood."

"Well, if you don't get out of our way, you will," said a third voice. And Jane lifted her head and stared at the door, which flew open a second later.

Standing in front of it were Victoria and Natalya. They were each holding a bouquet of long-stemmed roses, Victoria's white, Natalya's pink.

Jane got to her feet. She stared at her friends, and they stared at her. None of them said a word. It seemed to Jane that the entire building was holding its collective breath.

And then, with no warning at all, Jane took a deep, shuddering breath.

There was only one thing that could follow a breath like that. Tears.

"Don't cry!" Victoria yelled, crossing the distance between them and throwing her arm around Jane, not caring that her bouquet was being crushed by their hug. "You'll ruin your makeup."

Natalya raced over and put her arms around her friends. "Yes. Whatever you do, don't cry," she said, and then burst into tears.

"Don't *you* cry!" Jane protested, squeezing them both to her while blinking frantically. "Then *I'll* cry!"

"I'm so sorry," Natalya whispered into Jane's shoulder.

"No, I'm so sorry," Victoria said, pulling away to look at Jane and Natalya. "I'm *so* sorry. I totally let you down." As she spoke, her eyes grew damp and tears began to run down her cheeks.

"You guys, you have to stop." Jane pressed her fingers to the corners of her eyes. "I'm serious. And if anyone's sorry, it's me, okay? I'm sorry. Now stop crying!"

From the dressing room door, Wendy called, "Hippolyta, you need to get to your place."

Jane took a deep breath. "Oh god." She put her hands out,

and Natalya and Victoria each took one. They could feel how hard she was shaking. "Guys, I did such a stupid thing."

"What?" asked Victoria, eyes wide with concern.

Jane didn't say a word. She just stood there, feeling her friends' warm hands transferring their strength to her. She squeezed their fingers so hard it hurt.

"I'll tell you after," she whispered finally.

"Hippolyta, we need you onstage *now*. Curtain going up in two." Wendy beckoned Jane over frantically.

"Okay," said Jane, but she spoke to Natalya and Victoria, not Wendy. "Okay." She nodded firmly. "I can do this."

Abruptly, she released their hands. "Hold my roses for me, okay?"

They nodded, and she took a few steps in Wendy's direction, then suddenly spun around.

"Can I just tell you guys one thing?"

"Sure," said Victoria.

"It's like this . . ." She thought for a second, trying to find the words for what she'd recently discovered. "Sometimes . . . you're afraid to do something for a reason. Let's keep that in mind, darlings, okay?"

"Sure," agreed Victoria, grinning.

"Okay," echoed Natalya.

Smiling at the wisdom of her insight, Jane gave Victoria and Natalya a tiny curtsy, then turned to follow Wendy through the dressing rooms and into the wings, ready to take her place onstage.

Chapter
Forty-five

GA GA NOODLE WAS PACKED.

Jane, Natalya, and Victoria stared at each other in amazement, then looked back at the three long tables crowded with diners. The unfamiliar group took up more than half the room and was talking and laughing loudly enough for twice as many people as were actually there.

It was like the girls had walked into the wrong restaurant or something.

"Hello! Hello!" Tom rushed toward them carrying menus, then hustled them over to a small table they'd never sat at before. His cheeks were red and his forehead was coated with a thin sheen of sweat. "The usual?"

"Um . . ." Jane began, but before she could answer, another

waiter yelped out a command, and Tom nodded briefly before racing toward the kitchen.

"What the . . ." asked Victoria. The girls studied the noisy group gathered in the restaurant they'd always considered their own. A chair with its back to them had balloons tied to it.

HAPPY BIRTHDAY read one of them.

"Mystery solved," said Victoria, pointing at the Mylar bouquet. She turned back to her friends, grinning at Jane's still heavily made-up face. "It's too bad the party at the Met wasn't tonight. You could have been an Amazon warrior and just gone straight from the show."

"I could have *floated* from the show." Jane shook her head as she thought back to the play she'd just been in. Was it possible it was the same production they had stumbled through at Saturday's dress rehearsal? "It was perfect, wasn't it?"

"It really was," agreed Natalya. Her hands were still sore from clapping, and her ears rang from the standing ovation the actors had received.

Victoria had never seen Jane perform so well or be in such a professional production. "That was like Broadway. I can't wait for the next one."

Jane's face fell. "Guys, I don't know if there'll be a next one. I did . . . I did something pretty dumb." She toyed with the red paper wrapping on her chopsticks, then tore it off.

"What?" asked Victoria, concerned. "What are you talking about?"

Jane looked across the table at Natalya. "You were right. You remember, about chess?"

Natalya's eyes popped open. "Oh my god, did you two . . . ?"

"Wait, what?" demanded Victoria. She turned her head from Jane to Natalya. "What are you talking about?"

Jane gave a bitter half-laugh and ripped her chopsticks apart. "First of all, there's no 'you two.' There's just me. Being. A total. Idiot."

"Will someone please tell me what happened!" wailed Victoria.

Natalya reached over and put her hand on Jane's. Then she turned to Victoria to explain. "Jane likes—"

"Like*d*," Jane corrected.

"*Liked*," Natalya repeated. "Her director. Mr. Robbins."

"Oh my god!" Victoria's eyes opened as wide as Natalya's.

"And I think—" Natalya continued slowly, glancing toward Jane and trying to guess what might have happened.

Jane finished for her. "Mr. Robbins does *not* like Jane. Which Jane discovered when she asked him out for a drink—"

Victoria gasped.

"And he rejected her." Pressing her lips together, Jane clapped her hands and folded them in front of her at the conclusion of her sentence.

"I'm really sorry, Jane," Natalya whispered.

Victoria didn't speak.

"So basically, it's over for me," Jane explained, rubbing at an eyebrow with her finger and streaking her forehead with thick black paint. "I'm done at the Academy."

"Oh Jane, that's horrible," said Nat, shaking her head slowly and sadly.

There was a long silence, then suddenly Victoria spoke. "Oh, please," she snorted.

It was such an un-Victoria thing to say that Jane and Natalya just stared at her, too shocked to respond.

"I'm sorry, did you not hear what I just said?" asked Jane.

Victoria waved Jane's question away. "I heard you. But you're not done. No one as talented as you are is just *done*."

"I made a *pass* at my *director*."

Victoria shrugged and rolled her eyes. "Big deal. I was on the *cover* of a major *newspaper*. Holding a *banana* wearing a *condom*." At the word *condom*, she burst into laughter.

Jane stared at her friend. "I think..." She looked at Natalya, who was also studying Victoria, a bewildered expression on her face. Jane turned back to Victoria. "Have you maybe gone a little crazy?"

Victoria stopped laughing long enough to consider Jane's question. "You know something? I think maybe I have."

"Me too," Natalya informed them. She turned to Jane. "I think wanting to be friends with Morgan made me a little crazy."

Jane shook her head. "Don't talk to me about how wanting something can make a person crazy, okay? Because I could like, write a *book* about it."

"You should write a *play*," suggested Victoria.

"Maybe I *will*," said Jane. She smiled at the idea. "Maybe I'll write a play and *star* in it."

"I'll come!" promised Victoria.

"Me too," agreed Natalya.

"By the way, Mr. Robbins will *not* be directing it," Jane told them.

"That's probably for the best," agreed Victoria. As soon as she said it, she started to laugh. So did Jane and Natalya. They laughed so hard their sides ached, and just when they had almost caught their breath, Jane squealed, "Oh my god! I think I just peed!" and they laughed until they cried. They'd been laughing together for longer than any of them could remember. It should have felt totally normal. But tonight it felt miraculous.

"Anyway," said Natalya, finally wiping her eyes and putting her hand near Jane's, "I just want to say I'm sorry I let Morgan ignore you."

Jane squeezed Natalya's hand. Hard. "I'm sorry I gave you such a hard time for wanting to be her friend."

As she returned Jane's squeeze, Natalya thought about the apology she'd e-mailed Colin. It wasn't exactly a surprise that he hadn't responded.

Old friends forgave you.

But Colin wasn't an old friend.

Suddenly Tom appeared, carrying a tray of piña coladas that they hadn't ordered. He practically tossed them on the table and sped away. "I'll be back for your orders," he called over his shoulder.

Jane looked around the table at her friends, then pointed at their drinks. "Who remembers the last time we had these?"

All three of them thought back to their Labor Day lunch. Had it really been less than *two months ago*? Impossible.

"You guys," Victoria reminded them. "It's still *October*." She dropped her head down and banged her forehead lightly on the table. "We still have to get through the election next week!"

"I can't take much more of this," Natalya said, grabbing her hair. "My head hurts just thinking about it."

"Hey!" Suddenly Victoria looked up and shot an accusatory glance at her friends. "I just remembered something. You lied to me!"

"What?" asked Natalya. "What are you talking about?"

"Who lied to you?" asked Jane.

Tom and another waiter emerged from the kitchen carrying a cake laden with sparklers as the diners at the other table began to sing "Happy Birthday."

Victoria ignored the noise and looked off into the middle distance, as if a memory were playing on a screen somewhere between their table and the birthday party. Suddenly she swung her head around and pointed a finger at Natalya. "It was you!"

"Me?! What did *I* do?" asked Natalya.

"You promised nothing would change!" Victoria cried.

No one said anything as Natalya and Jane tried to remember the conversation Victoria was referring to. It all felt so long ago. Had Natalya really said that?

Jane twirled her cherry through her drink. A guest at the birthday party started to give a toast, but he spoke too quietly for the girls to hear what he was saying.

"I guess you can't promise something like that," Jane said finally.

"And anyway, would you really want *nothing* to have changed?" asked Natalya, elbowing her friend. "Would you want to have not met Jack?"

Victoria blushed as Jane demanded, "Yeah, what's the deal? One second you're all, 'Oh, I don't even like him anymore'; the next you're playing hide-the-banana on the cover of the *Mirror*!"

"Jane! That is *disgusting*," said Victoria, laughing.

"Well?" Jane demanded.

"I was going to tell you Friday—" Victoria started, but Natalya cut her off.

"Don't worry," she assured Jane. "You'll hear all about it." She turned back to Victoria. "My point is, without change—*Poof!* No Jack."

"I hate that." Victoria shook her head sadly. "It scares me." She shook her finger warningly at Jane. "And if you tell me to face my fears, I'm going to strangle you."

"Okay, *hi!*" said Jane. "Here's what you're not going to be hearing from me for a while: Do what you're scared to do."

Natalya considered Jane's words. "That means we need a new toast."

"To Jane!" Victoria said, lifting her glass. "Our star!" Automatically, Jane and Natalya lifted their glasses.

"To Jane!" echoed Natalya.

"And to us!" said Victoria.

"To us!" repeated Natalya.

"And to Nana!" said Jane.

"And to some things *not* changing," said Victoria, touching her necklace.

"Like being the Darlings," said Jane, touching hers.

"Like being the Darlings," repeated Natalya, holding hers up so it shimmered in the restaurant's bright lights.

Finally, they clinked their glasses together. They were ready to face whatever came their way.

As long as they faced it together.

ACKNOWLEDGMENTS

To paraphrase this book's epigraph, those listed below are people who let me be stupid with them. Some took the time to respond to a panicked e-mail or phone call while others read (and reread) multiple versions of this manuscript; I am forever in their debt. Thanks to: Jennifer Besser, Rachel Cohn, Ben Gantcher, Jodi Kahn, Bernie Kaplan, Rebecca Lieberman, E. Lockhart, Sarah Miller, Helen Perelman, Abby Ranger, JillEllyn Riley, Emily Schultz, and Angie Sheldon.

COMING SOON

The Darlings
in Love

Turn the page for a sneak peek!

WITH ITS WALLS covered in black-and-white Ansel Adams landscapes and Richard Avedon portraits, piles of photography reference books, and double bed blanketed with a soft red comforter, Jack's room was Victoria's favorite place in the world.

Too bad she almost never got to be in it.

Jack's mom taught preschool a few blocks away, so she was usually home in the afternoon. If she wasn't, his father, who played cello with the New York Philharmonic and had morning rehearsals and evening performances, was pretty much guaranteed to be in the apartment from four to six. When he'd been younger, Jack told Victoria, he'd loved that one, and sometimes both, of his parents picked him up from school and spent the afternoon with him. He'd always felt a little bad for kids who had to log after-school hours with babysitters because their moms and dads worked late.

But lately Jack didn't feel bad for those kids.

He envied them.

Jack's parents had made it clear: they did not want to walk down the hallway and find Victoria and Jack in Jack's room with the door closed. And Victoria's parents had made it equally clear that if neither of them was home, Victoria and Jack couldn't be at Victoria's apartment. Since her dad was basically living in Washington, and her mother worked until six or seven every day, they couldn't be at her apartment in the afternoons *at all*. (The one time they'd tried to take advantage of no one's being there, the doorman had inadvertently ratted them out by cheerfully telling Victoria's mom when she got home from work that she'd "unfortunately just missed" Victoria and her friend Jack.)

All of which made what they were doing right now practically a miracle.

Victoria lay with her head on Jack's stomach, their bodies forming a T across his bed. One of Jack's hands was running lazily through Victoria's hair, and the other was holding hers. The Hastings were spending the afternoon walking along the High Line before getting an early dinner in Chelsea with friends from out of town. When Victoria had turned on her phone that morning, there had been a text from Jack. Who has an apartment all 2 themselves this afternoon? Call me & find out.

It had felt like Christmas in January.

"I love Sweden," Victoria said.

"Why?" asked Jack, his voice rumbling gently against the back of her head.

"Isn't that where your parents' friends are from?"

Jack laughed. "They're from Denmark, actually."

Victoria laughed too, then rolled onto her side so she was facing Jack. He curled toward her, his face just inches away. "Denmark, Sweden," she said. "They're kind of the same, right?"

"Close enough," Jack agreed. He kissed her lightly on the nose. She raised her face so his next kiss found her lips. At first their kiss was gentle, but then he put his hands on her face, pulling her toward him, and it became deeper and more intense. Kissing Jack made Victoria feel like she was slipping out of her body, and at the same time, like she was slipping *into* it, really existing inside herself for the first time in her life.

He gently kissed her closed eyes. "I'm hungry, but I don't want to stop kissing you."

"Mmmm," Victoria sighed dreamily. "That reminds me, I brought cookies."

"Oh, no," Jack lamented, "the impossible choice. Your delicious kisses versus your delicious cookies."

She laughed as he traced the edge of her ear with his lips. "That tickles."

Victoria's phone buzzed. "Do you want to answer that?" Jack asked.

She didn't, really. She just wanted to be here. With Jack.

Instead of reaching for her phone, she pulled his lips back to hers. "I'll take that as a nó," he mumbled, through their kiss. She slid her arm around his back.

When his phone rang the opening bars of the Lost Leaders' "All the Stars," he groaned and pulled reluctantly away from her. "I just have to see if it's my mom. If I don't answer, she'll use her Spidey sense to figure out what we're doing, and she'll race home."

Victoria kissed him once, swiftly, then let him go. He got up and dug his phone out of his bag. "I *knew* it!" he said triumphantly, holding the screen toward Victoria so she could read THE MOM.

"Hey, Mom," he said. Propped up on her arm, Victoria watched as he sat on the window seat and toyed with the shade pull, appreciating how cute he looked in his jeans and soft gray sweater, the same color as his eyes. Sometimes when she saw Jack in the hallway at school, she couldn't believe he was really hers. It wouldn't have surprised her if their whole relationship turned out to be just a figment of her imagination, something she'd wanted so fiercely, she'd believed her own dream. Every time he saw her coming toward him down the hall, and she watched his face break into its slow smile of happy recognition, she felt the same glow of joyous surprise.

It's real, she would think. *It's really real.*

"When?" Jack asked. "Oh, yeah?" He stood up and strolled across the room to where his guitar leaned against the wall, then idly plucked at the strings before picking it up by the neck and sitting down in his white desk chair with the guitar across his lap. "Okay, Mom, I'm glad you called, but I gotta go." He listened for a second, then said, "At my desk." Something about the way he said it made Victoria's ears prick up. It was like he was lying or something, even though he really *was* sitting at his desk.

Jack's mom must have sensed something too, because whatever she said next, Jack responded, "I'm *not* lying," but he grinned and shook his head, mouthing to Victoria, *I'm a terrible liar.* "Yes, Mom, as a matter of fact, she is." He listened for a second. "Yes, Mom, I *am* impressed . . . Yes, you *should* work for the CIA . . . Mom, we're not doing anything untoward. I promise you won't have any grandchildren in the immediate future." Victoria felt her face grow bright red, and even Jack blushed at what he'd said. Despite being halfway across the room from the phone, Victoria could hear his mother's voice grow loud with annoyance. "You're right, Mother, that was a *completely* inappropriate thing to say." He put his hand on his heart. "I sincerely apologize . . . Yes, I do realize how lucky I am . . . It's true, you are much more permissive than most mothers." Jack rolled his eyes at Victoria, who smiled sympathetically. "Though, let me point out, not as permissive as some . . . Sorry, sorry," he added quickly. "No, I don't want you to come right back uptown this second . . . Okay, Mom. I love you, too . . . Yeah, see you soon . . . Okay. We will. I promise. Bye." He hung up and gave Victoria a sheepish look. "My mom says hi."

Victoria raised an eyebrow. "It sounds like she said a lot more than that."

"As you know, my mother is not one for brevity," he reminded her. It was true: Victoria liked Jack's mom a lot, but she definitely was chatty.

Idly, almost like he didn't realize he was doing it, Jack began picking out a tune. He had never played the guitar for Victoria before; she'd noticed the instrument in the corner and wondered if he played at all, or if the guitar was just something he'd planned on mastering and then given up, the way she had ice skates hanging in her closet, which she'd worn once and never put on again.

But clearly Jack had spent way more time with his guitar than she had with her skates. Victoria watched his agile fingers moving across the strings, then lifted her eyes to his, which were staring at her. She felt the melting feeling she always experienced when Jack looked at her like that.

Still looking into her eyes, he began to sing along to the tune he was playing. Jack's voice was soft but deep and sure, and he let the song unfold slowly and sweetly. The words were about swimming alone under the night sky, and they described a place so still and perfect and beautiful, Victoria wished she could be there.

Suddenly, Victoria felt her eyes filling with tears. Everything about this moment was just so perfect and beautiful. It was as if her whole self—her very soul—was standing on tiptoe with joy. Why did they call it falling in love? She didn't feel like she was about to fall. She felt like she was about to fly.

The silence that hung in the room when the song ended felt as significant as the music had. Victoria and Jack stayed perfectly still, staring at each other. Neither of them spoke. They didn't need to. To Victoria, it felt as if somehow they were communicating on a level deeper than language.

Jack spoke first. "I love you, Victoria." His voice was serious, his eyes dark and intense as they bored into hers.

Victoria felt her heart pounding in her chest. Jack put the guitar down, stood up, and walked over to where she lay on the bed. He reached his hand down to her.

Victoria let him pull her to her feet, and they stood facing each other.

"I don't want you to—" Jack began, but before he could finish, Victoria blurted out, "I love you too." As soon as the words were out of her mouth, Victoria realized she'd been waiting to say them, like they were a present she'd picked out for Jack months ago and had been carrying around with her as she waited for the right moment to give it to him.

He smiled and took her other hand, intertwining his fingers with hers. "I was going to say that I didn't want you to think you had to say it back."

"I know," Victoria whispered. "I said it because I wanted to say it." She stood on her toes and tilted her face to his. As his lips came down to meet hers, she felt the familiar soaring feeling she always felt when Jack kissed her, only now, after what they'd just said to each other, it was stronger. She was taking off. She was leaving the world far below.

She was flying in love.